Doubleday
Doubletake

Also by J.B. Manheim:

FICTION

The Deadball Files

Book 1: This Never Happened:
The Mystery Behind the Death of Christy Mathewson

Book 2: TheGameKeepers:
Whitewash, Blackmail, and Baseball's Darkest Secrets

Book 4: The Federal Case

SELECTED NONFICTION

Strategy in Information and Influence Campaigns:
How Policy Advocates, Social Movements, Insurgent Groups,
Corporations, Governments and Others Get What They Want

Strategic Public Diplomacy and American Foreign Policy

All of the People, All the Time:
Strategic Communication and American Politics

Doubleday Doubletake

One Ball, Three Strikes, One Man Out

BOOK THREE of The Deadball Files

a novel by
J. B. Manheim

MILFORD
HOUSE
an imprint of Sunbury Press, Inc.
Mechanicsburg, PA USA

MILFORD HOUSE

an imprint of Sunbury Press, Inc.
Mechanicsburg, PA USA

For information about special discounts for bulk purchases, please contact Sunbury Press Orders Dept. at (855) 338-8359 or orders@sunburypress.com.

To request one of our authors for speaking engagements or book signings, please contact Sunbury Press Publicity Dept. at publicity@sunburypress.com.

FIRST MILFORD HOUSE PRESS EDITION: July 2023

Set in Adobe Garamond Pro | Interior design by Crystal Devine | Cover by Lawrence Knorr | Edited by Sarah Peachey.

Publisher's Cataloging-in-Publication Data
Names: Manheim, J.B., author.
Title: Doubleday doubletake : one ball, three strikes, one man out / J.B. Manheim.
Description: First trade paperback edition. | Mechanicsburg, PA : Milford House Press, 2023.
Summary: Civil War hero Abner Doubleday was long credited with inventing baseball in Cooperstown in 1839. Now, baseball historians say he was just a foil masking a conspiracy by Albert Spalding and others to lay claim to the game. Baseball sleuth Adam Wallace is called on to put the Doubleday myth to the test. But he's not the only one on Abner's trail.
Identifiers: ISBN : 979-8-88819-080-7 (paperback) | ISBN : 979-8-88819-081-4 (ePub).
Subjects: FICTION / Sports | FICTION / Mystery & Detective / Historical | SPORTS & RECREATION / Baseball / History.

Product of the United States of America
0 1 1 2 3 5 8 13 21 34 55

For the Love of Books!

For those who still worship at the
Church of Baseball
And for those who have fallen away

The Lineup Card

Author's Note	ix
Of Grapefruits and Cacti	1
Opening Day	32
Mid-Season Form	53
The Trading Deadline	99
Rosters Expand	158
Wild Card Game	175
Casey, Mighty Casey	200

The Box Score

Acknowledgments	207
Pleading Poetic License	209
Notes	210
Sources Consulted	215
About the Author	218

Author's Note

As the third installment of The Deadball Files, this book brings forward the story developed in the two earlier titles, *This Never Happened: The Mystery Behind the Death of Christy Mathewson*, and *The GameKeepers: Whitewash, Blackmail, and Baseball's Darkest Secrets*. Readers of those volumes will find here a number of familiar characters as well as some additions to the cast. Like its companion volumes, this one reaches back into the early years of baseball for its point of origin, in this instance, to the attribution of the game's very invention to Civil War General Abner Doubleday. Modern historians have discounted this long-held foundational myth, in some instances going so far as to suggest it might have been the product of a conspiracy in which the early player, later baseball executive, and eventual sporting goods mogul Albert Spalding played a central role.

What is the truth of Doubleday's connection to the game, if any? Perhaps only Adam Wallace, with a little help, can answer that question. The conspiracy may or may not have been real, but as for the answer to the question proffered here, well, it is pure fiction. Indeed, though it draws on actual events in the history of the game and some real actors on that stage, our story is simply that—a story—and except where attributed to an identified source, the motives, actions, and conversations of these individuals as portrayed here, like those of the other characters in the tale, exist only in the imagination of the author and, it is to be hoped, in that of the reader. As for the rest, any resemblance to any living person or event is strictly coincidental.

In this book, there is an extensive treatment of the history and beliefs of Theosophy, a system of religious and philosophical tenets first developed in the late nineteenth century and still attracting adherents today. Though rooted in part in the established history of that movement, this story does not purport to be a true or accurate portrayal of that history, and at points steps especially far from it to carry forward the plot. In particular, The American Theosophy Circle, an invention of the author, is employed as a literary device, and neither that fictional entity nor the characters that lead and populate it are meant to represent in any way the Theosophical Society in America or its local or international affiliates or any real persons associated therewith. Again, any resemblance to either the Society or any living person associated with it is strictly coincidental. In other words, like its companion volumes, though grounded in some interesting and little-known facts, this is a work of fiction.

"When I was younger, I could remember anything whether it happened or not; but my faculties are decaying now, and soon I shall be so that I cannot remember any but the things that never happened."

—Mark Twain

Of Grapefruits and Cacti

Max Tomhoff looked out over the room with a weary eye. He was beginning to think he had been doing this job for too long. The Monets were starting to look like Manets. When the Kandinskys started to look like the Hoppers, he'd know for sure it was time to hang up his gavel. And it wasn't just the paintings, or even the art in general. After so many lamps signed by Louis Comfort Tiffany and American craft tables and chairs by George Nakashima and baseballs by Babe Ruth, it was all starting to run together. Then you had auctions like today's, auctions of undistinguished objects, insignificant documents, items of obscure origin. He understood that Marbury House could not live by reputation makers alone, that the firm still relied on basic retail auctioneering to sustain itself and that, in the absence of glamour, sheer volume had its virtues. But the thrill of the buzz, the chill of the tension, the utter exhilaration of bringing down the hammer on a multi-million-dollar transaction that would make *The Times* the next morning—even that was fading. And the several lots up for sale today did nothing to dispel his rising sense of ennui.

Consider: A Frederick Remington bronze that was, generously, not the artist's best work. An autographed, game-used sports jersey from a disgraced player in a discredited league in a sport debased by general thuggery. A collection of papers from an unknown follower of some obscure doctrine called Theosophy. A pair of jewel-studded handbags from the 1920s. A bawdy circus poster. Even the featured lot, a collection of gold dinnerware from the estate of the early Robber Baron Jay Gould, carried a sort of taint if one applied the sniff test too assiduously.

Still, it was Max's responsibility to achieve top dollar for the sellers of these and the rest of the items on the block today, and he would, as always, do his best to accomplish that. So, as it had been on so many previous occasions, once again it was Max Time.

The Remington went for about twice what Max thought it was worth, which, he guessed, was something of a personal triumph. The sports jersey, on the other hand, failed to make its reserve and was returned to the showroom, or perhaps, if there was justice in the world, to the laundry. By the time his attention turned to the collection of philosophical tracts, or whatever they were, Max was thoroughly resigned to the mundane nature of the day's offerings. But in the auction business, one never knows.

"This next lot comprises a collection of papers from the estate of Reginald Gilbey Maxwell. Mr. Maxwell was a student, as well as a practitioner, of Theosophy, a set of philosophies relating to spirituality and religious experience. Over his lifetime, he gathered together many writings on and about this subject, and it is the entirety of that collection that is before us today. Included, and as described in somewhat more detail in your catalogue, are some five hundred books, articles, tracts, letters, and other writings that Mr. Maxwell believed either to characterize or to illustrate theosophical principles."

There had been little to no interest online, and the phone bank remained silent, presaging a modest result at best.

"Let us begin the bidding at one thousand dollars. Do I see one thousand?"

A paddle was raised in the right rear corner of the room.

"I see one thousand—do I see two?"

A second paddle was raised, this one across the aisle and closer to the center of the room. This in itself Max found rather surprising. Actual competition?

"I see two thousand—do I see five?" he queried, pushing just a bit to see whether the bidding might somehow get interesting.

Right Rear raised his paddle.

"I see five thousand, do I see ten?"

Left Center weighed in. On it went, and before long, the bidding was approaching six figures.

"One hundred thousand dollars. Do I hear one hundred thousand?" Others in the room had begun to take an interest, though the number of bidders never exceeded two. This was clearly becoming a war of wills between two well-heeled parties, though, like Max, few in the room could imagine why. Still, many reveled in the sport of a good contest of wills, however obscure the prize.

Then, unexpectedly, a third paddle was raised. That could mean anything. Perhaps the well-dressed matron in row two had figured out what all of the fuss was about. Perhaps she simply wanted to pursue something that must have some value to someone. Perhaps she was simply juicing the action for her own entertainment, willing and able to take the risk of having misjudged the intentions of the two early bidders. Or perhaps she had merely been hanging back to let the game develop. Max had been around long enough to have seen all of these dynamics and others take over his auction room. And as far as he was concerned, the more, the merrier, regardless of motivation. Besides, her motives would resolve themselves soon enough.

"I see one hundred thousand—do I see one hundred twenty-five?"

"One hundred fifty thousand!" It was Right Rear, breaking with the traditions of the House and, not incidentally, breaking Max's rhythm.

But before he could react, Left Center shouted back. "Two hundred thousand dollars!"

The auction had gone rogue, and it was all Max could do to try and regain some modicum of control.

"I see—*and hear*—two hundred thousand dollars," he asserted loudly, to the general delight of the room. Row two matron was silent, but there was considerable stirring involving Right Rear and several people who must have accompanied him to the sale.

"Two hundred thousand dollars, once."

The stirring at right rear rose in pitch, becoming loud enough to attract the notice of patrons throughout the room who turned to observe.

"Two hundred thousand dollars, twice."

The scrum at right rear continued until, at last, one man—not the bidder—said loudly, "No!" Those clustered around him resumed their seats, looking angry and resigned.

Max paused momentarily, then announced, "Two hundred thousand dollars, fair warning . . . Sold to buyer number 297 for two hundred thousand dollars."

Left Center, a balding middle-aged man in a sports jacket and bow tie, was clearly quite pleased, and, as the staff rotated the objects on display, he rose from his seat, made his way to the center aisle, and walked to the table at the back of the room to conclude his purchase. At that, the entire phalanx of conferees at right rear rose almost as one and moved with what Max could only describe as righteous indignation toward the same table, there to confront the successful bidder.

"When are you going to stop this outrageous behavior?" shouted the group's apparent leader. "You are depriving us of our heritage!"

Every neck and pair of shoulders in the room turned to identify the disturbance. Even the matron managed to rotate in her chair, relieved, Max guessed, not to have been the object of this outburst.

Left Center, now better identified as Bow Tie, made to ignore his antagonists, continuing to complete the financial arrangements and the formal transfer of ownership.

This was more than the group leader could take, and he reached out, grabbed Bow Tie's arm, and spun him around to face them. "Why are you doing this? You are clearly not a believer! And yet you continue to spend these ridiculous sums to steal our very history from its rightful owners. Are you trying to bankrupt the Circle?"

This was too much for Max. He banged his gavel so hard he almost split the oak handle. "Gentlemen!" he shouted. "Release that fellow at once! May I remind you of where you are? If you do not desist immediately and move your disagreement into the outer lobby, or better yet, off the premises, I will authorize these gentlemen," and at this, he pointed toward four burly security officers who were already moving from their respective posts toward the source of the ruckus, "to remove bodily from the building those of you who do not have business to conduct, and you will be banned from any further participation in Marbury House sales. Do I make myself clear?"

The evident leader of the group released Bow Tie and, turning toward Max, said, "My colleagues and I apologize, sir, to you and to the other patrons in the room. Our behavior was unacceptable. Please forgive us." And with that, the group turned and left the room.

Chairs scraped and clothing rustled as everyone else turned forward and prepared for the next lot. The exception was a young woman of perhaps twenty-five, seated along the aisle at the rear of the room, who gathered her things, stood, and followed the disgruntled losing bidders through the exit.

"Oh, dear God," said Max to himself. That young lady was a familiar presence in the room, and he could only imagine what would follow. But that was a worry for another day. At the moment, Max needed to reclaim the room.

"Next on the block is this pair of jewel-studded handbags. . . ."

The group had reached the street and turned uptown before the young woman caught up with them.

"Gentlemen! Excuse me!" she called after them. One man turned and she waved for them to stop. They kept walking but slowed enough for her to catch up.

"Please," she said. "Please stop for a moment. My name is Holly Hayboro. I publish a weekly blog on the auction scene, OntheAuctionBlog. com, and I was just in the room at Marbury House. If you don't mind, I'd really like to ask you some questions about what happened there, what that was all about."

"I'm afraid that was terribly embarrassing," responded the leader of the group. "We don't generally act like that. In fact, we are against conflict in all its forms. Our emotions simply got the better of us for the moment. I'm Joseph Armstrong, by the way. I am the president of the American Theosophy Circle, and these are some of my colleagues and fellow members. I cannot apologize enough for our behavior."

They came to a small plaza just off the sidewalk and stepped aside, out of the ceaseless flow of New York City's pedestrian traffic.

"What was that all about? You were clearly very upset, and it looked as if you knew that man who outbid you for those papers."

"Indeed we do. As I said, we are members of the American Theosophy Circle. Actually, we account for about seventy percent of the Circle's

Board of Directors. Reggie Maxwell, the man whose papers those were, was, how shall we say it, a fallen member of our group. He was actually at one time the president of the Circle, as I am now, and a strong believer. But something happened, and he fell by the way. But when he was an active believer—subscriber might be a better term—he spent many years collecting everything he could find pertaining to Theosophy."

"Excuse my ignorance, but just what is that? What is Theosophy?"

"I'm sorry. I forgot for a moment just how little is known about us. I suppose you could say that Theosophy represents something of a middle ground between religion and science. We believe in universal brotherhood, we encourage our adherents to study the intersections of religion, science, and philosophy, and we try to understand the unexplored laws of nature and the unexplored powers of humankind. We are all students pursuing some form of higher truth, but none of us is so foolish as to believe we have found it. I expect that sounds rather strangely doctrinaire, but I assure you it is not. We are seekers."

"Okay, so you wanted to get these papers for your . . . Circle?"

"Yes. We maintain an extensive library here in New York and others in the major capitals all around the world. Our association is truly international and has been around for many years. We were generally familiar with many of the holdings in Reggie's collection from the days when he was active. Many are quite rare, even unique in some cases, and some represent knowledge that we have never had the opportunity to explore. Reggie was a bit of a researcher, you see, and he traveled widely, gathering unpublished materials and interviewing persons who had reported having certain kinds of experiences. Those papers would have been an extraordinary addition to our library. But now, like others in recent months, they are lost to us."

"But if you know that man who bought them, well, can't you still get access to them? What does he do with them?"

"That man, as you put it, is Professor Charles Dickens, if you can believe the name. Actually, Professor James Charles Dickens of Columbia University. He is on the faculty of engineering, of all things. And, as to what he does with them, we can only wonder . . . and hope that he preserves them. He makes these purchases in the name of the university, yet there is no archive at the university library nor any other public collection that we have been able to locate. This is the third time in the last half year or so that he has purchased materials like these that we were hoping to acquire. This is the first time it has happened at auction, but he has swooped in even to sales we were arranging privately and walked off with the prizes. He seems to know almost before we do when one of our members is disposing of an important collection, and his resources . . . well, they dwarf whatever funds we can marshal. It is a mystery to us, and not a happy one."

"Wow. This is some story. I wonder if maybe this Professor Dickens will talk to me. Worth a try. If he does, you can read about it on my blog, OnTheAuctionBlog.com. Is there someplace I can find you if I have some more questions?"

"Of course. Here's my business card," he said, handing her a handsomely embossed green card. "Our headquarters building is just a few blocks up, as you can see. You are always welcome to come ask questions or to browse our literature or visit our library. You never know, young lady. You just might be a Theosophist and not know it yet. Have a pleasant day."

And with that, they resumed their walk uptown, this time at a more normal pace.

<hr>

The Commissioner and his closest aid, Jim Prevost, were seated at the conference table and chatting over lunch. He missed the bean soup and the Capitol Hill club sandwiches of his Senate days, but after a bit of experimentation, he had come to appreciate the Tuscan white bean soup and the chipotle chicken clubs from the outpost of Brooklyn's Hale and Hearty in Chelsea Market, just off the lobby of his new digs. He had thus far managed to resist the temptation of the oatmeal raisin cookies, but he knew it was just a matter of time.

"CI," he began, using the nickname of the man who had long served as his chief investigator in the House and Senate and had made the move with him to Major League Baseball, "I have a job for you."

Prevost took the ever-present notepad out of his shirt pocket and grabbed a pen off the table.

"What is it, about five or six months since we moved up here from Washington? If I had known how much real work this job would be, I might have thought better of it." He smiled, and CI chuckled, appreciating both the irony and the insincerity of the comment. "It's taken a little longer than I expected, but I think I am getting a picture in my head of our first opportunity to have a little fun."

CI knew that, to his boss, the word "fun" usually had little to do with humor and much to do with money or other forms of mischief. It was the very glue that kept them together.

"I went out west and sat in that storage room for almost three whole days, and I worked my way through those boxes of documents, forward and backward. Mostly it was just a lot of ancient history—interesting, I guess, and some real inside dope, but not very relevant to anything that's going on today. But that one box—the one with the World War I military papers and the letters and the interview notebooks from that sportswriter—I tried to understand why anybody would have paid eight million bucks for a bunch of musty old papers. You can get Cobb and Rickey autographs for a hell of a lot less than that!

"Then it dawned on me just where the value was. It wasn't in the papers or anything in the box itself. It was the threat that stuff represented to the image of the game. I mean, I always knew that at some level. But the more I immersed myself in it, the more I came to fully appreciate it. Those guys paid eight million dollars for one reason and one reason only—to preserve their franchise, to preserve the grand image of their multi-billion-dollar cash machine—to cover up the cover-up. And it was cheap at the price. So, that got me thinking.

"I don't have to tell you that this little enterprise we're running is in the crapper. It's almost like they could have saved their money, given everything that's happened in the last few years. For me, it was all kind of symbolized by the Astros. Baseball players have been stealing signs and loading up baseballs and finding a hundred other ways to cheat ever since the world began. But that's a catcher standing on second, or a batter juicing or corking his bats, or an over-the-hill lefty looking for an edge to hold onto. It's penny-ante. Now, the thing about the Astros cheat is that it was a pretty complex scheme, what with the TV cameras and the garbage can lids, maybe even buzzers, and so many guys involved. It was systemic, it was institutional, it went on for a long time, and in the end, most of them didn't even show any real remorse. People looked at that and they got pissed off. They started asking questions about the integrity of the game. So my predecessor decided to solve the problem by stationing guards outside the video rooms and, eventually, bleeping out the catchers' signs from the feeds. He could've saved everybody a lot of trouble by just canning their asses and leaving Houston with what amounted to a Triple-A team for a few years. But that just wasn't his way.

"Then, in my humble opinion . . ." At this he looked up at CI with a twinkle in his eye, realizing that his aide was at least one man who would relish the irony inherent in any such expression of humility. His glance did not go unrewarded. "Then, he started really messing with the rules. Pushing the DH on the National League so maybe he could make a deal with the union where they got to add a body to each team, not to mention the rest of the damn concessions. And that didn't all go so well, anyway. And then there were all the other so-called innovations he was pushing: batters keeping contact with the batter's box, limiting mound visits, the pitch clock, the runner on second in extra innings, seven-inning doubleheader games, the three-batter rule for relievers, moving the mound back two feet, using the computer to call balls and strikes, limiting defensive shifts, softening the baseballs, letting batters steal first on balls the catcher doesn't catch, grabbing control of the minor league affiliates—which I have to say I salute him for—but then trading the traditional leagues for these soulless corporate regional divisions, and on and on. It almost isn't baseball anymore. And some of that stuff he even changed in the middle of a season. It was like he didn't believe there were any basic rules or customs he couldn't play with, and of course, truth be told, there aren't. But he forgot about one big thing. You have to bring the fans along. And after the way he handled the Astros, well, I think the fans just didn't trust him. It just built from there.

"In the middle of all that comes that damned virus, which, of course, my new colleagues handled with their customary aplomb. By the time they got their act together, they had used up most of whatever goodwill they had left, with the fans and with the players alike. I mean, sixty games if you can make it? And sixteen teams in some sort of playoff, and even the outlines of that continually changing? Who thought that was going to go well? Then they screwed up the testing, players were taking the year off, teams were refusing to travel, and politicians—hell, the whole country of Canada—wanted nothing to do with any of it. And when he survived all of that, what did he do? He refused for months to let teams know how the order of the '21 draft would be set, which left him with the power to pick winners and losers. And talk about picking winners and losers, the next year he actually had two different baseballs in play—a live one and a dead one—and never let on. Who knows what the effect of that was on the standings or player stats? There's no certainty anymore, no continuity, no sense of stability. It's like baseball is not a sport or an entertainment or a bundle of traditions or any kind of social event; it's just a commodity. I think he was getting close to selling horsehide like it was pork bellies, I really do. Just the guy you wanted in the labor talks the next year, right? Could have seen that coming like a freight train.

"On top of all that, of course, he decides to take sides in a squabble between the political parties, so he moves the '21 All-Star Game out of Atlanta at the last minute. There were even people running ads against baseball at that point, calling for boycotts. And for what? And when all of that got sorted out, what's the next brilliant innovation for the good of the game? They start putting sports gambling kiosks inside the ballparks. Inside the parks! Can you imagine how old Pete Rose must have felt when he heard that? What a bunch of hypocrites. And still, somehow, that guy hung on. Makes me wonder what kind of dirt he must have had on somebody and who that somebody was.

"And icing on the cake, he goes all NBA on us—starts kissing up to China and partnering with the Communist Party over there, building up a network of teams, doing deals with companies tied to the military. Talk about putting fan support at risk! I think he even got Rawlings to close up a plant in Minnesota and move the jobs to China. That one was enough to get my old colleagues in Congress into the act, claimed it was an outrage for the supposed National Pastime to pull a stunt like that. And *that* is exactly my point about all this.

"So here we are. Really, we did these people a favor by forcing the change and taking control. Unfortunately, in the process, we've inherited this pile of dung and we're supposed to make it smell like French perfume.

"But, you know, CI, sometimes it pays to have spent life as a politician. Because this kind of crap comes down every day in politics, so guys like you and me . . . we have some ideas about how to deal with it. In this case, what we need is some kind of distraction, something big that everyone can focus on, something that casts the game in a bright, positive light. And I think I know just what that needs to be."

Adam was restless. He had come to terms with what Liz and the Lizard had asked of him, or rather, asked him to decide for himself. He loved Liz, and there was a baby on the way, so there really had been no choice to make. And what was one book, more or less? True, it would have made a heck of a story—all those scandals woven together into one. And he had been conjuring up all sorts of ways to tell it. The secret history of baseball. The arrogance of the baseball powers that be. And that was just for starters. It was a writer's dream, that archive, and that made it Adam's dream.

But time had passed, and watching young Henry Fairchild Wallace, or Hef, as they had begun calling him, grow and learn day by day and month by month was almost distraction enough. Almost. Though they had kept his old apartment in the city, Adam and Liz had made their home on the Fairchild family farm outside Cooperstown, and he was learning to enjoy, or at least appreciate, the rhythms of farm life. But he was still, at his core, a writer, and in this new life, he could not help but feel just the slightest bit adrift. He needed a new project, and he had no idea where to find it. Just then, as so often, his moment of introspection was broken.

"Adam!" It was Liz. "You've got to see this!"

Adam moved toward the door to the porch and opened it just in time to see Hef, who was becoming surer of his footing as he learned to walk, wrestling with a hay bale across the yard as he tried to climb atop it. Suddenly the bale yielded to his weight and rolled away from him. But Hef held on and found himself rolling with it. Startled, he shrieked in panic, and Liz began to run over to him. But as the bale resettled itself on what had been its near side, leaving Hef perched somewhat precariously on top, his cry of fear turned to one of joy at his accomplishment. Liz and Adam almost fell over laughing. That was Hef in a nutshell—if you can't climb the mountain, just roll it over and hang on.

As he always did, Adam forgot his troubles. He went to collect his son before he managed to hurt himself.

———

Holly's post on OnTheAuctionBlog.com had all the elements of a good minidrama: money, conflict, a powerful university beating up on a group of philosophers, some weird history, and even a dip into the occult. If she'd had any readers—not counting her neighbors across the hall, six friends from college, and, of course, her parents—or if she had hired a consultant to develop the tags that could game the Google search engine, it would have attracted a great deal of attention, and might even have landed her a job interview at *Vanity Fair* or at least the *Daily News*. But none of that was to be, and, like so many others before and since, the story faded into the vast Googleplex. For a time, because of its recency, it might show up among the first hundred hits on Theosophy or James Dickey (one of those misdirected Google search suggestions, as in, do you *really* mean Dickens?) or maybe even Columbia University, but that would not last for long.

The question was whether it would still pop up by the time Adam Wallace began his research.

———

"Jimmy Dancer was in here the other day. You remember Jimmy, CI. Back in the day, when I needed to figure out how to beat the old man and take his Senate seat, Jimmy was the guy who came up with that idea about having voters from all around the state send him cases of energy drinks to help him perk up and get the job done. All of a sudden, people started thinking about how old he was and how tired he looked. And we didn't have to say a thing. Just needed to show up all over, looking vigorous, and the thing took care of itself.

"I had Jimmy do some polling for us, and what he found out was not good. We still have some diehard fans, but they're aging out and they're basically still living in the good old days. But a majority of everybody else who follows sports is of the opinion that baseball is stodgy, greedy, elitist, and self-centered. And that's the leagues, the teams, the players, and even the game itself. They've lost their confidence in the game, and they are losing interest. And we are really starting to see it on the bottom line. Ticket sales, concessions, the whole range of MLB logo goods. My god, I just had a look at the proposed TV contracts from the networks for the next five years. They claim the ratings have gone in the tank, and they've really cut their offers. It's a disaster in the making.

"Jimmy's thought was that what we need to do here is give people a simple reason to trust us again—not a rational argument at all, just a point of emotional connection. We need to get them refocused on baseball, not as a collection of fumbles and stumbles, but as the National Pastime. It's a phrase you don't hear enough these days. We need to change that. And he had an idea of how to do that. It's counterintuitive at first, but if you think about it, it just might work.

"Like I said, our core problem seems to be one of trust, and a big part of that is that we never seem to acknowledge our mistakes. We just move on and figure over time people will either forgive us or forget whatever our latest stupidity or transgression might have been. And until these last few years, it seemed to work. But now, not so much. So, Jimmy suggested that we need to reach back into our history, far enough back that nobody has any recollection of it, and find a place where baseball told a whopper and stuck to it for years. And we need to come clean in a big and very public way. Basically, it amounts to confessing our sin and seeking absolution, all the while making people think it's something they should care about."

"So, if I am hearing you correctly," CI interjected, secretly relieved to have even a small chance of interrupting the boss's narrative, "what you want to do is to go back and find some really big lie baseball told that is old enough that nobody really cares about it anymore, and make a big deal of fessing up. Basically, creating the appearance of a new era of openness and honesty, and then, what, marketing off of that?"

"Precisely."

"So what's the lie? Something about the Black Sox scandal? I mean, nobody gives a shit about that anymore."

"No, that's too obvious. And it's too negative about the game itself. I thought about the Cobb-Mathewson thing for a while, and it has some of the elements we need. Collusion with the government, a believable villain, a dead superstar. But in the end, I decided it was just too complicated of a story for this. We need something simple that we can spin the right way. And I think I know what it should be. In fact, it comes right out of Jimmy's polling. One of the things he asked about was people's favorable beliefs about the game, things they think are true and that they feel good about. And he found a good one. Abner Doubleday."

"Huh?"

"Abner Doubleday. The man, and the myth. I've been looking into this just a little, and I think this is the thing. Back in the day—and we're talking more than a hundred years ago—there was a big discussion about who invented baseball, the Americans or the Brits, or maybe even somebody else. Well, it was becoming the American national game back then, and people wanted to find a way of proving that it was an American invention. And it was pretty touch and go, because the truth was, the Brits had a pretty good claim of their own—even though most of them, if you didn't count this one sportswriter named Henry Chadwick, couldn't have cared less.

"So along comes this former player, Albert Spalding, same guy who started the sporting goods company, who by then had gone on to be part owner of the White Sox and one of the founders of the National League. Even wrote the first set of official rules for the Bigs, and he published some sort of annual review that a lot of people thought of as the Bible of baseball. He was a real take-charge type of guy, Spalding was. He had rules for his players, and he knew how to enforce them. Of course, back then, you could. Not like dealing with all these prima donnas and their agents today. Spalding actually had a rule that his players couldn't drink booze—even in the offseason. And he hired the Pinkertons to follow them around and make sure they didn't. Guy after my own heart.

"Well, he was really big on this idea of baseball being a red-blooded American sport. So on his own, he up and creates a commission to decide on the quote-unquote true origins of the game. I mean, who better, right? And he put the fix in. He hand-picked the members of the commission, and he let them know what they would find . . . that baseball was invented in a cow pasture in Cooperstown in 1839 by this local war hero, Doubleday. That's the gist of it.

"A lot of people know by now that it was total bullshit, and even the Hall of Fame, which was started in Cooperstown on the presumed hundredth anniversary of Doubleday's invention, has backed away from this myth. Apparently, though, a huge number of people don't know that at all, and they swear by the myth—see it as one of the things that paints a beautiful gauzy haze over the game. Doubleday *personifies* baseball. For all that, though, no Commissioner of Baseball has ever simply come out and said this was a purposeful misstatement designed to bolster the image of the game. In fact, Selig apparently believes the myth, or did, or at the very least devoted himself to aggressively selling it when he was in this chair. There's even a letter out on the internet where he says he really believes Doubleday's the guy. I looked in the files, and it's the genuine article. But Spalding was a liar. He may have been a liar with good intentions—making Americans feel a sense of ownership in their emergent National Pastime—but a liar nonetheless. And officially, baseball has let that lie fester since, what, 1907?

"Well, I'm the Number One Historian of Baseball now—the Number One Historian and everything else. I get to say what the history of baseball is. And what I want to do is to acknowledge the lie and do it convincingly in my role as commissioner. But then, I want to spin it. We don't need to rely on silly myths like this in the twenty-first century. The truth is, baseball is a quintessentially American sport. It has carried American influence around the world for more than a century, and everywhere the game is played, it teaches American values and honors American virtues. Maybe it's tofu or sushi here, or tacos and beans there—like that great scene in *The Scout* where there's a guy in the stands eating the leg of whatever animal that was—but it's still as American as hotdogs and apple pie. We really can take pride in the fact that this is our national game and that

15

it carries our culture to every corner of the world. And that's the history we should embrace, especially if we can hype it enough to get everybody's attention off all this other stuff they've been focused on. If we do it right, it'll bring back the gate, not to mention the ratings."

"You know, boss, I think that might really work. But it needs some filling out. I don't think you can just assert some of those things. You could probably name the same five or six sportswriters I could who'd jump at the chance to pick that argument apart, even while they accept the basic premise that Doubleday was a phony."

"I couldn't agree more, CI, and that's where you come in. I want to know everything there is to know about Doubleday, about Spalding, about his commission—all of it. Find me some real dirt that proves the fix was in, and if you can't find it . . ."

"Got it."

—⊂⊃—

Maria Hoffbert had just finished her last class of the day and was about to open her office door when she heard the telephone. She finagled the lock, set her books and notes on the desk, and grabbed the receiver on the fifth ring, knowing that the next one would send the caller into the English Department's labyrinthine voicemail system, known to one and all of the cognoscenti as Dante's First Circle, AKA, Limbo.

"Hello?" she said, somewhat breathlessly.

"Maria, is that you?"

"Yes, who's this?"

"Maria, it's Chuck Dickens. Did I catch you at a bad time?"

"Hello, Chuck. No, actually it's a good time. I just got out of class, and I was down the hallway when I heard the phone. It's been a while. How are you?"

"Good, I think. But honestly, I've been so busy I haven't had a chance to check for several weeks."

"Ha! Well, you'll be glad to know I have just saved you from a fate worse than death—the departmental voicemail. I think the 'new menu' of the week has fourteen options, none of which is particularly revealing."

"Oh, the Humanities," he responded, riffing on Herbert Morrison's famous commentary on the Hindenburg disaster. "Sounds like you folks could use some engineering over there." This was a standard line of banter between them.

"Thanks for the offer, Chuck. But you just keep your little machines stuck up there in 'The Mudd'—what did *The Times* call that concrete blockhouse of yours? 'An exercise in definitive ordinariness?'—while we deep thinkers breathe the clean air in Philosophy. We've even got that Rodin statue out front to prove it. Now, to what do I owe the honor? Not another University Senate committee, I hope."

"No, nothing like that. But I have a bit of a puzzle that I could use some help with, and, knowing your side interest in codes and ciphers, I thought you might find it interesting. Up for a little challenge?"

"Always. I could take a look now if you like. Want to bring it down the street?"

"Actually, I was hoping you might be willing to come up to the engineering school. The puzzle is fairly small, but there is some important context that you might find helpful. Besides, I am always coming down there to La-La Land. It's high time you visited my digs up here. I promise I have a better view than you do, or I would if I could find the window through all this clutter. Got some walking shoes?"

"Okay. Tell you what. I'll pick us up some salads for lunch on the way."

"Excellent. I'll arrange for a visa and travel documents to be waiting at the front desk, and I'll look for you in a half hour or so."

———

Maria made the four-block hike up Amsterdam Avenue toward 120th Street, taking a brief detour across the brick-paved plaza that bridged the roadway just outside her building to pick up a couple of Greek salads from Friedman's. To this point, as she'd teased Chuck, she knew the Mudd Building primarily as the ugliest and most utilitarian excuse for architecture on campus, an impression of which she was not disabused upon entering. She circled the building, went in through the entrance opposite University Hall, and approached the attendant at the welcome desk. *Geez*, she thought to herself. *Engineering has its own welcome desk*! Then she noticed that the welcome desk was actually staffed by a security guard with some sort of sidearm—a taser or something like that.

"Hi. I'm Professor Hoffbert to see Professor Dickens."

"Ma'am, may I see your faculty ID, please?"

She rummaged through her purse, extracted her wallet, and produced the card. As she was doing this, three or four students passed by, flashed their ID cards and some sort of plastic pass, and were buzzed through the turnstile that she now noticed separated this outer lobby from a bank of elevators.

Wow, she thought to herself. *Engineering actually has elevators*!

"Here it is."

The guard—and she was a guard, not merely a greeter—studied the card, consulted her computer, and returned it.

"Professor Dickens is expecting you. When I buzz you through, take the left-hand elevator to sixteen, then push the yellow button and insert this plastic key into the slot next to it. That'll take you up to the seventeenth floor. No room numbers up there. You're looking for the door marked Applied Human Potentiality. You can't miss it. And I'll need this back when you leave."

"Thank you," Maria said, reclaiming her card and accepting the proffered plastic tab. It struck her that Chuck almost wasn't kidding about visas and travel documents.

"What are you people doing up here on the north end of campus?" she asked once she had ridden to the seventeenth floor and found the aforementioned door. "And what on Earth is Applied Human Potentiality?"

Chuck Dickens smiled. "You made it!"

"And they even let me in! Armed guards. Elevators. I'm jealous. I guess that's what Chinese money will do for you."

"Ouch!"

This, they both knew, had been a running debate on the campus in recent years, and one that was taken at least somewhat seriously given the deterioration in US-China relations. The engineering school honored a Chinese businessman named Z.Y. Fu, who had given the school about $25 million back in the 1990s when his brother-in-law was a member of the faculty. So Columbia put his name on it—adding a word—so that it would not simply be the Fu School, which sounded odd to Western ears. It became the Fu Foundation School of Engineering and Applied Science. Dickens could have pointed out that Mr. Fu had actually established his giant trading company in Tokyo, not in his native Shanghai, but he was not in the mood to have this debate with Maria today.

"Well," he said, "if it's any consolation, my position isn't supported by the Fu Foundation endowment. And in a way, that's what I want to talk to you about. Have you ever heard of Paul Chi Mannington?"

"You mean *the* Paul Chi Mannington, as in Chi Square International?"

"Same guy."

"Well, of course I've heard of him. Isn't he, like, the fifth richest man in the world? You think something like that hasn't made it to the English Department?"

"Actually, he was sixth in the last list I saw, but that's not really the point. The point is, he has a lot of money. And it's his money that pays for the sign on the door, the furniture and equipment, my salary, and pretty much everything that goes on in this little corner of paradise."

"You have a grant from Paul Chi Mannington? That's the kind of thing this place would shout about, but I don't remember seeing anything about it. Wow! I'm impressed."

"Believe it or not, Paul is a very private guy. It's true that people talk about him a lot, but you hardly ever see or hear him talking about himself. He just doesn't like publicity."

"And you *know* him? You *know* Paul Chi Mannington? Well, enough to call him by his first name?"

"I guess you could say that. We were next-door neighbors growing up. My first fight? A big punch-up with Paul Mannington when we were both about four years old. I forget now what it was about. We played Little League together, we traded class notes, we dated the same girls in high school. We were best buds until about the second year at college when we just sort of drifted in different directions. Then he went off to business school at Berkeley and I went off to study engineering at Virginia Tech and Stanford, and I suppose you could say that each of us was successful in his own way, except that my success got me a full teaching load and his success got him a full bank account. Hell, who am I kidding? It got him his own bank, and that was just for starters. Paul has the best eye I've ever seen for anticipating where things are going in the future, the bucks to buy into whatever it is, and the courage of his convictions. I have never met anyone else like him. You know how he made his first fortune? Ever hear of a guy named Robert Abplanalp? He was in the news for a while a long time ago."

"Abplanalp . . . Wasn't he one of Richard Nixon's buddies? Was he in on the campaign slush funds for Watergate?"

"Don't know about that, but that's the guy. He was filthy rich, and you know how he did it? He invented the aerosol spray valve, the tiny thing that regulates the spray when you push down on an aerosol can. Well, every time somebody bought an aerosol can, old Robert A. saw a tiny green light flash in his bank account. Year after year, those little green lights flashed every time somebody bought a can of spray paint, or deodorant, or furniture wax, or bug spray, or whatever. And that added up pretty good for Robert A.

"Well, Mannington was kind of like that, with a modern twist. He wrote some really short computer algorithm, some strip of code, that ended up being essential to pretty much every online transaction in the world. Do a credit card transaction at the store? Ka-*ching*. Transaction with your bank? Ka-*ching*. And he had the good sense to get a patent. It took years for the computer folks to figure out a way around his algorithm, and for all those years, every online transaction flashed one of those little green lights. Of course, he's branched out since then.

"But to get to the point, or at least closer, a few years ago, I was teaching at Purdue when I heard from Paul out of the blue. Actually, a fellow showed up at my office one day and said that Paul would like to see me and could I go for a short ride with him. As it happened, I wasn't doing much that day, so I agreed. We got into this limo, and the next thing I know, we're at a little general aviation airport somewhere in Indiana. The limo pulled up right next to a big private jet, and the driver just pointed to the stairway and said, 'That way please, sir.'

"Now if this was the movies, the part of Paul would be played by some gorgeous actress named Paulette instead, who would be a former girlfriend of mine, and the plane would whisk me off to a fancy resort where she was waiting for me with champagne in hand. So the movie part kind of ends at this point. But I went up into the cabin of the plane, which was every bit as leather-fancy as you might expect, and sure enough, there's old Paul, looking dapper as hell even if he was twenty years older. So of course, we hugged, and arm wrestled, and did all the customary old guy friends reunion stuff for a few minutes. But then he got serious.

"'Dickie,' he says. He always used to call me Dickie. And I'm going to paraphrase here and it'll still sound like bragging, but he really did say this. 'Dickie,' he says, 'I have a proposition for you.' And he tells me he's been following my career for a long time, and he's pretty impressed. That back when he was doing my spelling homework for me—and I was doing his Spanish—he wouldn't have guessed I'd ever be able to string together a coherent sentence, let alone write a bunch of books on problem-solving with engineering and science. He says I have this way of letting people in on the secrets so they can understand what's being done and why. And he's kept track of my research projects as well. 'I am pretty sure,' he says, that I have the particular set of skills he's looking for. Plus, I'm the one person in this world other than his folks that he trusts like he trusts himself. And they're not engineers. Then he says, 'I think there is an amazing opportunity opening up that's going to change life as we know it, and I really need you to help me test it out and develop it.' Now, I'd be lying if I didn't say I was pretty flattered.

"So Paul has me sign this nondisclosure agreement—guess he didn't trust me that much, but I understood—and then he lays out this idea of his and the years of dedicated research it's going to take to bring it to fruition, if that ever actually happens at all. And he tells me that he wants to create this institute at Columbia, because he has an office in the city, he wants to give it an unlimited budget, and he wants me to run it. But he doesn't want to make a big deal of it. Most people would say he was simply crazy, and the rest would be pressuring him to let them buy in, or they'd try to do the same thing in competition with him. Did I think we could make that happen?

"After giving this a great deal of thought . . . as much as a person could in less than ten seconds . . . I told him I thought we could probably make the logistics work fine, especially if there was enough money on the table. I mean, what university wouldn't jump at that. Controlling the publicity might be a little bit tougher, but there was probably a way. Then I told him I thought the whole thing was nuts. If it worked, even to a limited degree, it would be extraordinary. But the chances of that happening, I told him, were close to nil. I'd be lying to him, I said, if I took his money and told him I could make it work.

"And you know what he says? He says he's glad that I told him that, because he knew it to be true. And he wanted my skepticism. He wanted my deepest doubts. It was an area chock full of true believers, and he thought their belief got in the way of good science. It was enough for them, but he wanted something else. And only someone who did not believe it could be true could produce the desired results.

"So we struck a deal. Columbia bought in, as you might expect, and I moved across the country and set myself up in Seeley Mudd on a floor that most people don't even know exists. Actually, I keep an office and a lab next door with the bio people in the Fairchild Center, too. That's where I take any outside meetings, and it's the one listed in the directory. But that's a little off-topic for today."

"Speaking of," Maria finally interjected as Chuck caught his breath, "what *is* the topic for today? What is this big idea that's going to change the world?"

"Ah. We have come to the awkward moment in our conversation. I mentioned a moment ago that Paul, literally my lifelong friend, had me sign a nondisclosure agreement before he would tell me what he was doing. And now, Maria, I must ask you to do the same. I know it's an unusual request, though probably more so in your field than in mine. But it's simply the way of the world. Anything you and I discuss from this point forward must be held in confidence. It's a rule that Paul established for just this kind of situation, should it arise."

With that, he took a paper from the corner of his desk and placed it in front of her. "Please take a minute to look this over. You truly do not have to sign, but I hope you will, because I think you may be able to help us solve a very interesting little problem."

Maria read over the two paragraphs of the agreement. Perhaps it was simply her curiosity overwhelming her judgment, but she saw nothing in the language that was constraining in any way that wasn't directly related to whatever it was she was about to hear. She signed her name and handed the paper back to Dickens.

"Excellent," he said. "I will make you a copy of this before you leave."

"So," she replied, "what's the great mystery up here in your little engineering penthouse?"

"Have you ever heard of something called Theosophy?"

"Theo who?"

"Theosophy. It's this weird-sounding blend of Eastern religious beliefs like karma and reincarnation, some ancient European traditions, a couple of ideas you could best characterize as being from the occult, and a lot of classic human brotherhood and social emancipation stuff. Best I can tell, and if there's anybody who's made a study of it from the outside, I'd be the guy, it's not exactly a religion, but close, and not exactly a stand-alone philosophy, but close. It looks to outsiders to be a little like a cult, but again, not really."

"Okaaaay," Maria replied, drawing out the word. "But this is the Fu Foundation School and you're an engineer. What's any of that got to do with you?"

"Well, that's where Paul's big idea comes in. As far as I can tell, Paul is not a Theosophist. I don't think he subscribes to all these beliefs, and maybe not any of them, but he stumbled across them at some point. I don't know if he met somebody who was proselytizing, or if he read something, or if he just walked past a billboard in some wacko city like Portland. But Paul's a reader, always has been, and once he gets interested in some topic, he'll read about it and read about it until he feels he has a solid grasp. And that's what he did here. I know this because, if you take a look at the left-hand bookcase over there," he pointed across the room, "you'll see about four shelves of books that he passed along for me to read. And I can tell you, those people don't write like engineers. It's some of the most arcane and convoluted text I have ever seen. And they go on forever. But I made my way through it, and by the end, I could just begin to see what Paul was getting at.

"If you are willing to posit that there are still some mysteries in life, still some things that we don't fully understand, or may not even recognize—and I don't know of a single scientist who wouldn't sign on to that, and maybe even a few of your poets—then part of the joy of inquiry is figuring out what they are and where to look for them. And buried under all of that gobbledygook rhetoric in all those books are some ideas that, if they were discoverable and replicable and scalable, well, they just might change everything. It's not a question of belief. There are apparently lots of believers, either in Theosophy itself or in one or another of the belief sets it draws from. It's a question of validation. So the question Paul posed to me is this: Are there aspects of theosophical belief that are testable, and if testable and supported, that are reproducible, and if reproducible, susceptible to replication through some yet-to-be-developed technology? In other words, if good or bad karma exists and can be quantified, can we devise a technological means of generating it on demand? If reincarnation, in any form or any degree, actually occurs, can we capture the process in a way that allows us to initiate or control it? And so forth."

"My God," Maria interjected, "and this is what you are studying up here on the roof?"

"It's what I am trying to study," he continued. "And like I said, I am highly skeptical. And yet . . . And yet, every once in a while, I see some bit of writing or some piece of evidence that I must confess gives me pause and makes me wonder whether I'm overlooking something. For example, and this will at last get us to the reason I asked you to wander up north here among the practical-thinker types, this Theosophy, as I have learned, is a truly global movement that's been around in more or less its current form since about the 1870s, and there have been scholarly and other intensely curious people over the years, all true believers, who have collected not only books like the ones over there, but also what they have regarded as examples and case studies of theosophical beliefs at work.

"One of the things Paul has had me doing for the past few years is going around and buying up as much of this material as I can when it becomes available. In fact, I just bought a collection at an auction here in New York a few weeks ago. It was put together over the course of an entire adult lifetime by a fellow named Reginald Gilbey Maxwell. He was clearly really into this stuff and actually headed up the New York branch of the Theosophy Circle for some period of time. His estate was selling it off. Paul's idea, and I think it makes perfect sense, is that science is based on data, and regardless of how loose their methods may have been or how excessive their own interpretations of what they found, some portion of the collections these Theosophists have gathered may contain actual data, data that we could not hope to collect ourselves, and that we ought to mine them for that. So, down the hall, we have a storage room with boxes full of books, papers, drawings, objects, and you name it, all things that some Theosophists believed proved *something*. And it was while taking a first cursory look through the Maxwell papers that I came across the thing I wanted to talk with you about."

CI had just seated himself in one of the leather club chairs in the corner of the Commissioner's office.

"What have you got for me?"

"I'm about a third of the way through at this point. Basically I've been looking mostly at Doubleday since he seems most central to the myth. He was actually quite something. You already know some things about him, but let me start at the beginning and lay the whole thing out. You just never know which little fact will be the key to something like this."

"Sounds reasonable. Enlighten me on our erstwhile inventor."

"Well, he actually was something of an entrepreneur, but I'll get to that. Doubleday was born at Ballston Spa in New York on June 26, 1819. That's about eighty miles or so north and east of Cooperstown. If there were roads between the two back then, which I don't know, that would have been a three- or four-day walk. He came from what passed in those days for a military family and a political one. One grandfather was at Bunker Hill and Valley Forge, the other was a messenger for George Washington himself, and his father was in the War of 1812. After the war, his father was a publisher, and he also served a couple of terms in Congress. Doubleday grew up in Auburn, New York, which is between Syracuse and Rochester. There's a state prison out there—it's where they did the first execution using an electric chair, though of course that was much later—and I think his father was the warden at some point.

"He did go to school for a time in Cooperstown, at a place called the Cooperstown Classical and Military Academy, but things get a little hazy here. Doubleday was appointed to West Point in 1838, and he went there after Cooperstown. But I found an old advertisement from the local paper announcing the formation of the Cooperstown Academy and laying out the curriculum and calendar, and that was dated January 28, 1839. So it's not clear if the school even existed when Doubleday supposedly attended, and if it did, he would have been around twenty and in a new school in the very year when he supposedly invented baseball. And he would not have been there for any length of time. Adding to the confusion, there appears to be some correspondence from the officer in charge of the West Point Archives in 1977 stating that Doubleday did not leave West Point between August of 1838 and the time he graduated in 1842. It's not clear if that means he never left the grounds during those years, or simply that he did not interrupt his education. Finally, it appears that, when it credited Doubleday with inventing the game in 1839, the Mills Commission, the one that Spalding set up, relied on a letter to a newspaper from a guy named Abner Graves, saying that he had been in school with Doubleday in Cooperstown in that year and had seen him making drawings laying out the field. But then I read that Graves would have been only five years old in 1839. The bottom line is, there is a near zero likelihood that Abner Doubleday invented baseball in Cooperstown in 1839—or any other time.

"So the question becomes, why would Spalding say it was Doubleday? I want to wait to answer part of that until I know more about Spalding, but at least part of the answer is clear. By the end of his life—and remember that he was long dead when Spalding made the claim—Doubleday was a heroic figure and an entrepreneur of sorts. He fought in the Mexican War and he fought against the Apaches in Texas. Then he actually mapped the Florida Everglades and the area that is now Miami for the Army. He was at Fort Sumter when it came under fire at the start of the Civil War, and apparently fired the first cannonball against the rebels in reply. He was in most of the major battles of the Civil War, including the defense of Cemetery Ridge at Gettysburg. There's even a statue of him there. His hand was crushed under his horse at Antietam, and he suffered a neck wound at Gettysburg. After the war, he commanded some units in San Francisco and in Texas, and also wrote a couple of books about his experiences. While he was in San Francisco around 1870, he owned a patent for the cable cars that are still there, but when he was reassigned to Texas, he signed away his rights. He retired from the military in 1873, and he and his wife moved to New Jersey. They had no children. He died there on January 26, 1893. He's buried in Arlington.

"So, basically, Doubleday had the kind of military record that made him look heroic, at least at a distance. He had managed to occupy some level of command everywhere there was action. I did see that he had a nickname in the Army—'Forty-Eight Hours'—that was not intended as a compliment. He apparently had a reputation for being indecisive. But that was about the only negative I found.

"There was one sort of weird thing. Doubleday was pretty religious. You know, didn't drink, didn't cuss. And after he retired and moved to New Jersey, he got interested in this kind of religious cult called Theosophy, which apparently had some strange ideas about seeking the one great Truth. In fact, he joined the Theosophical Society in America in 1877, and he was its president for some period of time. Now, Thomas Edison was a member of this religion, too, so it's not clear just how far outside the mainstream it was. But it was out there somewhere on the fringe."

The Commissioner had listened closely as CI recited his findings. "Okay, so we have some things to work with already. Not least, it was almost impossible that Doubleday was even in Cooperstown when this supposed invention of the game occurred, and so far, there is almost no supporting evidence for the claim. That's a good, solid fact base, and I know it's pretty well documented. More to the point, he had some reputation issues that haven't been fully exposed, and he was apparently a leader of some obscure religious movement. We might want to find out more about that. All in all, CI, this is a great start. Why don't you move on to Spalding and his commission and see what else you can find."

⎯⎯◆⎯⎯

"Maria, take a look at this," said Dickens. "I found this tucked inside a book flap in the Maxwell collection. There were some notes with it indicating that Maxwell had obtained it from some local Theosophist out in Ohio way back around the 1930s. The paper is not dated, but according to the notes, the fellow in Ohio claimed that he had interviewed a young local boy of ten who had never traveled more than five miles from his home, was barely literate, and was having strange visions. He reported that the boy's birthday was January 26, 1893, and that he seemed to be in good health at the time of the interview, though he displayed a large wine stain mark on his neck and complained of stiffness in his right hand. Those are pretty common notations in these kinds of files. Reportedly, in the course of his interview, he gave the boy a pen and asked him to write or draw the first things that came to his mind. This is what he produced."

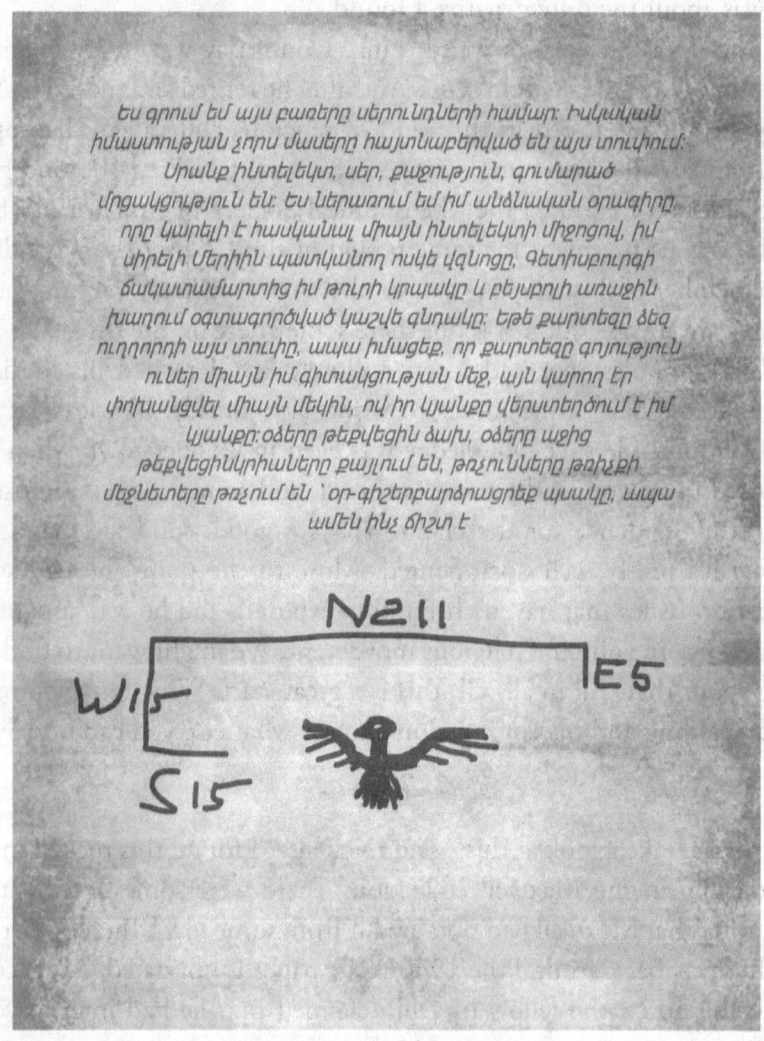

"What the heck is that?" she asked.

"You've got me. It doesn't look like any language I've ever seen before, so I assume the text is some kind of code. There do seem to be some standard, or at least repeated, symbols, but beyond that, I couldn't even guess. And the notes that Maxwell made at the time he acquired it described it simply as a nonsense scribble, plus a picture of a bird of some sort.

"And I would have let it go at that and not given it a second thought. But since we have all these resources and we are trying to be systematic about everything, we do keep a database of all the materials we review. And when I went to enter this page of gibberish into the database, the kid's birthdate and the picture of the bird triggered a link to another item. It was in a different collection, one that we picked up way back when we were just getting started, which might be why I didn't remember having seen it. That one came from a girl of fourteen who was born and had lived her entire life in Manchester, England. Both of her parents worked in local factories making cloth for export, and according to the doctor who interviewed her, she, too, was virtually illiterate. She had a scar on the right side of her neck but no recollection of an injury. Her parents were worried because she had begun speaking in a strange tongue, and they thought she might be bewitched or cursed. Apparently, it was their employer who talked them into taking her to see the doctor, who, as it turned out, was also a Theosophist. He gave the girl an instruction similar to the one in Ohio, and this is what he got. He has noted that as she wrote, she complained of stiffness in her hand. Recall that she was barely able to read simple words in her native English.

"As you take a look, the thing you need to keep in mind is this: This incident took place sometime in 1908. And the girl's birthday was January 26, 1893."

"What?" Maria exclaimed as she looked at the second piece of paper, then back to the first. "Except for the spacing and a few . . . words, I guess you'd say . . . these look almost identical, except for the hand and the drawing style. And the second one looks like it has a name . . . Ab somebody. Was that the name of the girl? Maybe she was a bit more literate than you think. Chuck, you're putting me on, aren't you? You're thinking, 'I'll show that silly Humanist a thing or two.'"

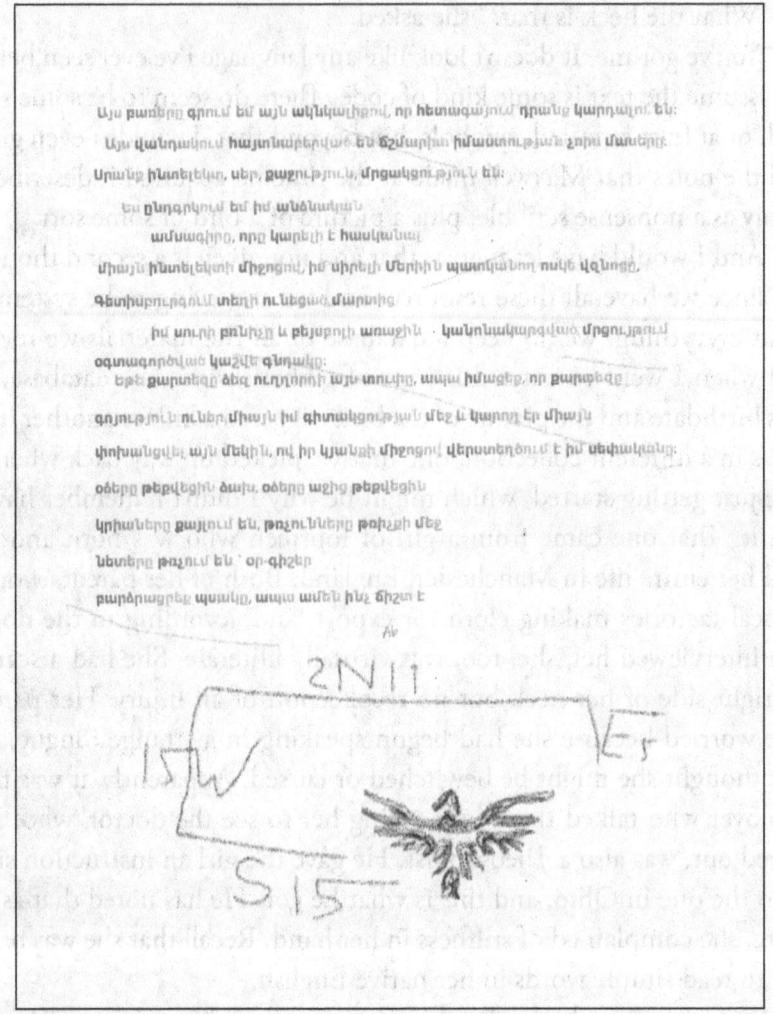

Dickens smiled. "Alas, Fair Maria, I am not putting you on. These two papers were created independently, as far as I have been able to ascertain, and lay for almost a century in one case, longer in the other, in two unrelated collections on two continents. I looked at the paper chemistry of both, and both seem to be right. Same for the ink on the first one. The second one, being in pencil, is harder to date. Now, is it possible that these two original collectors were trying to perpetrate some sort of a hoax? Absolutely. But if so, there doesn't seem to be anything in our archive here to suggest that they ever went public with it, or even that they knew each other. I looked for any cross-references between the two in their own materials or elsewhere, and there was nothing. And neither document is referenced in any of the literature in our collection or any file of correspondence or notes, so that would have been an unlikely mechanism for copycatting. I haven't told Paul about this yet, but I'm going to have to do that pretty soon, and when I do, I'd like to have every bit of information I can put together to try to make sense of it all. And that's where you come in.

"I'd like you to take copies of one or both of these papers and play around with the symbols to see if you can decode them or make any other kind of sense out of them. I'll arrange a generous honorarium out of my budget to make it worth your while. But I do need to have your assurance that you will not share or discuss these things in any way with any other person without my prior approval. In fact, before you would do that, I'd need to run all of this past Paul for his okay, because this just might be the key to the one big thing we've been looking for.

"Interested?"

"Are you kidding me?"

Opening Day

"Chuck," she said into the telephone, "it's Maria. How are you?"

"I'm doing well. I was wondering when I might hear from you."

"Sorry, but I wanted to have something firmly in mind before I got back to you."

"And do you?"

"No. Not really. But I am almost certain that this is not a code. I separated the individual symbols, which is the usual first step for something like this, and then I put together a frequency distribution to see if I could figure out what letters they might represent."

"You are starting to sound like an engineer."

"Well, I'm not totally mathematically illiterate. But that *was* about as far as I could go. So I used the standard frequency characteristics in English. You know, 'E' is the most common letter, followed by 'T,' then 'A,' then 'O,' and so forth. And I tried plugging that in, substituting letters for the symbols based on their relative frequencies, and it didn't give me anything. Then I made a few substitutions up or down, you know, like switching off 'E' with 'T' and some other adjacent pairs since no single text will necessarily match up precisely with the averages. And that didn't work either. I've kept at it for a while now, but it's starting to make me crazy.

"In any event, after all that, I am led to one of two conclusions. One is that whatever is in this text has a very unusual linguistic profile. That is, there are a lot of letters that are used in ways very different from their average frequencies in general usage. I cannot rule that out, but it just seems unlikely to me. Of course, that's exactly how it would seem if that were the case.

"The other possible conclusion is that this document isn't encoded at all, but instead, it's written in a very arcane language with unusual symbology. It's not ideographic, like Chinese or Japanese. It's more like Hebrew or Arabic, or even Sanskrit. It may not be a language currently in use, or it could be so limited in reach that most people, including me, simply don't recognize it.

"So, what I would like to do is show these examples to one or two colleagues in Languages or Classics to see if anyone recognizes the characters or maybe even knows the language. It might be simpler than we think, if only we can get it in front of the right set of eyes. And as we agreed, I wanted to get your permission to take that step."

"Actually," Professor Dickens replied, "as I have continued to look at these exemplars, I was drifting toward a similar conclusion myself. I went ahead and spoke with Paul about it. And what you are suggesting is similar to his own thinking. So what we would authorize you to do is take one or the other of those pages, but not both, and make a photocopy that does not include the drawing at the bottom, and show that to anyone you think can help. But you may not tell them where or how you got the paper, only that someone passed it along in the hope that you might be able to figure out what it says. You can show others the paper, but do not, under any circumstances, leave the paper or a copy behind. If you find yourself in a situation where doing that seems fruitful, excuse yourself and check with me first. You with me? Will that work for you?"

"I am. We are basically taking this one step at a time, and that makes complete sense to me. I'll keep you posted."

"Albert Spalding was a very interesting man," CI said to open the conversation. He was reporting to the Commissioner on the second phase of his investigation.

"I'm going to call him A.G., because that's what he went by. He was a hotshot pitcher back in the early 1870s. Guy won 54 games in 1875 after going 52–16 the year before. Started out in Boston, then jumped to Chicago in 1876, and the next year he and his brother started a store there that sold baseball goods. That was the seed that grew into the Spalding company today. They made the first official Major League baseball in 1876, the first glove in 1877, and published the first official rule book in 1878. On top of that, A.G. himself, along with a guy named Hulbert, formed the National League, and A.G. eventually became the captain and the manager of the White Stockings, then the club president and principal owner. That team won pennants in five out of six years in the 1880s. Spalding also apparently was the one who started spring training in 1886, and he sponsored a world tour of ballplayers in 1888-1889. When the players formed a sort of union around 1890, he opposed it and did his best to undermine them. So this fellow had serious credentials within the game, and he also had a strong commercial interest in its success. All of that helps to explain why he later did what he did.

"Spalding pretty clearly wanted baseball to be All-American in every sense. Maybe it was a patriotic thing, or maybe just good marketing. Probably some of both. Anyway, to accomplish that, he felt like he had to make the game American in every sense. Back then, there was a prominent writer—a Brit named Henry Chadwick—who claimed that baseball was actually derivative, that it came out of an English game called rounders. As it happens, Spalding and Chadwick were friends, and Chadwick was for a time the editor of an annual Spalding publication called the *Official Base Ball Guide*. So he actually worked for Spalding. But they developed this dispute over where the game originated. Seemed to be more important to Spalding than to Chadwick, although that's beside the point. It became a point of pride for Spalding. However, then he had to prove it, and that's when things got a little . . . political, if that's the word.

"The other thing to keep in mind about Spalding was that he had a strong view that sport was essential to society, and that sporting competition was the crucible in which young men prepared for life's challenges. And you have to remember that now we're getting into the years of the Spanish-American War and Teddy Roosevelt and the start of American empire building. Nationalism was a big thing, as was the rigorous outdoor life, and it looks like Spalding was all in for that.

"But there was something else going on in his life, too, and you're going to love this. In 1899, Spalding's first wife died, and a couple of years later, he remarried, this time to a woman with whom he had apparently had an ongoing affair for some years, not to mention a son. And this second wife—her name was Elizabeth—she was really big into . . . Theosophy. She studied directly with this Russian woman named Madame Blavatsky, who was the big name in this thing, and after Madame died, Elizabeth got connected with a big Theosophy colony out near San Diego. So after the wedding, she talks A.G. into moving out to California, and she hooks him on this Theosophy. And that seems to have really amplified his existing philosophy on the importance of sport in national character, though I couldn't tell you how the two were connected. Anyway, by the time he died in 1915, he and his wife had put together a really extensive library on Theosophy. And in the meantime, Spalding apparently also paid for building several large temples and other structures for the Theosophical Society out there on the West Coast. So he was really into this stuff.

"Now, sometime around 1903, Chadwick writes this article saying that baseball isn't American at all, but is just an extension of two British games, cricket and rounders. Again, this is the middle of the Teddy Roosevelt era, and Spalding's been out living in this philosophical colony for four years or so, and he decides he needs to respond to his old buddy by creating a purely American origin story for baseball. Good for the country, and certainly good for the sporting goods business. And he probably knows he needs two things: a real American hero to credit with starting the game, and some kind of institutional justification for picking him. I guess you could say that he was doing kind of the same thing for baseball back then that you're trying to do today.

"Anyway, I haven't found a time yet when Doubleday and Spalding actually met, but at the very least, Doubleday would have been the kind of man he was looking for. Distinguished military career, lots of visibility, national reputation, business-minded. And Doubleday had two other traits that must have proven attractive: he was also into Theosophy, as we found out a few days ago, and he was dead, so he couldn't deny, or even be asked about, the origin myth Spalding was about to spin. At the very least, living among some real Theosophy fanatics in San Diego, it's a name he would likely have heard mentioned. And there might have been more to it than that.

"As for the commission, I know some basics about it at this point, but I want to nail down some specifics in the context of Doubleday and Spalding before I pass that along to you, if that's agreeable."

"As always, CI, this is great stuff. When you're ready, give me the rest, and we'll figure out how we can put all of this to productive use."

———※※———

"Liz, hi. I'm Tres, and I guess you know what that means." He had knocked lightly and peered into her office since no one was at any of the desks in the reception area. Liz noticed he was carrying a briefcase.

"Come on in. Nice to meet you. So," she offered him a knowing smile, "what have you got to say for yourself?"

He smiled back. "He melts rainbows paying heed."

"Devilish journeymen toil," she responded.

"I rented view plus Uncle Hooch."

"Oh battle unhappiest."

With these formalities concluded, the two sat down on opposite sides of her desk. "It's nice to meet you, too," said Tres. "I was sorry to hear about your dad. I can't say I knew him well, but I always enjoyed our brief visits together. I know my own dad felt the same way."

"So," she said. "I guess it's something of a family business for both of us."

"Apparently that's the way they wanted it. I'm the third, and you must be, what, the fourth, I think. It all seems passing strange to me," he added, not being exactly truthful, "but I guess we each have our respective legacies to serve."

"Looks that way. So, how can I help you today?"

"The usual way, I guess. I'll need the keys."

Liz opened the long desk drawer, opened the old metal lockbox, and handed Tres the keys, not realizing that in so doing she was giving away information—the location of the lockbox—that her progenitors had usually chosen to hold unto themselves. If she was curious as to the contents of the briefcase, though, she gave no outward sign, and in that she held true to their ways. But then, in his full view, she released the hidden catch and pulled the wheeled bookcase forward, revealing the doorway.

"Take your time," she said. "I'll just be up here working."

Tres thanked her, used the first key to open the metal door, closed it behind him, and disappeared into the passageway. He was gone for the better part of an hour. Then, without any warning sound, the door opened, startling Liz, and Tres emerged from the darkness. He pulled the door closed, pushed the bookcase back into position, an action that was accompanied by an audible click from the adjacent unit as the latch found its home, and returned the keys to her.

"One more thing. We have a change in the roster. The way that works is I just tell you who the other three people with access will be going forward, and you make a note of them in your log."

"Okay. I needed to list your visit today anyway . . . Here it is. So . . . what's the change?"

"Straight Arrow is out, and the new name is Legal Eagle. So the three names would be Lot Lizard, First Fan, and Legal Eagle."

"Got it," said Liz. "Can I offer you some iced tea or a soda?"

"No. I've got a long drive and I'd best get going. It's been a real pleasure meeting you. And thank you."

And with that he was gone.

Liz picked up the phone and dialed Adam's cell.

"Guess what just happened," she burbled when he answered. "We just had a visitor. One of them."

"Really," Adam replied, drawing the word out just a bit. "Was it that Lizard guy?"

"No, this was Tres. He seems to be the messenger. Made some reference to his father having done the same job. In fact, if I heard him correctly, his grandfather, too."

"I wonder what it was this time," Adam said. He knew they had promised never to use the keys again themselves, a promise they both felt honor-bound to keep. And he knew he was not supposed to speculate about these visits, which they knew to expect from time to time. But he could not help himself. Something had just been added to the archive of baseball horror stories, and he could not help but wonder what it was.

"What do you think?" Adam asked. "Maybe the company they picked to do all of that virus testing a couple of years ago was paying off somebody to get the contract? Or maybe it had to do with that free-agent thing last year. Or some kind of under-the-table deal with the union. Or some super-agent colluding with one of the clubs. God! It drives me crazy not knowing! Sometimes I think I was better off before I knew about all that stuff down there."

"Well," Liz offered, "just put it out of your mind. We made a deal, and we need to stick to it. Goodness knows we benefit, and Hef will, too, when he grows up. You just need to find something to write about that doesn't have anything to do with baseball or with that vault. Stop baling hay and start making some before you drive *me* crazy, Author Man."

"Rosie? Hey, it's Maria. Have you got a minute?"

Rosie was Rosalind Lindholler, Professor of Classics, whose office was on the sixth floor of Hamilton Hall, a building just down Amsterdam and across the College Walk that split the campus north from south at what would otherwise have been 116th Street.

"Hello! How are you?"

"I'm great, actually. Just finished grading a stack of freshman essays, and I'm afraid I've arrived at the usual question. How did all of these people manage to get admitted to Columbia? And of course, four years from now we'll have developed every one of them into a genius and gladly pass them out into the world, right? Just what society needs . . . more English majors."

"Just try placing Classics majors, sweetie."

"Point taken. But speaking of Classics, and specifically of your own forte, classical languages, I wonder if I might drop over and show you something. I'd like to pick your brain about what it might be."

"Of course. Want to just meet at the wine bar in twenty minutes or so?"

"I'd love nothing more. But in this case, I think it will be better if we just do it in your office. Do you have a line of students waiting?"

"Maria, this is the Classics Department, not English. We probably haven't seen a line of students outside a door here since they held the lottery to hand out Greek letters to fraternities and sororities in whatever century that was. Come ahead. I'll make us some tea."

Maria made a copy of her copy of the page filled with mysterious writing, careful to remove any trace of the drawing at the bottom. She placed the altered copy in a new manila folder, then dropped the folder into her new leather briefcase with its shiny brass fittings—a birthday gift from her husband—grabbed her umbrella as protection against the threatened showers, and headed downstairs and out of Philosophy Hall in the direction of Hamilton. If Mudd was the dreariest place on campus, Hamilton at least had some character. It was one of four similar buildings at the heart of the campus that seemed to stand guard at the four corners of the Campus Walk. She thought of those four buildings as sentries. From the look of their interiors, though, they had been manning their posts without relief for quite a long time. And as for its character, to Maria, Hamilton was arguably one of the most architecturally pretentious buildings on campus, with its triple-double-doored entrance, its Greek columns, fancy lintels, and old Alex himself, Columbia's most famous dropout, standing guard in weathered bronze silence out front. It was the perfect place to house the Dean's office, which it did. The Classics and Foreign Languages offices were relegated to the upper reaches of the edifice.

"I hope Earl Grey is okay," Rosie said once Maria had arrived at her destination, shaken out her umbrella in the hallway, and come into an office she had to admit was a good bit cozier than her own, which is to say, smaller.

"Earl Grey will be delightful." And so it was.

The pair sipped in silence for just a moment.

"Okay! You're toying with me! What have you got that I need to see?"

Maria lifted up her briefcase and modeled it slowly from left to right as if the case itself were the prize.

"Oooo. Where'd you get that?"

"David gave it to me for my birthday last month. Isn't it classy?"

"You've got that right. Look at the light reflect off of that latch!" Now Maria knew she was being mocked. "But something tells me that's not why you're here, because you could have flashed that academic bling at me at the wine bar. Am I right?"

"As usual, you are." At that, she opened the case and pulled out the folder, which she handed over to her friend. "What do you make of that?"

"What is this?" asked the classicist, considering the proffer. "Where did you get it?"

"For all I know, it's just a random piece of paper. A fellow I know passed it along and asked me if it looked like any sort of code I was familiar with. It didn't, unless it's some sort of third-order substitution cipher, in which case it might as well be written in algebra. But after I studied it for a while, I thought it might actually be in some ancient language. Obviously not Hebrew or Arabic, which I'd probably recognize, but maybe something more obscure. Old. Arcane. I thought instantly of you." There. Things were even.

"You always were a dear," Rosie replied. "Let me look at this. . . . Okay, it's not Greek, but you know, it may not be that far away from Greek. It does seem to have repeating characters, so it's probably a language of some sort, though maybe not as many characters as some of the more modern Western languages. But it's difficult to be sure. And if some of these subtle differences are grammatical markings, there might even be some remote link to ancient Hebrew or one of the Middle Eastern languages, where every little dot or squiggle means something different. But you know what? I'm going to go in another direction. I think this might be some archaic form of a language from further north, perhaps one of the Slavic languages. Are you up for climbing some stairs?"

───── ═══ ─────

"Okay, boss," CI began, "here's the next installment. The Mills Commission was a put-up job from start to finish. It was actually kind of a National League conspiracy to cement the American roots of the game. Abraham Mills was Spalding's pick to chair the thing. Both, by the way, went by 'A.G.' But they had something else in common. Remember that Spalding was once president of the National League. Well, so was Mills, who also drafted the National Agreement that laid out the modern business structure of the game. And among the other members, so were Nicholas Young and a pair of US Senators—Arthur Gorman and Morgan

Bulkeley—all were also past presidents of the league. The secretary was James Sullivan, who earlier had run Spalding's publishing operation. Alfred Reach was yet another business associate—Spalding bought his competing sporting goods company in 1889, and his name, Reach, was the trade name on American League baseballs clear up to 1976. The last member, George Wright, was the brother of Harry Wright, a player-manager in Cincinnati and Boston, who had been the guy who had convinced the young Albert Spalding to turn professional, a decision that would eventually lead him to the Hall of Fame, and who then served as his mentor.

"Gorman is kind of interesting, even aside from the weird fact that he was yet another guy with the initials A.G. He was one of the founding members of the first official baseball team in the US, the Washington Nationals Base Ball Club. That was in 1859, and by 1867 he was a star player. That's when he led the Washington team on their first trip out West, really to the Midwest, where they beat every team they played except one, from Rockford, Illinois. Rockford had its own young star, a pitcher named Albert Spalding. So these guys went way back.

"Also, as it happened, when Mills was in the Army in the 1890s, he actually served in the honor guard when Doubleday was buried at Arlington.

"Now, the story is that all of this got started at a big, fancy dinner at Delmonico's in New York in 1889. There were a bunch of very prominent players who had just come back from a world tour showing off the game. Spalding was the guy who organized the tour, which he saw as a sort of patriotic mission. Anyway, you had Mark Twain at this dinner, and Teddy Roosevelt, so it was a big deal. And it was all about Spalding's mission of using baseball as the American goodwill ambassador. So a lot of the speakers—and they had a lot of speakers at the big dinners in those days—took the theme that baseball was an American game and not a descendant of rounders, the Brit game, like Henry Chadwick and others had been claiming. Apparently, every so often, the diners would break out in shouts of 'No rounders, no rounders!' Chadwick, by the way, wasn't invited.

"This all added momentum to an apparently good-natured debate between Spalding and Chadwick that went on for years until, in 1903,

Chadwick published an article showing in detail just how baseball owed its origins to rounders, and he published it in the *Spalding Guide*, where he was still the editor. The next year, he doubled down with another article making the same case. That's when Spalding decided he needed to do something, so he wrote to a bunch of his old baseball buddies asking for evidence of the American origins of the game, then he wrote his own piece in the 1905 *Guide* in which he said he would put together a commission to decide the matter. That's when he had Sullivan advertise the commission in papers around the country, and Graves, the guy who claimed he saw Doubleday invent the game, was responding to one of those ads. By the way, there's even a ball that somebody later claimed had belonged to Graves and that was supposedly used in the first game. It's a beat-up old leather thing, and it's actually been on display at the Hall of Fame, even though they have backed away from the Doubleday story itself.

"In any event, the whole thing was pretty moribund for the next couple of years, but Mills, prodded by Sullivan, eventually realized that they had to issue a report. So at the very end of December in 1907, he wrote a letter to Sullivan that started out sounding like he was accepting the Chadwick story but ended up backing the Spalding view and, based largely on a pair of Graves's letters, one to the editor of the newspaper where he read the commission's call and the other to Spalding himself, concluded that Doubleday was the inventor. Let me read you part of what Mills wrote:

"I can well understand how the orderly mind of the embryo West Pointer would devise a scheme for limiting the contestants on each side and allotting them to field positions, each with a certain amount of territory: also substituting the existing method of putting out the base runner for the old one of 'plugging' him with the ball."

"Okay," said the Commissioner, who had been listening attentively to his aide. "So it was a put-up job, and that might be useful. Anything else?"

"Well," said CI, "there is one other thing. It seems like Abner Graves, the guy who supposedly singled out Doubleday, might have been a closet Theosophist. And there were some things about the way the whole writing of his letters was done that seemed kind of hinky. I haven't been able

42

to nail it down, but it could be that Charles Knight, the editor of the Akron paper that published Sullivan's ad and Graves's response the very next day, was also a Theosophist and that Graves was sent to Akron on a mission of sorts. In fact, I read one book by our own former historian, John Thorn, that I think hinted that the whole thing might have been cooked up as much to save Theosophy, which was starting to be marginalized in the US even as it was expanding, as it was to claim American roots for baseball."

"CI, you old son-of-a-bitch. You were holding out on me!" Both men smiled.

"Lud?" It was spoken to rhyme with "hood."

They had climbed one flight to the seventh floor, the Slavic Languages Department, and Rosie was pushing on a partially opened office door. Stenciled on the glass was the name and position of the resident, *Ludomir Bondarenko, Professor of Slavic Languages.*

"Yes, come in," came the accented reply. "Ah! Rosalind, it is you!"

"Lud," she said, pushing the rest of the way into his office. Seated behind the desk was a man in his fifties, more or less, square in the face, with short-cut hair that was once black but was now shading to gray. "So nice to see you. I'm glad we caught you in. I'd like you to meet my friend Maria Hoffbert. She's ventured down to see us from the English Department. Maria, this is our distinguished colleague, Ludomir Bondarenko."

"My dear Professor Hoffbert, it's an honor. I have read of you from time to time in *The Spectator*, if I am not mistaken. I, myself, advise *The Birch*, our little Slavic culture journal, but I don't know if that ever gets beyond the building here."

"It's so nice to meet you, Professor."

"Lud, please."

"Lud. And I'm Maria. Honestly, I'm not sure I have ever seen an issue of *The Birch*, but now I know to be on the lookout for the next one."

"So," said Lud. "To what do I owe the pleasure of a visit by two such brilliant and, dare I say, attractive colleagues?"

Rosie turned to Maria. "As you can see, Lud is very, ah, old school."

"European, Rosalind," he responded. "I prefer the term European. But my question remains unanswered."

"Lud, we've brought you a piece of paper. An acquaintance passed this along to Maria, thinking it was perhaps a code of some sort. She has an interest in linguistics and ciphers, and he—or she, I don't really know—thought that she might be able to work it out."

Maria picked up the narrative at that point. "I thought it might be some sort of substitution code using strange symbols, so I tried all the usual tricks for figuring that out, and nothing worked. Eventually, I decided it might not be a code at all but some sort of obscure or archaic language that I simply did not recognize. That's when I called Rosie here, figuring the answer would be found in classical languages. I won't make the hackneyed old crack about it all being Greek to me, but it turned out it wasn't actually Greek to anyone. But Rosie had a suspicion that it might be something Slavic, or even proto-Slavic. So here we are."

"You have my undivided attention. May I see this mystery missive?"

Maria passed the paper across the desk. He looked at it for just a moment, then smiled broadly.

"My dear Rosalind, you were half correct. The language is indeed obscure, but it is far from extinct. This document is written in Armenian, which, as you can see, has its own rather distinctive alphabet. More specifically, it appears to be written in what is called the classical orthography of Armenian. I won't go into all the details, but there are two basic versions of the language, and this appears to be in the older form. It suggests that the document was written by someone in the Armenian diaspora, rather than by someone resident in the region at the time. The language actually does have some historical connections to Greek, perhaps more than to most Central European languages, but it is rarely seen or spoken outside of the Caucasus, although many Armenian communities around the world do try to preserve it through ritual use, especially after the Hamidian Massacres of the 1890s and the genocide by the Turks not long after. It does not surprise me that neither of you would have been familiar with it. Indeed, even here, we do not have either faculty or courses devoted to this particular language, which is related to the Slavic tongues but is not itself one."

"Does that mean you can't tell us what it says?"

"Rosalind, Rosalind. You classicists are always in such a hurry. An amazing trait for students of cultures that have been lost for a thousand years and more." It was said with good humor, and taken the same way, in a manner Maria sensed was merely a continuation of a line of cross-disciplinary repartee.

"I said it was rare. And I said we do not have faculty or course-work devoted to this language. But I did not say I could not translate it. Growing up as a young lad, and the way things were at that time, it was not possible to even encounter persons of different cultures and experiences, let alone different languages. The Russians were not only firm masters of the Slavic and Transcaucasian states, but they had certain prejudices that reinforced many indigenous ones, and political needs that restricted travel or even communication. But when I was at university, I encountered for the first time others who, like me, were learning about one another and beginning to break down some of those barriers. Then, of course, the entire edifice collapsed, leaving us free to, shall we say, exchange many things, including our languages.

"It was then that I met a delightful young woman from Yerevan, which is now the capital. My Anush. It means sweet, and that she was. And a real beauty. We were lovers for two years, more or less, and in that time, I made a point to learn Armenian, just in case, you understand, I might have occasion, someday, to meet her parents. She left me for an Italian, of all things. Sergio or Silvio or one of those ee-oh names. Never got over it. But at least I kept the language. Would you like me to translate?"

"I would like nothing more," said Maria.

"Very well. It is rather long, though, and I am rather rusty after all these years. Would you mind very much leaving it with me for some period of time?"

Maria thought for a moment, recalling the very specific instructions Chuck had given her.

"Yes, I would like that very much. But as I said, this document is not mine. I don't want to give offense, but would you mind if I stepped out into the hallway for a few moments so that I can call the owner for permission to leave it with you?"

"Yes, yes. That would be the honorable thing. I'm sure Rosalind and I will find some fascinating topic to fill our time while we wait. Rosalind, have you yet seen the latest Russian translation of the *Journal of Slavic Linguistics*?"

They all had a laugh and, concern abated, Maria left the office to call Chuck. She hoped he would answer, a hope that was fulfilled on the third ring.

"Hi, Maria, what's up?'"

Maria explained the situation and gave him a brief sketch of her two colleagues, with special emphasis on Professor Bondarenko. As it turned out, Chuck had run into the Slavic specialist over drinks at Faculty House two or three times when both had come unaccompanied.

"Lud's a good fellow. And I think he'll honor a request for confidentiality. So yes, I'm on board with that. But please don't tell him the source of the document. It's not a discussion I ever want to have with him. Okay?"

"Got it. I'm not sure how long it will take him to do a translation, but I'll keep you posted. Gotta run. I don't want to make this seem mysterious." Maria ended the call and returned to Professor Bondarenko's office. There was a burst of laughter just before she knocked and re-entered, so she was pretty sure they were not reviewing the Russian translation of the journal.

She was mistaken about that, as it turned out, and Lud set the journal down as she entered. Neither he nor Rosie chose to share the joke, whatever it had been.

"Sorry for the delay. The owner says that he would be both delighted and grateful if you were able to prepare a translation. I must ask this, though. Because this document is not mine, and because I have no idea what it says, I must ask that you not make any copies for any reason, and that you not share the contents with anyone else. I know that is unusual, but. . . ."

"Say no more. I understand completely, and I am happy to comply. I must confess, now, that I am most curious myself. Please leave the paper with me, and I will endeavor to determine its contents. It may take some time, depending on the match between my remembered vocabulary and that of the author. But I assure you I shall not forget the commitment. May I call you at the number in the online directory when I am finished?"

"Yes, that would be excellent. Thank you, Lud. It really has been a pleasure making your acquaintance."

With that, Rosie and Maria took their leave and headed back downstairs for a second cup of tea.

"Commissioner, it's Jimmy Dancer on line one. Shall I put him through?"

"Yes, Diane, by all means." He waited for the call to forward to his phone. "Jimmy? Nice to hear from you. Have you had a chance to think about the results of CI's little inquiry?"

"Commissioner, good morning," responded the communication consultant. "Indeed I have. And I agree with you that there is some material to work with. But if you are serious about what you hope to accomplish, I think you'll need something more . . . shall we say, concrete."

"How so?"

"Well, it's pretty clear that no one who has given it any thought really believes the old Doubleday myth any longer, if they ever did. The Hall of Fame, which might have been the principal beneficiary in some ways, has walked away from it. At least one of baseball's leading historians has discounted it and, if CI has it right, even pointed to the potential for a bit of a conspiracy involving some old religious cult. Lots of historians of all stripes laugh it off as ridiculous. There's even an alternative theory about this other fellow—Cartwright, is it?—having done the deed earlier. That one seems to have been discounted lately as well. And then there is old Henry Chadwick's original argument about rounders, whatever that is, or was. So honestly, I can't see you getting a lot of mileage out of joining the fun and simply rejecting the Doubleday story as phony. I think you need more. I think you need something far more odious, even corrupt, that you can not only reject but strongly recant. Baseball should be ashamed that after so many years and so much contrary evidence, we still seem to wink, nod, and pay lip service to this absurd, and maybe in its day even dangerous, creation myth. That sort of thing. And then you make the point about the centrality of the game to the American culture and its spread across the globe as the real thing that makes baseball All-American in every way.

"To do that, you need to open a closet, move a pile of dirty laundry, find an old pair of socks, and air them out in public, if you catch my meaning. This Doubleday thing has to be seen as important in some fundamental way, as self-serving to the game, and so disgusting or threatening in its implications, even today, that you, as Commissioner, have an obligation to address it. That's your chance to be seen as decisive and forward-looking in claiming the moral high ground. In political terms, you need to create some kind of an enemy for people to rally against, get them stirred up. And that enemy can be the Doubleday myth if you juice it enough. *Then* you can ride to the rescue."

"Okay, Jimmy. I'm with you so far. It's certainly a game that you and I have played often enough before. But how do we do that? How do we give something that old juice? Any ideas?"

"You need something physical, something explicit. Something that reeks to high hell, and that makes Doubleday, who had the good fortune to be dead anyway when all of this happened, look like a pawn in a larger game. Something to make the American people look like dupes back in the day and maybe even now. Make 'em mad. Then stand up for them by doing the right thing. You remember the Zimmerman telegram?"

"That rings a bell," the Commissioner replied. "Give me a second. World War I, right?"

"Right. Back in 1917, the Germans sent a telegram to their ambassador in Mexico offering Mexico financial aid and the chance to reclaim the whole damn southwest if they'd attack the US from the south and keep the Americans pinned down at home so they couldn't get behind the Allies. Now, the Mexicans at that point really resented the Americans. As they saw it, not only had the US bought or stolen half of their land, but it was only a couple of years since Black Jack Pershing and a bunch of yahoo troopers had gone romping around northern Mexico, chasing down Pancho Villa. Plus, Americans tended to treat the Mexicans like second-class citizens in general, even in their own country. The Germans figured they could take advantage of that anti-American sentiment.

Unfortunately for them, the telegraphic traffic in those days passed physically through England, where the transatlantic cable hub was, and the Brits intercepted the thing and deciphered it. They secretly shared it with the Americans, who in turn released it to the public. Boom! Germany became an enemy overnight, and the US government had the excuse it needed to enter the war on the other side, which it did about a month later. That's what you need."

"A Zimmerman telegram?"

"Functional equivalent. Some document or set of documents that make the Doubleday thing out to be a deception intended to fool or manipulate Americans in some important way. Not just a baseball thing, but something bigger. I don't have enough information at this point to say what that might be."

"All right, I hear you. And that's very helpful. I know just what to tell CI about next steps. Send your invoice to me at my personal post office box, will you? Not the office. I think you have that from before. Still the same."

"Will do. Let me know if you need anything more. And if I come up with anything really diabolical on my own, I'll let you know."

"Ladies and gentlemen," intoned Joseph Armstrong, "please come to order. This emergency meeting of the Board of Directors of the American Theosophy Circle is called to order. Without objection, we'll dispense with the reading of the minutes of the last meeting.

"I need not tell you how grave a crisis we confront. A force unknown appears to be working hard to deprive our movement of its essence through the expedient gathering and burying, or perhaps even destroying, of records produced over a hundred and fifty years. We know the face of the effort, the esteemed, and I hope you detect a note of intense sarcasm in my choice of words, the esteemed Professor James Charles Dickens of Columbia University. But we know nothing of his motives and less still of the source and extent of his resources, except that they have been proven quite ample. Chances are that Dickens is merely a front for some other person or organization bent on our annihilation.

"The purpose of today's meeting is to formulate whatever manner of defense we can and to agree upon a course of action to preserve the Circle and, more importantly, to secure the movement. The floor is open for your suggestions."

"Mr. President," rang out the voice of Vivian Vance-Victor, one of the Circle's principal sustaining members. "It seems to me there are three things we must do immediately. The first is to broaden our own base of resources by reaching out to the full membership of the Circle with a clear appeal for funds, as well as bringing the situation to the attention of our international colleagues. Frankly, if this continues the way it has thus far, we'll need more money if we are to compete in the marketplace when necessary. Second, and not a distant second, I believe we need to find out as much as we can about this Professor Dickens. Forgive me, but who is this man and what the dickens is he up to? I don't mean just reading his work or looking up his biography somewhere. I mean that we need to hire one or more investigators to learn everything we can about his motives, his resources, and yes, also his vulnerabilities, in case we should be positioned at some point to exploit them.

"Finally, Mr. President, we need a counterstrategy. We need to have some plan of action rather than just sitting back in meetings like this— and I mean no criticism, as such things must start somewhere—but we cannot afford to be passive. In times past when our movement was passive, its adherents suffered, and when it was assertive, they—we—have prospered. We need to reclaim the initiative here, if we can, or to identify actions we can undertake in our own interest.

"Recall, if you will, those times in our history when such need has arisen. I think, for example, of the problem of the Hodgson Report of the Society for Psychical Research in 1885 that attacked Madame Blavatsky personally as perpetrating a fraud through false claims of psychic phenomena, which was then, on her urging, rejected by another member of the same Society as fundamentally flawed. Shortly afterward, there came the issue of the Esoteric School and the leadership succession when Madame Blavatsky left this plane. It took two years, from 1891 to 1893, to resolve that matter, and success was dependent on recognizing that H.P.B. herself had left a plan of succession in place through the understanding of W.Q. Judge. Or those of the modern era who would label us Nazis, racists, sorcerers, necromancers, and antisemites—even today in Germany, for example—which allegations are routinely refuted and never left to stand. We have no choice but to be proactive."

"Here here!" shouted several voices around the table.

"I think . . ." It was Jeremy Shirokan, one of the newer members of the Board but an active one nonetheless, "I think we should organize ourselves for action in precisely the ways Mrs. Vance-Victor has suggested. In the course of my work in the law, I have had occasion to contract with private investigators of various stripes. I would be glad to take the lead in identifying one or more whose services we could employ."

Armstrong reclaimed the floor. "That sounds to me like a volunteer to chair a working committee to investigate Professor Dickens. Are there others of similar interest?"

And in that manner, three separate committees were formed, the others to focus on finance and strategy.

"If there is no further business, this meeting stands adjourned."

"Hello, is that Madam Professor Hoffbert? Here is Professor Bondarenko telephoning."

Maria was charmed by Lud's not-quite English. "Lud, yes, hello. It's Maria speaking."

"Ah, Maria. I have for you the finished translation of your document. I apologize that it has taken so long. It is, in its way, a little, ah, unusual, one might say. Shall I dispatch it to you through the campus mail?"

"No," she replied. "Best not do that. Let me come up and collect it from you. When might I do that?"

"I am in my office the entire day from now. Any time will be convenient. I have many manuscripts on my desk for review, and any distraction would be welcome, let alone one from such a lovely lady."

Still very old school, she thought. What she said was, "I'm taking a bit of a break myself. Why don't I come up now?"

"That would be a delight. I shall expect you."

Maria made the short walk to South Campus and the climb to Lud's office, where she made the expected small talk and collected both the copy of the Armenian-language text and Lud's translation. Knowing now what it said, he was curious as to what it might mean, but she was truthful when she told him she had no idea whatsoever. After a few minutes, she left and hastened back to her own office, where she immediately picked up the phone and reached out to Chuck Dickens. This time he picked up on the first ring, and it took precisely one exchange of sentences for him to ask Maria to bring the translation to his office at her earliest convenience. So it was that, a mere ten minutes later, she found herself on the seventeenth floor of the sixteen-story engineering building.

"Here it is. Lud seemed pretty sure of the translation. He obviously spent some serious time on it." With that, she handed the document to Chuck.

"I'm sure he did," Chuck said. "Listen. I know exactly what Lud likes and what he wishes he could afford. Could I prevail on you to buy him a bottle of vodka—Beluga Gold Line—as a thank you? It'll set you back a hundred bucks or so, but we'll pick that up as an expense item."

"Absolutely."

"Oh, God. A vodka pun." They both chuckled, he that she would even think of it, she that he would pick up on it. "Now, let's see what we've got here. . . ."

With that, Chuck read through the translation, and as he did so, he could feel his blood pressure rising and his pulse quickening.

"Damn, Maria! This could be it! This could actually be it! These two little pieces of paper we happened upon more or less by chance could be the key to the whole thing. Paul's going to be really excited about this translation. Obviously, we need to figure out who this 'A' or 'Ab' is, and see if we can put this map to use in a real location. Actually finding this box that's referenced and seeing what's in it would be the cherry on the sundae! I need to call Paul right away. Would you mind?" He pointed toward the door. "And thank you. Thank you!"

As an afterthought on her way out the door, Maria turned back and mentioned, "If you need somebody to track this down, I might know just the person." And she was gone.

Mid-Season Form

"Maria, it's Chuck. How are you?"

"I'm doing well. And you? It's been, what, three hours since I last saw you?"

"True. True," he said. "But they've been hours well spent. I did catch up with Paul and we talked about the notes and the translation. As I suspected, he got very excited about everything. And he wants to pursue it, if you'll excuse the expression, balls to the wall."

"Guess that lets me out," she quipped. They had a good laugh.

"Well, not entirely. You mentioned that you knew someone who might be able to figure out this little puzzle. What is he? Or she?" It was a quick recovery. "Some sort of treasure hunter? Detective? Researcher?"

"Actually, he's a writer."

"Ah. Now that could be a problem. You know how Paul is about secrecy. But if I might ask, just who is this fellow?"

"His name is Adam Wallace. He—"

"The guy who did that baseball book? The one with the Hall of Famers and the crazy journal?"

"That's the one."

"I read that book. Honestly, it left me wondering how much of that story was true and how much was marijuana-induced. How do you know him?"

"Adam used to live in the City. Until very recently, as a matter of fact. He and my husband are good buddies. Met at the gym or something, I'm not sure. But you mentioned that crazy journal, as you called it."

"Yeah."

"I was the one who interpreted that hobo code for Adam and his friend."

"No kidding?"

"Cross my heart."

"Okay, so leaving aside, for now, all of the issues with hiring a writer to track down this thing, why do you think Adam Wallace is the guy to do it?"

"Well, if you think about it, Adam and his buddy started with a suitcase full of papers, and they had to make sense of everything. Then they had to locate that journal and find a way to make sense of that. Enter yours truly for a cameo. I expect to be played in the movie by Julia Roberts, made up, of course, to look much younger. But then, and this is really important, at least to me, when they had figured out the whole thing and when Jason—that was Adam's friend—could have found a way to claim maybe millions in recovered value, they both chose to do the honorable thing. They went to the Hall of Fame, which they had determined was the rightful owner, and not only told them the whole story but offered to help them retrieve the papers. Even handed over Jason's granddad's journal. That all really happened, Chuck. At least that's what my husband tells me, and he would know.

"But there was one more thing. There seems to be some baseball connection here of some sort. Something lost in history, most likely. And Adam now has just a bit of expertise in chasing down baseball-related mysteries. At this point, none of us really knows who or what this is all about, and in the end, it might just be the military angle that plays out. But even there, that dimension was present in the journal episode as well. The guy is simply good at what he does, and honest as the day is long."

"All right, I hear you. And that's very helpful information. I still have to worry about the fact that he's a writer. Maybe he can separate his skill sets, maybe not. I'll talk with Paul about it and see what his take is."

<hr/>

Jeremy Shirokan opened his office door to greet his visitor, a rumpled man almost looking the part of the stereotypical investigator. Or, he thought, college professor.

"Jeremy Shirokan. Pleased to meet you."

"Mr. Shirokan, I'm Mike Chaney. Just call me Mike. I was very pleased to get your call."

"Have a seat, Mike. You come highly recommended. I've worked with several investigators over the years, but I have to say I was not familiar with your firm."

"With respect, Jeremy—if I may—that is by design. We try to remain under the radar, whoever may be operating it. Our phones are unlisted, our offices are unmarked, and we never advertise our services. Everything is word of mouth, and I won't ask you who mentioned us to you."

"Excellent. It is precisely that sort of discretion we are after. I represent the directors of the American Theosophy Circle. Have you perchance heard of us? Or perhaps of Theosophy?"

"No, sir, I can't say that I have." Chaney tilted his head to the right and his face took on a quizzical expression.

Shirokan proceeded to set out the connections of his movement to various Eastern religions, its many centers of study around the world, and its thousands of believers. "Our ideas are not as widely accepted as some others," he continued, "especially here in the West, and some look upon us as a marginal religion or even a cult. But we are serious and open-minded people who have simply come to the conclusion that human beings are not yet fully aware of their inherent capacities.

"Now, because we have had so many adherents in so many lands over so many years, many of them intellectuals of one stripe or another, much has been written by and about Theosophy. And because we are driven by a fundamental scientific curiosity, and because we strive to understand the human condition in all of its many dimensions, down through the years many Theosophists have performed research and gathered data testing the limits of our beliefs. Some of them have amassed large collections of such materials. Also, like Circles elsewhere, we maintain a large and publicly accessible library here in the City where our members, but also members of the general public, may come to read and think. Over the years, many donors have contributed their own libraries and research to our collection.

"It is the view of members of our Circle, and, I should add, of our counterparts around the world, that, as they change hands through death or other circumstances, these additional diverse books, papers, and the like ought to become part of one or another established theosophical library so that all may benefit from them. We would, of course, welcome them as outright donations. But we realize that some deceased members of our movement are not positioned to make such offerings. So we maintain an acquisitions budget that, until recently, has proven adequate to obtain them at prices judged fair by all parties.

"I say 'until recently.' Within the last few months, one man who is not a member of our Circle and, insofar as we can tell, is not himself a Theosophist, has traveled the world purchasing such collections as have become available, either privately or at public auction. His funds appear to be, for all practical purposes, unlimited, which is to say that he is easily able and quite willing to outbid us and our colleagues elsewhere. Our entreaties to this man have had no effect on him.

"We do not know what his purpose may be. We do know that, over our history, Theosophists have been singled out in many ways for verbal and other forms of abuse, accused of being everything from Nazis and antisemites to necromancers—lovers of dead bodies—*none* of which, I can assure you, is true. Our fear is that this man may be planning a similar attack, and given the breadth of his acquisitions—few of the contents of which are known to us—he may be contemplating such an attack on a vast scale. You know the old saying: a lie is halfway around the world by the time truth gets its boots on. That is what we fear here—that we will be under an attack so fierce that we may not have the time or opportunity to counter it with truth. And if that is not his purpose, then what is? The sums he is expending are enormous—already well into the millions of dollars."

As he paused for a moment, Chaney interjected, "Okay. I'm getting the picture. Where do I fit in?"

"I was just coming to that. We know very little about this man. His name is James Charles Dickens, and he is a Professor of Engineering at Columbia University. He has a *curriculum vitae* online, so we obviously know the public side of his biography, which seems mundane and, frankly, unrelated to this entire matter. Two of our members, who are themselves engineers, have undertaken to read his publications, and they, too, report no apparent connection to Theosophy. So there must be something more. That's what we want you to find out.

"We want you to develop a profile of this man that goes beyond the obvious. See what you can learn about his finances, his personal life, that sort of thing. See whom he talks with and, if possible, what they discuss. In sum, give us whatever information you can glean that might help us understand this man in ways we might then use to our advantage in countering his activities."

"What kind of time frame are we talking here? Days? Months?"

"Something in between, I should think. To our knowledge, there is no imminent rush. At the same time, we cannot be sure when the next important collection might become available, and we would hope to have our plan of action in place before that happens. The damage to our interests is cumulative, or at least potentially so. And the sooner we can stanch it, the better."

Adam reached across the table for his cell phone as it rang. He'd been dozing on the sofa and was lucky he hadn't banged his head when he awoke with a start. The number flashing on the Caller ID was unfamiliar, but in his world, one took those calls. Some of them proved interesting.

"Hello?" His voice was a little groggy.

"Adam, is that you?" The female voice on the other end was vaguely familiar.

"Yes. This is Adam."

"Adam, hi. It sounds like I woke you. I'm sorry. It's Maria. Maria Hoffbert."

"Maria? Hi. Ah, is Hoffy okay? Is everybody all right?"

"Yes, yes. We're all fine here."

"Well, okay then. Glad to hear it. So what's up?"

"I was calling to give you a heads up. Sometime later today, and maybe fairly soon, you're going to get a call from a guy named Paul Mannington. I wanted to tell you that you should take the call."

"Mannington. Never heard of him. Only Paul Mannington I know of is that tech guy, Paul Chi Mannington, and he isn't going to be calling me. So who is this guy with the knock-off name?"

"Actually, his full name is Paul Chi Mannington. And he *is* that tech guy, as you put it."

"Are you putting me on? Come on, Maria. Did Hoffy put you up to this? I'd have to be completely asleep and dreaming to fall for this one."

"Adam, that's the reason I am calling. David doesn't even know about this—and you must never tell him. When you talk to Mr. Mannington, you will understand. All I can tell you is that I suggested that he call you. What he wants to discuss with you is real, though I do not know exactly what it will be, and if you choose to do what he proposes, you will find it very interesting. Beyond that, I am not in the loop and probably never will be."

It was not twenty minutes later that Adam's phone rang again, this time showing that his Caller ID had been blocked. *Gotta be the guy*, he thought to himself.

"Adam Wallace."

After a brief pause, a woman's voice came on the line. "Hello, this is Rachel. I've been trying to reach you. I'm calling to let you know this is your last chance to extend the warranty on your car. To speak to an agent, press one."

Again! Rachel and her friends were frequent callers and unwilling to take no for an answer. So over time, Adam had begun creating increasingly bizarre narratives to engage the nameless voices who picked up at extension one. He figured he might as well cost them some time and money rather than just hanging up. But today he was expecting a call, so he cut corners and ended the call.

Not a minute later, his phone rang again, and again the Caller ID was blocked. *Great*, he thought. *I've offended poor Rachel and she's calling to let me know.*

Resignedly, he answered. "Adam Wallace."

"Mr. Wallace. This is Paul Mannington. May I assume you were expecting my call?"

"Yes." Adam recovered his wits quickly. "Yes, I was. Maria Hoffbert had given me a heads up."

"I apologize for doing that and also for blocking my number, which you probably noticed. I have found that when I don't have someone clear the way like that, people I don't know whom I cold-call like this, well, they tend to consider it a crank call, and it's hard to convince them otherwise. I guess they just don't believe that I make my own phone calls. Always have."

"Well, I must say," Adam replied, "that would probably have been my first reaction as well, so it's good Maria called ahead, though I admit I am quite curious as to how the two of you know each other."

"Actually, we've never met. But that is for another time."

"Fair enough. How can I—" Adam began but was interrupted. Sometimes cell service was oddly unidirectional, what they used to call in the old days half-duplex. Sometimes callers liked to act as if it were. Hard to tell the difference.

Mannington was in mid-sentence. "—your book on your friend's grandfather and his rather strange journal. I understand that Maria interpreted that for you. And she swears that the story is true, even though it reads like page-turner fiction."

"Oh, yes. It really happened, or something pretty close to it. Poetic license here and there, I'll admit."

"I have to say I was left with the impression, though you never said it in so many words, that the people at the Hall of Fame were the ones who bought those papers at the auction and that they have hidden them away from public view. Do I have that right?"

"Well, you're right. I didn't say it, but I did have my suspicions. As it turned out, though, which I didn't find out until a couple of years later—after the book was published, in fact—I was wrong. It was actually part of something else altogether, and they weren't even involved. Wish I'd known."

"Now *that* sounds like a story I'd like to hear."

"Unfortunately, it's one you never will. After the book came out, I was made privy to some additional information, but I took a vow of silence on that, and I like to keep my vows. Sorry."

Mannington ticked off the last mental box on his list. "Actually, I'm really pleased that you won't tell me. But we'll get to that. Have you made nice with the people at the Hall? I see that you actually live up in Cooperstown now. That could be awkward."

"Yeah, I moved up here from the City a year or so back. And it could really have been awkward, because my wife is a local, and her family has been here since about the 1930s. She runs the family landscaping business, and the Hall is one of their clients.

"When I realized the mistaken impression I had—and, if you are any indicator, had created—I reached out to Roger Coppersmith, the head guy over there to make things right. They were quite gracious about it. As you can imagine, their first reaction when the book came out, as he told me, was outrage. But then they started noticing that people were bringing the book into the museum with them and using it as they looked at the exhibits. And there seemed to be a modest bump in their attendance, and some of the researchers from places like SABR—that's a group of thousands of baseball nerds—were making requests for records that seemed tied to the book. So they decided it was a marketing opportunity for them. They hosted a book signing, which I thought was really nice of them, and they started selling the book in their own bookstore. So, as it's turned out, everything is very friendly."

"Excellent. That's good to know. Now, let me tell you why I've called. I may have a business proposition to put to you, one I hope you will find attractive. For several reasons, I don't want to do that on the telephone, so I'd like to come up there and meet with you one-on-one. Would you be open to that?"

"Are you joking? Of course!"

"I thought you might be. I am actually a major sponsor of the Fenimore Art Museum up there, specifically of the indigenous arts and artifacts collection. But I've never actually visited either the museum or Cooperstown. So I have a built-in excuse for coming up there.

"Now, I have found that when I travel someplace, I tend to attract attention. It simply goes with the territory. But I do need privacy at times, either for meetings or for some personal matters. And I have learned over the years that the best way to hide is often in plain sight. So here's what I'd like to do. I want to drive up there, as that seems to be the only way in, and make a giant spectacle. I want everybody to see me;

basically get it out of their system. So, I'll make a very public visit to the museum, maybe lunch with the director and the curator of that arts exhibit. I'm pretty sure they'll make an accommodation for me even on very short notice. Plus, I really want to see their holdings, which I've heard great things about. Might walk over and do a turn at the Hall of Fame. Give everybody the Paul Chi Mannington treatment, if you know what I mean. But then, I want to sneak away from the hotel and do our meeting. I have ways to do that. But is there someplace in town where we can get together without attracting notice?"

"We can do better. Liz and I actually live on a farm just outside of Cooperstown. It's a ten-minute drive, and once you get off the main road, it's pretty isolated."

"Perfect. I hate to ask this, but will it be possible to meet without your wife present? I really don't want anyone to know about our conversation at this point."

"Ah, sure. Like I said, she runs a business in town. If we do it, say, midafternoon, maybe around two, she'll be hard at it. I'll have some babysitting duties for our son when the nanny gets overwhelmed, but he's not old enough to have any idea what's going on. There might be a couple of interruptions, but that's it."

"Accepted. I'll give you a private email address, and you can send me the coordinates. I'll also send you a cell number where you can reach me if necessary while I'm in town. One last thing. I can put my staff on this, but I have learned to value local knowledge. As I said, I've not visited Cooperstown before. Is there a particularly good place you'd recommend to stay?"

"Actually, a perfect one. The Otesaga Resort is right in the middle of town. It's a lovely spot right on the lake—very picturesque. It's where all the bigwigs and inductees stay when there's big doings at the Hall. Rooms are nice, food's great. Goes way back. I think it opened ten years or so before my wife's family moved to town. I always feel like I'm playing a part in *The Great Gatsby* when I'm in the place. And if you're a golfer, bring your clubs. I don't play, but their course is eye candy."

"Never had the time for golf. But the hotel sounds perfect. Is there a big public parking lot, or just a garage?"

"It's all outdoors and public. Plus the museum is maybe two minutes down the road by car, and the Hall is maybe ten the other way by foot. The walk takes you right through the center of the Village, which sounds like it might fit your scheme nicely."

"Indeed. Let me have my aide set this all up for, shall we say, next Tuesday and Wednesday, and you and I can meet on Thursday. Will that work for you?"

"Absolutely."

"Great. I look forward to meeting you. Cheers."

And just like that, he was gone. Adam's curiosity went on a sugar high.

Mike Chaney turned to his colleague with a puzzled expression on his face. "You ever seen anything like this?"

"Not really. I mean, usually we can find something just by hanging around. But not this guy."

"Okay, so he's a Columbia professor. But hardly anybody on campus seems to know him. We think he has an office in the engineering school, because he seems to go there every morning and leave every evening, but he's not on the building directory. And we can't just roam around the halls looking for him, because the place is guarded like Fort Knox. So we follow him after work, and he lives in a nice brownstone on the West Side, but we can't find a neighbor willing to take a little compensation to talk about him. He never seems to shop, so somebody must do that for him, but we don't know who or where or what for. He's not a pretentious dresser or a big drinker. Never talks on his cell while he's outside, or at least not that we've seen, so we can't intercept his SIM ID to listen in. I hate to say it, but I think the only thing we have left to try is a honey trap."

"You thinking of Margot?"

"Too young. Especially if we tried to set it up on campus. Something tells me this guy would steer away from anybody who looked young enough to be a student. I think we have to look early thirties or something close to that if we're on the low side. Maybe Francine. But not yet.

We're going to have to come up with a really solid cover and backstory. We're only likely to have one shot at this, and I don't want to rush into it and make a mistake."

"It's always possible he likes boys, you know. Well, men. I don't think we can rule that out at this point, do you?"

"No, but it does give us something to watch for. On the tails, let's make a point of noting anything that turns his head, that sort of thing. And in the meantime, we can start building a persona, one that can go either way when the time comes."

"You plan to run this past the client?"

"Nah. Something tells me they wouldn't want to know about this. They seem pretty straight-arrow when it comes to surveillance techniques. Want it done, but don't want to know how. You know the type."

"Like most of our clientele. If only they all knew what a dirty business this can be."

"I, for one, am not telling."

"Albany Tower, this is Gulfstream November 1674 on final for runway one zero. Request permission to land."

"November 1674, Albany Tower. Clear to land runway one zero. Visibility 4 miles, winds one one zero at 12 knots. Contact Ground on 121.7."

"Albany Tower, Roger. November 1674."

And just like that, the silver-gray Gulfstream G700 with the burgundy Greek letter Chi on the tail touched down, taxied to the right, and came to a halt in the general aviation area. Paul Mannington removed his headset, unstrapped the belt, and pulled himself out of the left-hand seat, while his regular copilot, Scott Witten, flipped the switch to open the forward door and lower the stairway. Paul left the flight deck and exited the plane. Scott would later taxi the Gulfstream to a more remote parking area that he had prearranged with the airport manager.

At the foot of the stairs, he watched as a sturdy-looking young man outfitted in what might best be described as dress coveralls, or at least a finely pressed set, removed several large protective padded bumpers, pulled the fitted cover from the vehicle on the flatbed of the specially outfitted standard-duty Jerr-Dan car carrier, tilted the bed to the pavement, and ever so carefully released the tension on the hoist that had held the vehicle in place for the drive up from the City. He detached the hook from the special fitting on the underside of the car, then retracted the hoist chain and lifted the flatbed back into position in preparation for his return down the interstate to the Apex rental facility in the City. Even Paul did not know exactly where the Apex garage was located, a wise precaution given their fleet of truly special vehicles. On the tarmac stood the precise vehicle he had requested: a new Bugatti Veyron Super Sport, matte black over orange. 1,200 horses, 1,500 Newton meters of torque in the critical RPM range, zero to 100 in two and a half seconds if you could shift gears that quickly, and capable of a speed approaching the cruising speed of the Gulfstream. It was a real eye-catcher and, equally important for the present mission, the exhaust did not hide itself when the sixteen-cylinder, 8,000-cubic-centimeter engine revved up. Anybody driving this vehicle on or off a race track was certain to be noticed. The perfect apparent toy for one of the world's richest men to seem to be showing off his wealth.

Paul signed papers for the young man, who then passed him a set of keys. He offered the Apex driver assurances that he was familiar with the particulars of the Veyron, which earned him a knowing smile in return. "You drive safely, now, sir."

"Thank you. I'll see you back here Thursday evening, day after tomorrow. I'm not sure yet what time, but someone will call that in."

Paul tossed his carry-on bag and briefcase onto the passenger seat and slipped into the well-padded driver's seat of the vehicle—it didn't seem right to call a machine like this a "car"—and turned over the ignition. The engine roared into action. He loved these Bugattis. Had two of them at home, in fact, though none in this particular color scheme, which he found to his liking.

Paul navigated his way down Old Naskayuna Road, around the traffic rotary at Watervleit Shaker Road, and down to Albany Shaker Road, where he made the right and the left that got him onto the southbound Northway. Between the Indian names and the old Dutch names and going south on something called the Northway, he thought, it's a wonder these people could find their way around at all. At least the airport was west of town, and he didn't have to try to protect the Bugatti in downtown traffic. He picked up the thruway west and, after that, selected the southern route across the state on I-88. And suddenly there he was, with 1,200 horses under bridle and spur and almost no traffic on the highway. He reached into his briefcase, felt for his portable radar detector, and placed it on the dash. Then he activated the configuration that Bugatti blithely referred to as "handling," which opened the front diffuser flaps, shifted his way up to seventh, and off he went. Twenty-three minutes later, he was in Colliersville and watching for the Route 28 turnoff.

Route 28 offered its own delicious challenges. It was a relatively narrow two-lane highway, so Paul put the radar detector away and dropped his speed back by nearly three-quarters. But the road was anything but straight, and he used the opportunity to power the Bugatti through the curves and test its handling. For all practical purposes, the road ended at Cooperstown, and he flashed into town in an orange blur, downshifting to break his speed in the noisiest possible manner. Next best thing to Jake Brakes.

Paul followed his GPS guidance through the lefts and rights that took him into the very center of the Village, then on to the hotel. Even purring like a mama lion, the Super Sport drew attention. Purrfect.

As Adam had said, all of the Otesaga parking was outside, off to the left of the hotel itself. There was a long circular drive in front of the building and, doubtless, bellhops and a valet parking service. But Paul worried that a valet might try to hide the car out of sight to protect it from prying eyes, something that, in other circumstances, he would greatly appreciate. This time, though, he wanted the car to be seen, especially when it was sitting out in the parking lot. So he found a space near the building but in full view, one with a curb to one side and open parking on the other, and parked it himself. He grabbed his bag and briefcase, locked the Bugatti, and headed for the nearest entrance to the building. That proved to be nearby on the ground floor. He went in and, following the signage, took the elevator up one level and turned right to the front desk. Before he could take more than three steps, a woman stepped out from behind the desk and walked toward him.

"Mr. Mannington! Welcome to the Otesaga. I'm Charlotte Webber, manager of the hotel. We're honored that you are staying with us."

"Thank you. That's very nice."

"No need to check in, sir. Your staff already took care of all the details by phone. We have you in our Grand Lake View Suite. I hope that will be satisfactory."

"I'm sure it will."

"James will take your bags and show you the way. James!"

A bellman in his middle years approached, key in hand, and reached for Paul's bag and briefcase. "Do you have any other luggage, sir? I can have someone collect it for you."

"No, this is all there is. But thank you."

The pair made their way to an expansive suite with a view of the lake beyond the hotel. James went through his customary welcoming spiel, making sure to demonstrate the many features of the suite and to advise the guest of dining and other options. All of these, of course, were also covered in the hotel literature, which is where Paul, like most guests, would eventually seek out any information of real interest. As James made to leave, Paul did what billionaires are supposed to do and slipped him a crisp hundred-dollar bill. As he did so, he wondered what the competition had been like to be the bellman assigned to this particular guest.

"Thank you very much, sir. And if you should need anything else, please just dial the bell captain. There's a designated button on the phone." And with that, he was gone.

Paul smiled, kicked off his shoes, cracked the bottle of Pappy Van Winkle's Family Reserve that had been placed on the wet bar on the instructions, no doubt, of his travel staff, threw some cubes into a glass, poured a generous portion, tested to find the most comfortable chair, and sat down to unwind. So far, everything was going exactly to plan.

"Gotcha!"

It was Chaney himself who picked up the tell. Dickens was headed for the Broadway IRT stop just outside the university's main gate at 116th when he passed a slim brunette on the sidewalk headed in the other direction. If he'd been tailing from behind, the old-fashioned way, he never would have caught the sideways glance and appreciative smile. But Dickens's one flaw so far was his predictability, and after a couple of weeks, that had allowed the team to anticipate his movements and, as in this case, tail from in front, or really from the side at various well-chosen waypoints. Finally they had something they could work with.

He texted his trailing operative: **Brunette, 25ish, slim. Observations and photo ASAP. M.** A block back, a man in a tan London Fog raincoat read the text, identified the young woman as she approached him, secured three photos, and studied her with a practiced subtlety. She walked on, never realizing she had been the object of so much attention or, for that matter, of any.

After seeing their quarry home and safely under wraps, the three investigators gathered over dinner and draughts at a pizza place near the professor's apartment. As always, Chaney led the conversation.

"Okay, forget Margot and Francine. This girl is almost a dead ringer for Bethany. Let's get it set up.

"We need to do this someplace where he's entirely comfortable. I think maybe that campus dining room he goes to for lunch three or four times a week could work. Anybody can walk in there, and there's enough tables to try a targeting setup. Girl sits alone facing boy, empty table nearby, that sort of thing. We'll need an interesting name, something even an engineering geek would perk up at. How about . . . Dakota?"

"Man, *I'd* want to pick up a Dakota!" offered one of his companions.

"Agreed," said his colleague.

"Okay," Chaney resumed, "so Bethany, with ID for Dakota something . . . Dakota . . . Rand! Dakota Rand. Rand is suggestive without saying 'randy,' which is just what we need. Now, what's she doing at Columbia? From someplace out West . . . Utah, I think. Colorado's too obvious. Nice dresser, not fancy, not provocative, but maybe just a little cleavage or leg. Glasses, I think, so she looks anything but aggressive. Frames will have to be carefully chosen. Bethany has the goods, and she'll know how to play it. Came into town to meet her younger brother, who's a doctoral student in . . . ornithology, or something like that that's obscure and not anywhere near engineering. Make sure they teach it somewhere at Columbia. Got to town, only to discover that he's off in Africa on a field trip for the next . . . year. Let's make it a year, so no chance he'll drop out of the sky. Staying at the . . . Beacon. That's at Seventy-Fifth and Broadway, right? Not next door, but easy walking distance from his place. Sitting there confused, and disappointed, and trying to decide what to do. What do you guys think?"

"There's a reason you're the boss, Mike. How do you do it?"

"I live a rich fantasy life, boys, a rich fantasy life. Unfortunately, this is the only way I get to do it in the real world." They all laughed.

"Cheesecake," he said, addressing the rumpled man who had taken the photos, "you make this happen within about three days, right?"

"You got it, Mike."

"And make sure you get her a prepaid cell and a Gmail address. This could run for several days, and we need to have comms covered. I'll call Bethany and clue her in, tell her you'll be calling. That way, she won't think you're just hitting on her. Another round, boys?"

When Paul had turned the key to the Veyron at the airport, it was the familiar vibration of a warming powerhouse that he felt. The rumble of the engine had been lost among the taxiing jets and other airport noises, or at the very least, had seemed of a place. But here, in the parking lot of the Otesaga, with the reverberation off the side of the building, it was the rumble of those sixteen cylinders, deep and pure, that struck the senses. And not merely his own senses. As he started the Bugatti, several heads turned, and as he crawled through and out of the parking lot, an equal number of heads turned. Once again, mission accomplished.

He made the requisite right turn and drove the short mile down the road to the Fenimore Museum. When his staff had made the arrangements for this quick visit, the museum director had offered to provide VIP parking, but on Paul's instructions, the offer was declined. The general public parked on the long circular drive in front of the building when visiting, and that was precisely where he wanted to leave the Bugatti. *Look at that car! I heard that Paul Chi Mannington is in town. I wonder if he's here at the museum.* Exactly.

A luncheon in Paul's honor had been arranged on short notice, and with the weather cooperating, it was held in the rear courtyard of the museum, which offered Paul a sweeping view of the extensive, perfectly landscaped grounds and of the placid waters of Lake Otsego beyond. It also offered strollers on those grounds a view of Paul himself, which served not only his purpose but that of the Fenimore, which could show off and photograph its prominent benefactor—good for the museum's standing and a potential attraction for other prospective donors. After lunch and a few brief words all around, Paul toured the indigenous arts and artifacts collection with the director and the curator of the collection and found it to be every bit as impressive as he had expected. When his guides offered to continue the tour by visiting the other areas of the museum, however, Paul demurred by the simple expedient of saying that he had been so taken with what he had seen so far that he had lost track of time and needed to move on to his next commitment. Everyone thanked everyone, Paul handed the director a personal check with six zeroes on it, pocket change, absorbed a minute or two of groveling, and off he went.

The Bugatti went back to the hotel parking lot, this time in a more exposed space some distance from the building. Paul went back to his suite to catch up on texts and emails and spend a few minutes relaxing, then it was on to phase two of hiding in plain view. He changed into jeans and some L.L. Bean Trail IV walking shoes, and headed out through the lobby, down the circular walk to the left, and on a zigzag course to Main Street and along a couple of blocks of shops and restaurants until he came to the other large museum in town, the National Baseball Hall of Fame. Never much of a baseball fan, he'd not visited before, but when in Rome, as the saying went. Besides, he was enough of a history buff that he figured he'd find a few things of interest.

He climbed the steps, passed through the great door labeled "General Admission," and found himself in a large lobby area with a couple of admission counters off to his left. If Paul had been in stealth mode, he could have pulled a baseball cap down over his face, paid a small admission fee to cover the day's visit, and walked through to the collection, all very anonymous. But today he was in show mode, as he thought of it, so instead he purchased a "Benefactor" membership, which cost a grand but, more importantly, required that he provide some identifying information. The clerk looked up when he did this but completed the task at hand without comment and issued Paul his membership card. Accepting this with thanks, he moved beyond the check-in point to begin his tour of the plaques, gear, and other reminiscences.

While the admissions clerk may have remained calm in the moment, she sprang into action as soon as Paul had passed through the entrance to the collection and down the hall to the right. She was immediately on the phone to the museum director's office, and soon he was on the floor and tracking his quarry. He caught up with Paul on the second level, in front of the glass case featuring some of the oldest items in the collection—Christy Mathewson's glove, a ratty and browned-out remnant of a baseball, and some others, none less than a hundred years old and some much older. He seemed particularly interested in the old leather ball.

"Pardon me for interrupting, but you are Paul Chi Mannington, are you not?"

"Guilty as charged," Paul replied.

"Please allow me to introduce myself. I'm Bill Walsh, director of the museum. I understand that you have just become one of our Benefactor members, and I wanted to catch up with you so that I could offer my personal thanks. We are very honored to have you in our Hall of Fame family."

"Well thank you. I figured if I was in Cooperstown, I couldn't leave without a visit over here."

"If there's anything I can help you with, just say the word."

"Actually, there is one thing. What's the story with this old baseball here? Was this the ball Abner Doubleday used for the first baseball game?"

"Ah," replied Walsh. "I'm afraid that's a long and winding story. The long and short of it is that, back when the Hall was founded, the belief was that Doubleday had set down the structure of the modern game here in Cooperstown back in 1839. The Hall was opened precisely a hundred years later, so you can see why that story was appealing. Over the years, though, many people criticized that story and, in candor, largely disproved it. But back around 1900, Albert Spalding wanted to claim the game was completely American and not a spinoff from an earlier English game with similar play. So he sponsored a commission to investigate, and the commission got a letter from a fellow named Abner Graves, who said he was here in Cooperstown when Doubleday did the deed. Doubleday was something of a war hero, you know. That was all they needed. They decided Graves's claim was both true and determinative. Now, Graves was an odd duck, and he didn't offer a lot of proof. But years after he died, somebody else sent in this baseball, claiming they had found it in an old house Graves had once occupied. They claimed it was the Doubleday ball. So we presented it that way for a while. But as you can see, we now treat it simply as an old ball, and it surely is that."

"Fascinating. Fascinating. Thank you so much."

"Mr. Mannington, would—"

"Paul. Please, just Paul."

"Thank you. Paul . . . would you mind if I put in a call to our COO, Roger Coppersmith? I'm not sure he's in town, but if he is, I'm sure he'd love to meet you."

"Well, sure. Okay. I hadn't planned on raising a fuss when I came in," said Paul, savoring the little white lie, "but that'd be okay, I guess. But just a hello. Nothing fancy, if you know what I mean. I'm just here for the collection."

"Absolutely. And you enjoy the rest of your visit."

Walsh was gone, and not three minutes had passed before an older gentleman in full business attire replaced him. So it was in the land of the rich and famous.

"We're all set up, boss. We've got a couple of video positions so we can follow the action, and Bethany is wired. We've got her over toward a corner, and there are two empty tables, one on either side. Dickens isn't there yet, so we have a guy in a maintenance uniform stationed in a spot where he can discourage anybody else from using those empty tables. He'll tell them he's waiting for a supervisor to decide how they should clean up from something that happened earlier. That ought to do it."

The text reached all of the members of the team a minute or two later. The subject was entering the building and heading for the restaurant.

Almost at that moment, he came into view, then headed for one of the self-service stations, grabbing a tray and some utensils as he went. Obviously a practiced routine, and a man who knew just what he wanted for lunch. There was a bit of a line at the serving station he had chosen, so it was nearly five minutes before he made his way to the cashiers and paid for his food. Then he emerged into the dining area and looked around for a place to sit.

Just then, a raised hand and a wave caught his eye, and he moved off to the left to join some colleague or student he obviously knew who, as it happened, was seated at a table with an empty spot.

"Damn!" The same word simultaneously escaped the lips of three operatives scattered around the room.

Bad luck. Shut it down. We'll try again tomorrow, read the text to the group. Suddenly, the maintenance problem seemed to have been solved and the spotters began to gather their things to make an exit.

For her part, however, Bethany remained in her place, where she turned more directly to face the room.

"Hold it!" exclaimed Mike to a colleague who had just joined him.

"What the hell is she doing?"

Both turned to the one video feed still operating.

"Damn it. She's working the room. Kenny, get over there before she gives some math wonk a heart attack. Shut it down, and tell her from me that nice girls from Utah don't do what she just did, and if I see it again, she'll never work in this town. Got that?"

"Got it."

From the girl's-gotta-try shrug and half-smile Bethany flashed at the camera, Chaney concluded that she had clearly heard the words but also that he might have to have a talk with her himself before the next morning's setup.

<hr>

Thursday morning dawned gray but not wet. Paul hung the Do Not Disturb sign on his door, and for good measure, called both the front desk and housekeeping to make the point that he had important work to do and that he was not to be disturbed under any circumstances. Then he pasted a mustache on his lip, threw on a well-worn pair of jeans and a plaid shirt, donned a pair of large, dark Reebok sunglasses, and pulled the previously eschewed, nondescript baseball cap low over his eyes. After checking the mirror and making a couple of adjustments, he grabbed the ice bucket from the wet bar in case he needed it as a cover, opened the door to check the hallway, and, finding it clear, chucked the ice bucket back into the room, pulled the door closed, and headed for the stairwell nearest the parking area.

Once there, he checked to make sure the Bugatti was in its place. After all, if the orange and black Bugatti was in the parking lot, Paul Chi Mannington was obviously somewhere in the hotel. He then headed for a far corner of the lot, where he found the magnetic gray metallic Toyota Highlander that had been stashed there by prearrangement. The key was hidden in the agreed spot, and in well under a minute, he was in the SUV with the engine purring. It was the perfect vehicle for its purpose—nice enough that it was not out of place in the resort parking lot, yet mundane enough that no one would give it a second glance. It was time to go to work.

Once again, everything was in place. Chaney had made clear to Bethany for a second time the nature of her role play, and even though she was dressed to attract, she looked somehow more demure, at least to his eye. The "maintenance specialist" had managed to chase away three or four students from the empty tables, including one young man who clearly had his eyes on Bethany and was reluctant to go elsewhere. The rag scented with Deer Scram that had been provided for just such an occasion made quick work of the young man and his libido. So far, so good. Dickens had just been spotted entering the building, and the lines were shorter today as well. Mike felt like a NASA flight controller waking up on launch day to find that the winds had died down and the clouds had cleared. Their luck held, as the professor drifted to his right this time, looking for a safe landing zone. He noticed Bethany and the adjacent tables just as maintenance completed its work, and ever so subtly but decidedly worked his way in their direction. He sat down half facing her and set the book he had been carrying on the table. It was just as he opened it and began to read that the attractive young lady at the next table sobbed ever so quietly. He looked up just in time to catch her dabbing at her eyes with her napkin.

"I don't mean to intrude, miss. But is everything all right?"

She looked up, and as New Yorkers are trained from birth to do, started to pick up her things and walk away. Then she slumped back into her chair. Chaney could not help but admire her work. Bethany knew just how to set the hook.

"Sorry," said Dickens and turned back to his book. A moment passed.

"No," she said. He looked up. "It's okay. It's just . . . It's my brother, my little brother."

"I'm sorry. Did something happen to him?"

"Happen to him? No. He's probably as happy as he can be. That's the problem. He's a grad student here, working on a Ph.D. in ornithology."

"Ornithology?" Dickens asked. He meant simply to make sure he had heard correctly, but she took it as his not knowing the word.

"Yes, you know, bird studies. He got into birds in high school. God knows why. Real geek about it. Carried around a pair of binoculars, which was way past weird, and I don't know how many science papers and projects he did—always on birds. Everybody took to calling him Bird Man, at least the ones that didn't call him Bird Brain. You know how high school is. Studied geography in college, I guess, so he could learn where the birds live. Who knows? Then he got accepted at Columbia and he ended up where he started—ornithology. Ecology, Evolution, and something-something, but basically, birds."

"Sounds quite dedicated."

"Yes. I'm sorry. I love him to death, and I don't mean to rag on him like this. He found what he enjoys in life, and he's going after it in a big way. Lucky him. No, the problem is, I just flew into New York from home to surprise him. I haven't seen him in a couple of years, and I thought we could have some fun, see the sights. You know. So I booked a hotel for three weeks, and I got a deal on airline tickets and here I am.

"So this morning I showed up at his apartment, but he wasn't there. Then I came over here to try to find him, and I did find this little shared office space he has. But this woman he was sharing it with looked at me like I was crazy. 'Ethan?' she says. 'Don't you know that Ethan is in Eswatini?' she says. 'I don't even know how to mix an Eswatini,' I told her, and she curled up her lip and looked at me like I was the most ignorant person on Earth, and she says, 'Eswatini is a place. You might still know it as Swaziland. It's over in Africa. You know that big continent just below Europe? He has a grant to study the birds living along the big bend in Great Isutu River.' By now, I am really not liking this person, but I still had to ask one more question. 'Do you know when he'll be back?' So she says, 'Duh. He just left last week, so he'll be back in one week less than a year.'

"I just looked at her and turned and left. I guess if I was from New York, I'd have handled it differently, had some quick come-back to put her in her place. But where I come from, well, people just don't act like that. I just didn't know what to do, so I left. Started walking around, and ended up in here. It was a place to sit down, at least, over in this corner where nobody else could . . . could . . ."

At this, she teared up again.

"Come on. Not everybody in New York is like that. She was probably just having a bad day. Or maybe she was jealous of your brother. Sounds like he's pretty successful, and she's spending the day in a dreary cubicle. At least I assume it was dreary. Most of the grad cubicles on this campus are."

Bethany smiled a little and sniffled. "I guess. Thanks for trying to cheer me up. But I'm afraid it doesn't solve my problem. I've missed my brother and won't see him for at least another year. And I am stuck in New York for three weeks and I don't know a soul, and the one person I did meet was a . . . was a . . . was a bitch. There, I said it. Sorry."

Chuck smiled. "Hey, it's New York. No offense taken!"

That produced a smile in return.

"Besides," he added, "you do, too, know someone in New York. I'm Charles Dickens. Don't ask. Chuck to my friends." He reached out his right hand.

"Dakota. Dakota Rand," she said, smiling at him and gently shaking his hand.

"Dakota. That's an interesting name. Is that where you're from?"

"No. When I was a little girl, my parents used to tell me that they were sitting around waiting for my mom to, you know, start her contractions, and when it happened, they were watching some movie about outlaws in the Black Hills. And they liked the movie so much, or at least the setting, they decided to name me Dakota. When I was a little older, I got the real story. Turns out they were vacationing in the Black Hills when they, well, you know. And they decided to commemorate that when they named me. Can you believe that?"

Chuck laughed. "Well, I like it. And I love that story. Where are you from?"

"Utah, actually. Tiny place called Evanston. Hour and a half or so east of SLC. Sorry, Salt Lake City. My folks run a restaurant there. I teach third grade."

"Utah. I don't know if I have ever met anyone from Utah before. Lot of Mormons there, right?"

"Yep. Not us, but there are surely lots of them. What about you? You work at the university? I guess so, since you're in here."

"Yeah, this is kind of my go-to spot for lunch. I'm afraid I'm something of a geek, too. I'm in the engineering school."

"What do you engineer?"

"Oh, you name it. If it's something obscure, you can bet I'll try to figure out how it works."

"Sounds fascinating."

"So you're stuck in town for three weeks. Where did you say you're staying?"

"I didn't. It's a little hotel down at . . . Broadway and Seventy-Fifth? The Beacon. I figured Ethan was living up here close to campus, and I could just run up and down on the subway to spend some time with him."

"Broadway and Seventy-Fifth? Really? Listen, that's only a few blocks from where I live. I'm in the eighties. How about I pick you up at your hotel at, say, 7:30 this evening and we can find a place to grab some dinner. At least you won't be alone on your first night in town."

"Actually, I got in last night. But I have a better idea. I told you my folks are in the restaurant business. Well, I know my way around a kitchen pretty good. How about we pick up some supplies and maybe a bottle of wine, and I cook you up a nice dinner at your place? I really would feel at home getting into a kitchen. It's kind of where I go when I need to relax, and I need to relax a lot after dealing with thirty or so third graders all day. Oh, jeez, I just realized. This is New York. Does your place even *have* a kitchen?"

Chuck could not believe that the gods of fortune had chosen to shine so brightly upon him. "Oh yes, I have a kitchen. I have to run. But I'll pick you up at the Beacon Hotel at 7:30 and we'll walk our way up Broadway with a shopping bag."

"I'll be there with bells on," said Bethany/Dakota, smiling broadly. *And very little else*, she thought to herself. A moment later she glanced across the room to see Mike Chaney grinning from ear to ear.

The Highlander was a capable vehicle but inevitably a constant, boring reminder to keep both his head and his speed down. Paul programmed Adam's address into his portable GPS and followed the turn-by-turn directions until he reached the highway, then watched for the landmarks as he neared the turnoff for the farm. As Adam had said, precisely 1.7 miles down that last country lane, he came to the turnoff for Fairchild Farms. A second sign with an arrow pointed to A. Holt Greenstick Landscaping. A smaller sign below read, Shops and Greenhouses Only. He turned in and continued to the farmhouse ahead on the left. Leaving the Highlander parked beside the road, he climbed to the porch, with its rockers, gliders, and what looked like a giant inflated . . . *what is that*? He knocked on the door, which was opened almost as he touched it.

"Saw you coming," said the man who answered. "You must be Mr. Mannington."

"Paul," he replied. "And I assume you are Adam."

They went into the cozy living room and nestled into a pair of comfortable chairs.

"Sorry for the mess," said Adam. "One-year-old and stay-at-home dad. Enough said? Can I get you something to drink?"

"A soda would be nice. Almost anything. Or, you know, just some plain club soda over ice if you have that."

"I'm pretty sure we do."

They did, and once the drinks were sitting on a pair of coasters that Liz would have insisted he use if she were home, they settled in to talk.

"Paul, I have to say, you have my curiosity running in high gear. It's not every day we have a guest of your stature in our living room."

"Actually," said Paul, "I've been looking forward to this ever since I read your book."

"Baseball fan?"

"No, not really. But I love a good story, especially if it involves a measure of mystery, and I must say, you left me wondering there at the end. Still won't tell me what you found out later, even after I flew all the way across the country to talk with you?"

"Paul, I wish I could. But I'm just not free to do that. It would be a violation of trust."

"Good answer, and that, along with the way you and your buddy Jason figured out that puzzle his granddad had left him, is pretty much the reason I'm here.

"I have five documents with me, and two of them, unfortunately, we have to talk about right now off the bat. The first one's a nondisclosure agreement. I imagine you're familiar with them. In fact, it sounds like you might have signed at least one of these things not that long ago. In any event, if we continue our conversation, I'm going to end up sharing with you some information that you must never, under any circumstances, reveal without my personal, written permission. Now to be clear, I am not saying you can never reveal it, but I am saying that you must have my written permission before you do, and you must abide by any restrictions that I put in place at that time. Can you agree to that?"

Adam thought for a long moment. "Paul," he said at last, "I'm a writer by trade. It's what I do. And—"

Paul held up his hand. "I know. I get it. And that's why I included a carve-out for future release to the public. I actually want you to write about your experiences as you follow up on our conversation. And I may very well want you to publish some or all of that work. So that gets me to the second document." He laid a second sheaf of papers on the table.

"This is a personal services agreement. You can take some time to read it, but basically it says that I am contracting you to perform certain personal services for me. Those services include, but are not limited to, preparation of a book-length manuscript of publishable quality. There's a list of other work I'll want you to pursue. I will agree, through one of my companies, to serve as the publisher of said manuscript, but I will reserve the ownership and the exclusive and unappealable right to decide whether or not to publish the completed work in whole or in part. In effect, the book will be work for hire, so your name will be on it, but I will own all of the rights. In exchange for this, I will pay you a fixed minimum fee and, if the book is published, this fee will convert automatically to a de facto non-refundable advance against royalties. So you can never be worse off than the amount we agree on, and if we publish the book and it's a best-seller and maybe even a successful motion picture, well, you might do much better still. Does this sound like something you can live with?"

"What it sounds is complicated. Let me take a few minutes to read through all of this and make sure I understand it."

"Of course. Take all the time you need. And when you get down to the end, you'll see that the minimum fee I propose is $200,000. And of course, you will be reimbursed for any and all expenses."

———

Chuck had found himself all but totally distracted when he returned to his office, so there was little lost productivity when he decided to leave early—around three-thirty, in fact—to head back to his place and tidy up. A lot. He hoped it was enough, that he had not missed some isolated pocket of grossness that Dakota would stumble upon. He made the bed, tidied the living area, scrubbed the pots, made sure the wine glasses were spotless, checked the silverware for residual grunge—in sum, all the things he seldom attended to under normal circumstances. Then he showered, shaved for a second time that day, and dressed in a pointedly casual outfit. That took him until about seven, so he headed downstairs, walked up to the corner, and hailed a cab to take him the few blocks down Broadway.

The Beacon Hotel was not, he concluded, much to look at, and as he sat in the small lobby, he detected the slight mustiness and look of decay that was part and parcel of almost any older building on the Upper West

Side. But when she appeared in the lobby a few minutes later and they exited to the street, Dakota assured him that it was not that bad. Quite nice, she said. At least on a Utah teacher's salary. Once again, the hook was set, though, to his credit, Mike was not listening in this time.

The pair worked their way up Broadway, picking up odds and ends. At Eightieth Street, she was curious about Zabar's, which she said she had heard of, so they went in and had some fun selecting cheeses and a few other specialty items. And when they reached Eighty-Second Street, they detoured across to Amsterdam and the West 82nd Grocery, where they did some serious provisioning. From there, it was back to Broadway and a short walk uptown to his apartment, which was, in reality, the entire second floor of a brownstone on West Eighty-Fourth just off Broadway down toward the river.

"Wow," she exclaimed as he went to set the bags down on the kitchen counter. "This is gorgeous. How long have you lived here?"

"Couple of years. The house is kind of a condo on a small scale. I was able to buy the second floor, and I fixed it up, but just a little. These brownstones in this neighborhood are classics, and you don't want to mess with them too much."

"That must have set you back! Sorry, I don't mean to pry. It's just that you hear so much about the cost of New York real estate. Even out in Utah."

"Well, I've been lucky, and I was able to do it. I enjoy my work, but it's a nice place to come home to."

"How about some wine and a tour?"

"You bet. Red or white?"

"Umm. Lamb for dinner. That's kind of neutral. Red, I think."

"Perfect. I have a couple of bottles of a '16 Robert Mondavi Oakville Cabernet that is really delightful. Cab work for you?"

"Absolutely."

"The '16 Oakville it is. Want to cut the cheese?" They both realized the double meaning of what he'd said at the same instant and broke out laughing. Chuck turned just the littlest bit red.

"You are starting to look like the Cab," Dakota observed. Good for another laugh. Chuck was starting to like this girl, and on top of that to think that she might like him a bit as well.

"Tell you what. I will *prepare* the cheese to be served with those crostini we bought at Zabar's, but first I want a tour of your castle. I'm curious about the turret in the front there. What's that about?" Bethany had been in any number of these old brownstones, and she knew exactly what it was about.

"Oh, that's the master bedroom. Actually, for me, the only bedroom. I use the other one, in back, for an office of sorts. I hope it's picked up enough so I won't be embarrassed."

"I'm sure it's fine."

And with that, they took a walk around the apartment. While Dakota pretended to study the art on the walls, he pretended not to study her. They did exchange glances while in the turret, and a giggle, but neither was anxious to make a move on the other. They peeked into the room used as an office, which featured an Apple Mac Pro with an enormous monitor, a multifunction printer, a small writing desk, and several boxes which she assumed were filled with papers.

"You do much work here?" she asked.

"Sometimes I'll bring something home. But most of my work can't leave the office."

"Sounds mysterious," she teased.

"Nah. Pretty tedious, really, and like I said, I like to come back here to escape."

"I just noticed. You don't have a television!"

"Caught me. I just don't find very much there that I want to watch. It's all sports and movies they've shown twenty times before. But I confess, I do like to stream some of the newer ones on the computer. Reason I got that big screen. It has amazing resolution. I can show you later if you like. There are just so many streaming services these days, you really don't need a dedicated TV."

"Boy, you really are an engineer!"

Another shared laugh, and he liked that it was on him—that she felt sufficiently relaxed in his presence to make a joke at his expense. This could be a most interesting three weeks.

Bethany/Dakota was not kidding around in the kitchen. She really was quite a gourmet cook. As they both sipped their wine and nibbled at the cheese, she did things to lamb he had never imagined, and when the food was plated and they were digging in, he thought his taste buds had died and gone to heaven.

"Is this what the food is like at your parents' place in Utah?" he asked.

"That's where I learned to do it," she replied. "People actually drive out from SLC to Evanston on a weekend just to come to the restaurant."

"I might have to do that myself!" Chuck exclaimed. She just smiled.

***

Adam read through the nondisclosure agreement and the contract, trying to focus on the language but admittedly distracted by the sum Paul had named. And he was torn. He had perhaps five minutes to make a decision before he risked offending his would-be benefactor/client, and suddenly he realized he was being forced to choose among the motives that drove him as a writer. Discovery. Creativity. Social Gratification. Money. Obviously, Paul Mannington was offering money, and it sounded as if discovery might be another possible reward. It was hard to say about creativity, though he clearly would be expected to write *something*. Unclear just what, though. And as for social gratification, as for connecting with an audience and feeling appreciated, well, that just might be off the table.

That is when Hef wandered into the room. He'd been napping two rooms away and had somehow managed to edge off the small youth bed they had moved him to recently, escape from captivity, and find his way to the living room.

"Aha!" said Paul. "The young Mr. Wallace approaches!"

Adam was a little embarrassed, but Paul put him right at ease. "I love kids, as long as they're not mine and I don't have to tend to them."

"Well, I'm afraid I do. But I'll just be a minute or two." He lifted up his son and carried him back into the depths of the house.

There was obviously someone else back there, out of sight and earshot, and Paul could just barely make out the sound of a brief discussion, but not the content.

"Sorry about that," said Adam, returning. Hef's unexpected appearance had broken his concentration, but it had also solved his dilemma.

There was college to think about, for Hef and any brothers or sisters he might chance to have. College, and braces, and weddings, and who knew what else. *I can't live off my wife and her landscaping company forever*, Adam thought.

"Paul," he said. "This is all very generous, and I confess it sounds intriguing. Let's do it." And with that, he signed both documents.

"Excellent," Paul responded. "I was hoping you'd say that. So let's get down to business. As I said earlier, I brought along five documents. We've taken care of the two least interesting ones. Let's get to the others."

With that, he opened his briefcase and pulled out the two documents, separated in time and space, that contained nearly identical messages written in Armenian, and the English translation that Dickens had obtained for him through the good offices of Maria Hoffbert. He passed the first two of these across to Adam.

"For now, at least, I don't want to say anything about where I obtained these or why they interest me. If you need to know that later, then perhaps we can discuss it. But for now, I think not."

Paul was all business now, a side of his personality that Adam had not yet seen, but one that would hardly have surprised him.

"If you look closely, you'll see that, though they are written in different hands, both papers contain what is, for all intents and purposes, an identical message. The language here, for reasons I have yet to determine—and perhaps in the course of your inquiries, that is a question you'll answer—is Armenian. Apparently, the Armenians have their own alphabet, and it looks like this. Both papers also have a drawing at the bottom, and the drawings, too, are quite similar, enough so that one might reasonably conclude that they, too, are identical. Beyond that, aside from some smudges and minor variations, the papers differ only in that one contains what appears to be a name or part of a name at the end, perhaps that of the author, while the other does not. I believe, and this is now confirmed, that the drawings in question are, jointly, a map of some sort. Of what and to what—that's where you come in.

"Now, this last paper represents a translation of the first two into English. Your friend Maria was of assistance in that process, and she has seen the translation. Beyond Maria, only the Columbia University professor who did the translation of the document on your left and a colleague of my own have seen it. The Columbia professor has promised confidentiality and, in any event, did not see the drawing or map and has no context for the translation.

"Why don't you take a moment to look through the translation before we go on. There seem to be some small differences between the two Armenian texts, and this is based on just one of the two, so we can't be sure there are no errors here. But then, who would know?"

Paul held out a single page of what appeared to be heavy bond paper on which a carefully aligned transcript had been rendered in an elaborate and yet quite precise hand. Adam accepted the paper and read it.

Approximate Translation of Armenian Text to English

Prepared by Ludomir Bondarenko (Professor)

I write these words in the expectation that they will be read in the future. In this box are found the four parts of true wisdom. These are intellect, love, valor, competition. I include my personal journal, which can be understood only through intellect, a necklace of gold belonging to my darling Mary, the handle of my sword from the battle at Gettysburg, and the leather ball used in the first regulated contest of base ball. If a map guided you to this box, know that the map existed only in my consciousness and could only be conveyed to and through one who, through his very life, recreates my own.

the snakes turn to the left, the snakes turn to the right

turtles walk, birds in flight

arrows fly day and night

raise the crown, then everything is right

Ab (final word not in Armenian characters)

ƒ

"What the hell is this?"

"That, Adam, is what I hope you will help me to determine. We have done a little preliminary research on the matter, enough to make us believe that the purported author, and I use the word 'purported' advisedly, is one Abner Doubleday. Doubleday was a field commander at the Battle of Gettysburg, and his wife's name was, indeed, Mary. And, of course, it was the baseball reference that set us on that track in the first place. Lastly, Doubleday was a follower of a kind of religious philosophy of his day called Theosophy, and one of the central beliefs of Theosophy is that of reincarnation. They take after some of the Eastern religions in that way. They believed—actually still do, because this movement is still around— that people, or souls, or some form of aura, I'm not really sure, come back after they pass to some other plane, which is their way of saying, they die. And you can see that whoever did write this might have held such a belief. And maybe that's how all this stuff at the end about snakes and turtles and birds and such will make sense. Reincarnation? People coming back as snakes, or snakes as people? Your guess is as good as mine.

"The thing is, of course, that stuff like this gets faked all the time. Mediums and palm readers and seances and phony documents—they are classic opportunities for scamming people out of their money. And that could well have been the purpose of these two documents in Armenian, which I can tell you, both date to the early 1900s. But then, there is this tantalizing little detail, the map. If someone could solve the map and find whatever is at the indicated location, if anything is, well, depending on what that is, it could be very, very interesting."

"And that's what you want me to do? Figure out this map and find this . . . what, hidden collection of Doubleday memorabilia?"

"Yes, precisely. And don't forget about the writing. I want you to chronicle the whole, what shall we call it, the whole quest. I like that. The Doubleday Quest. Maybe that's your title!"

"Maybe. But I don't even know where to start. And I don't know that I can do this alone. I might need some help."

"Understood. So here's the deal, and it's something I anticipated in the NDA you signed before. There's a paragraph in there that allows you to tell anyone you need to—*if you must do so in order to proceed*—in general terms what you are after. Just say some old Doubleday artifacts you think might be around. And, more to the point, you can share with a fellow quest seeker, if you need one, and also with your wife, since you may need to explain some absences, more about the task you have been set, but if you do that, and if anyone in whom you confide should break that confidence, you will be personally responsible for returning the entire personal services fee to me. The whole $200,000. No exceptions. So you are free to take on a partner, for example, but you assume all of the risk should they prove unreliable."

"Okay. I can live with that."

"Oh, and there's one more thing."

"What's that?"

"Remember. Abner Doubleday died in 1893, years before the two Armenian documents were ostensibly created. So there's that."

"Okay, so let me recap this. You want me to find the baseball that Abner Doubleday used the very day he invented baseball here in Cooperstown in, what was it, 1839?"

"Yes. Among other things, of course."

"And you know, I assume, that Abner Doubleday didn't really invent baseball, in Cooperstown or anywhere else. I mean, pretty much everybody has rejected that myth—even the guys over at the Hall. Hell, even the Village fathers, and mothers, of Cooperstown. Nobody believes that anymore, if they ever did!"

"Ah," said Paul. "But that is the question, is it not?"

That gave Adam some pause.

It was Day Five for Dakota and Chuck, and more precisely, the morning thereof. More precisely still, the *early* morning thereof. Things had developed very much to plan, though as of yet, there was little to show for it. After their first evening together, Bethany had reported to Mike what she could—basically that Dickens seemed like a nice man, very much to the character of what you'd think an academic and an engineer might be. He obviously had money—enough to buy into a West Side townhouse—and in that townhouse, he kept an office. She'd not yet had time to investigate the office, and she surely would as things moved forward, but he had told her that he hardly ever brought his work home, so she was not sure what that search would yield. On their second night together, she had hinted more strongly about the shortcomings of the Beacon Hotel, and he had taken the bait, suggesting that she might want to move her bags to his apartment for the remainder of her stay. Late in the afternoon of Day Three, he had left work early to help her do just that, and she had checked out of the hotel. Day Four was her first alone in the apartment, and it was then that she had a chance to look through the numerous papers in his office. There were piles of bills, bank statements, and other financial papers, though nothing she could find that identified a source of income other than his Columbia salary, which was surprisingly large, and some trivial royalty payments he'd received. Most of the boxes were filled with technical papers and old journals, and she didn't even try to understand any of that. And as for his computer, it was, not surprisingly, password protected, and she had no clue where to begin with that. She asked Mike if he wanted her to bring it out one morning so they could get inside and copy the hard drive, but that was further than he was prepared to go, at least for now. That left only his office at the university.

So on Day Five, rather than lounging in bed, when Chuck rose to dress and head to work, Dakota got up with him and cooked eggs and toast for breakfast. Then she set the next trap.

"Honey," she purred, "I was thinking about you up there all day in some stodgy old office, and I thought it might be fun if I made you something good for lunch and brought it to you. If it's nice out, we could go outside and have a picnic. And if not, we could just camp in your office and who knows what." The forecast, as she well knew, was for a day of rain, heavy at times. "I'm dying to see where you work, anyway, and you've been so nice about letting me stay here instead of that smelly old hotel. Can I bring you some lunch?"

Chuck thought for a moment and saw no harm in the offer. To the contrary, lunch would be nice, and the who-knows-what could be even nicer. Chuck, too, had seen the weather forecast.

"That," he said, "would be really fun. Here's what you need to do." And he proceeded to tell Dakota how to find the building, which entrance to use, and what to tell the security guard. He promised he'd arrange a building pass before she arrived.

"Did you hear who was in town this week?" Liz asked when she got home from work. "Paul Chi Mannington. A couple of my guys said they saw him running around yesterday in some sort of Ferrari or something, and Eddie said he saw it in the lot over at the hotel when he was working over there."

"Really?" Adam replied. "I would have liked to see that car!" After giving the matter some thought, Adam had decided he would not mention Mannington's visit or the task he had agreed to take on to Liz until he'd had a chance to plot a course of action. He hoped that would not take long, because he knew what her reaction would be once he revealed the secret, especially now that she had opened the subject.

He had set about the project in earnest almost as soon as Paul had walked out the door. He knew something about Abner Doubleday, of course, but not nearly as much as he would need to, and he wasn't sure at this point just how much of what he thought he knew was actually true. That was probably task one. He might need to know something about how the Doubleday myth was created and took root, but he wasn't sure whether that would be central to his quest or peripheral. He suspected the latter, so he put that further down his list. More importantly, he should study up on what baseballs might have looked like in 1839 and learn what he could of Civil War swords, specifically their hilts, just in case he might need to evaluate a find, on the off chance that would occur. Adam confessed to himself that he was not optimistic on that score, and he might well fail in his mission. But there would be a book in that as well, and maybe one Paul would be more willing to let him publish.

That was a question mark, too. For all he had read over the years of Paul Chi Mannington, and for all Paul had told him during his visit, Adam still had no real idea of Paul's motive for this project or of what his true interest might be. Until he had a better sense of that, he concluded, he would be well advised to proceed with caution.

It was easy enough to find the basics about Doubleday, who had been a prominent figure of sorts in his own time. Born in 1819, died in 1893. He was in the military and seemed to have a knack for being where the action was, anywhere from Fort Sumter at the start of the Civil War to Gettysburg, where he was something of a hero at Cemetery Ridge. But he didn't get along with some of the brass, notably the very powerful General George Meade, who did not like Doubleday and who, rather than promote or otherwise recognize his role at Gettysburg, appointed another officer over him. The next year, though, he had a chance to get even when he was invited to testify before a joint congressional committee investigating the conduct of the war, and he took it, offering harsh criticism of Meade's leadership, including that at Gettysburg. He stayed in the Army until about 1873, with postings in San Francisco and Texas, among others. And not long after that, he retired to a small town in New Jersey called Mendham.

All interesting enough, but it was Doubleday's early years—he would have turned twenty in 1839—that Adam felt he needed to study up on. And that's where he ran into some confusion of facts, indeed, the very confusion of facts that led to the early, and the later, questioning of the Doubleday myth itself. Everybody agreed that he was born in Ballston Spa, New York, over in Saratoga County, and he grew up in Auburn. But then it got a little murky. Some accounts had him studying at the Cooperstown Classical and Military Academy, where he would presumably have "invented" baseball, in 1838 and into 1839, but West Point records show that he enrolled in the Academy in 1838 and stayed there throughout his cadet years. If that were true, he could not have possibly been in Cooperstown in 1839 to do the fabled deed. And then Adam came across another account suggesting that the Cooperstown school itself did not even begin operations until 1839, when Doubleday was presumably already at West Point. A tangled web indeed, but only if you assumed that Abner Doubleday invented baseball in Cooperstown in 1839. Take away that assumption, and the rest makes no difference at all.

So, what was Paul trying to prove? And why was he trying to prove it?

And then there was the map. That might be the key to the whole thing. It was simple enough, laid out in the cardinal directions with numbers that might represent feet, yards, paces, miles. But that map could make sense, if at all, only with the one piece of information he did not have: Where was the starting point?

Finally, there was the very odd fact that the original documents had been written in Armenian. It almost looked like they had been dictation copies, so maybe there were two secretaries writing while Doubleday dictated the document in Armenian. But Armenian? Come on now. Why Armenian? He wondered if there was any record that Doubleday had ever traveled to that part of the world, or, alternatively, if there was some big Armenian settlement someplace near where he had lived.

It was that last thought that finally gave him a sense of direction. Whether it was his schooling, his career, the map, or even the Armenian connection, Adam needed to know where Doubleday had been living at various key times during his life. He had a good start: Ballston Spa, Auburn, Cooperstown, West Point, San Francisco, Texas, New York City, New Jersey.

Most of these were pretty close at hand, so he might as well get started.

"Man, what have you guys got in this place?" Dakota wanted to know. "Armed guards, secret passwords, unmarked elevators to nonexistent floors. Who are you?"

Chuck laughed. "That security is mainly for some guys downstairs. Honestly, I don't know what they are working on. But ever since 9/11, I think—and I wasn't here then—the building has been locked up pretty tight. The rest of us just learn to live with it. The people who find it really obnoxious are the students. Only place on campus, I think, where they can't just wander in and out at will."

"And the secret floor?"

"Oh. I was a latecomer, and I needed a lot of space. Seemed like the only way to get it was to build it, and there's not a lot of ground-level real estate open on campus. So they went up."

He cleared a space on his desk by pushing stacks of papers to one side and the other, and she pulled several plastic containers, along with a couple of plastic forks and napkins, from the bag she'd brought along. She began to peel the tops from the containers, but it was the subtle scent of her perfume, and not the delicious odors of the revealed delicacies, that he noticed. She could have brought peanut butter and jelly sandwiches for all he cared. He nuzzled her neck affectionately, and she responded with a peck on the cheek and a hug.

"Food!" she said. "I slaved in the kitchen all morning, and I lugged all of this food up here, and by God, sir, you're going to eat it!"

She pulled up the seldom-used visitor's chair, first removing yet another stack of papers, and they sat down to a varied repast of cheeses, salads, some kind of flatbread, some Greek olives, and two splits of white wine she had picked up along the way.

"What are all these papers?" she asked, waiving her hand around the room for effect. "Have you read all of these?"

"Read them? I wrote them all!" he replied. They giggled at the obvious lie. "Actually, I have a grant that lets me collect a lot of old studies from all over the world. My job is to read them all and see if there are any ancient engineering secrets we can extract from them. Maybe somebody had a better way to build bridges, and it got lost to history. That sort of thing. I mean, think about the Pyramids or the Taj Mahal. How did they do that? It's not clear that we could build those things today with all of our technology, but they did it thousands of years ago."

"Or how about something really ancient, like . . . Chaco Canyon? Would that be the sort of thing you look at, too?"

"You know Chaco . . . oh, of course you do. You're from Utah. That's an amazing place, to be sure. But so far as we know, the Anasazi, or whoever built it, didn't have a written language. They had those glyphs, of course, but if there's a way to make sentences out of them, nobody has found it yet. But ancient languages, anything like that, or just old documents . . . if there is a written record of how something was done, well, that's the sort of thing I'd be interested in."

Dakota picked up a book that was close at hand and read from the cover: "*Western Esotericism: A Guide for the Perplexed*, by Wouter Hanegraaff." She pronounced it "Wowter Handicraft."

"Okay," she said, turning toward Chuck with her best doe-eyed expression, "I'm perplexed. Can you think of a way to guide me?"

Ballston Spa. It was the starting point for Doubleday's life, and the starting point as well for Adam's quest. It was an easy drive from the farm, so he had packed a lunch, gathered up the map, and hit the road. Ballston Spa turned out to be a village not terribly unlike Cooperstown, but a little bigger, at least now. Back in 1819, it was apparently a typical spa town, with a couple of hotels. It was named for some eighteenth-century preacher named Ball, which struck Adam as appropriate given the nature of his search.

Adam's operating theory was that the map had something to do with a place where Doubleday had lived or a place that was highly significant to him. So his real objective that first day was to find the house where Doubleday had been born, or whatever sat on that spot today. As it turned out, the actual house was still there, at the corner of Washington and Fenwick Streets and pretty close to the center of town. Not surprisingly, the house had been through some changes in the last hundred-plus years, but Adam was nevertheless somewhat bewildered to find that it now served as the home of the Real McCoy Beer Company, something of which teetotaler Abner Doubleday would not have approved. He knew he had the right spot, or was close, when he noticed that the gift shop next door was called "A Day at Abner's." Then he saw the historic marker:

> **Birthplace**
> **Major-Gen Abner Doubleday**
> **Ballston Spa June 26 1819**
> **founder of baseball 1839**

Obviously, he thought, *somebody didn't get the memo.*

Adam pulled out the twin maps to see if he could make any sense of them at that location. He was in trouble from the outset, he figured, because the maps looked as if they started out going east, and the brewhouse faced south. Taking the numbers on the map as paces, which he thought was the best bet, he tried walking off the lines, but he was in the middle of a contemporary commercial center, and if there had been anything at the end of the map, where the bird was, it was long gone, and with it any hope of discovery. Then it occurred to him that he might be working from the wrong end of the map, so he went back to "go." This time, he started south, taking fifteen paces before turning west, and then north, and then east, but that did not seem to improve the result. Adam spent some time at the village hall, parsing old property records to see what might have been in these spots back in the day. But in the end, he simply gave up. *Besides,* he thought, *why would Doubleday return to his birthplace, which he might not even have remembered and may never have ever revisited, in order to secret his box of memorabilia?* Back to Cooperstown he went.

The day had gone a little longer than Adam had anticipated, and by the time he made it back home, Hef had been fed and Liz was waiting for him with dinner.

"I wondered if you'd show up," she said. "Where've you been?"

Adam decided that the moment had come to let his wife in on the deal he had made.

"Remember the other day when you said that Paul Mannington had been in town. Fancy car and all that?"

"Yes." Liz felt her curiosity rising.

"Well, he was here to see me."

"Excuse me?"

"Paul was here to see me."

"So it's *Paul* now? Do you *know* Paul Chi Mannington?"

"Well, I do now. But I can't tell you any more—and there is a lot to tell—unless you promise to keep it to yourself. It's like your thing with those baseball guys and the vault, where you told me and I have to somehow keep that secret forever? Well, this is the same kind of deal, but the shoe's on the other foot, my dearest. Do you promise?

———

"So," Mike said to Bethany as they sat down over coffee and danishes at an East Side hangout where there would be almost no chance of discovery by anyone who mattered. "It's been what, six days? You're costing me a fortune. What have you got so far?"

She thought for a moment before replying. "Okay, so I finally had a chance to go through the apartment pretty thoroughly, finances, personal papers, and such. The guy's pretty well off, like I thought, but there's just not much there about where it comes from except for that nice salary. I'm pretty sure that's a dead end. I've been up to his office twice now. It's impossible to be in there alone unless I slip him a mickey, and I won't do that."

"Wouldn't ask," said Mike, nevertheless thinking it was an interesting idea.

"That said," she continued, "I have been able to get an idea of what he's got up there. And it's pretty weird, considering the guy's an engineer of some sort. There are a bunch of really esoteric books on philosophy, which is odd enough. But then he's got papers all over the place that claim to be studies of reincarnation and some other bizarre shit. He doesn't seem like a wacko, but those papers are pretty far out there, at least from some of the titles.

"Only other thing is that he keeps talking about some kind of room down the hall where he must have some other stuff stashed, and some lab in another building. It's all kind of in passing, so I really don't know any more about that."

"Kiddo, this is really good. How are *you* doing?"

"You know, I'm okay. It's been almost a week now, but he's a nice enough guy and the digs are not bad. I'm good to keep going if that's what you want."

Chaney thought for a moment. "Tell you what. It sounds like there's not going to be a lot more you can find out. But let's do this. Go up to the office one more time, because from what you say and what my guys have seen, there's no way we will be able to black bag it without a helicopter, and they tend to draw attention. Take a shot at getting him to show you the storage room or the lab, or even both. But don't push it. Don't be obvious. Just see what happens. The other thing is—and you ought to be able to do this—see if you can grab one or two of those papers you were talking about. Nothing he seems to be working on right now, but something off a stack somewhere. Sounds like this guy has a lot of stacks, so something he's not likely to miss, or if he does, maybe just wonder where the heck he put it. Go for the reincarnation angle or something else that strikes you as similar. "Give that one day, maybe two at the most. When you have it, or if you decide you can't get it, give me a holler. That'll be the time for your mother to get sick back in Utah and need you to come home early. But not until we talk again."

"We doing okay?" Bethany asked.

"Doing great," came the reply. Chaney rose from the table and left Bethany to finish her danish in peace.

<hr />

"My God, Adam. That's quite a story. Are you sure you're not making this up?"

Adam stood and walked into the room he used for an office, returning with a piece of paper in hand. It was the check for $200,000 that he had yet to deposit—mainly because he knew he would need to explain it to Liz when he did. He set it on the table in front of her.

Liz looked at the check. "Kind of takes your breath away, doesn't it?"

"Left me almost speechless," he replied. "I can tell you that."

"Well all right, cowboy, you'd best get to work! What's next on your list?"

"Auburn, I think. That's where his family moved after Ballston Spa. His dad was a printer and ran a newspaper up there. There's a historic district in town—I think William Seward lived there, he of the Folly, and Harriett Tubman had a place there and she's even buried there. Oh, and there's a prison where the first person ever was executed in an electric chair. Edison, of all people, arranged that. But all of that's much later. I haven't been able to find any indication of a family home or anything else from the 1820s or '30s. Still, the town named their baseball team after Doubleday, so there might be something up there. Seems worth a look, though it's as much of a longshot as the Spa was."

"Want some company?" Liz asked. "It sounds like there might be a couple of things to see, and it might help to have another set of eyes to help you look around for traces. I could take a day off, and we could bundle up Hef and drive up there. That's over past Syracuse, right? Might even stay the night."

"Excellent idea, hon. Say the day after tomorrow? That will give me time to troll the web just a little more, just in case."

With a plan of action agreed, Adam went back to his computer, hoping that Auburn might yet reveal a hidden remnant of the young Abner Doubleday. The result was discouraging. He was able to find one reference to the location of the bookshop owned by Ulysses Doubleday, Abner's father, which appeared to have been across from an old hotel, the Western Exchange, at the corner of Genesee and Exchange Streets in the middle of town. Apparently, the hotel rated a state historic marker, but the bookshop did not. Beyond that, Adam learned that the most prominent citizens of early Auburn, which had about 4,500 residents when Abner was growing up there, tended to live in homes close to the center of town on South Street. Looking at the map, he saw that this area was an easy walk from the shop's location and might be the most fertile ground on which to center their search.

"Chuck?"

"Hey, I didn't expect to hear from you until noon. Everything okay?"

"Actually, no," Dakota replied. "That's why I'm calling. I just had a phone call from my dad. It seems Mom has taken ill. They don't think it's life-threatening, but it was serious enough that they want me to come home."

"That's awful. Is there anything I can do?"

"Not really. I'm a mess, but I'll be fine. I'm packing up my things even as we're talking. I need to catch the first plane back to Salt Lake. I'll call Dad with the details, and he said he could come and pick me up to get back to Evanston. I feel really badly, like I'm running out on you. I'll try to pick up the place a little bit before I leave."

"Don't be silly. I just wish there was something I could do. Can you get to the airport okay?"

"Last time I looked, they have taxis in New York," she said, making sure it was clearly a joke and not a swipe at Chuck. "I'll be just fine. I just have to figure out whether LaGuardia or JFK is the best bet. I'm going to miss you. Hopefully this won't be a long thing, and I can come back here over the next school break."

"Or I can come out there. In fact, why don't I do that? Maybe I can help out in some way."

"Uh, no, I don't think that's a good idea. As far as my folks know, I've been here visiting Ethan. In fact, my dad asked me to get in touch with him since they haven't been able to reach him. Tell him about Mom. I'll have a hard enough time explaining that to them without having to explain that instead of visiting my little brother, I shacked up with the first person I met, some random college professor. I'm going to need a little time to break that part of the news. I'll just say I was here anyway, so I decided to see the City for a couple of weeks. They won't be any the wiser. You have my cell and my email. We can always do video calls or something. Let me get settled, and I'll be in touch and we can figure it out from there."

"I know it's only been a few days, but I'm really going to miss you."

"Me too, babe. Gotta run."

Bethany had made the call from the back seat of Mike Chaney's car. When it was over, she handed him the phone, which he opened to remove the SIM chip, then discarded into a handy trash bin. The Gmail account would be shut down within the hour. They had to remember that this guy was an engineer, and if they didn't cover their tracks promptly and thoroughly, he might figure it out once he realized that Dakota Rand had disappeared without a trace.

She opened her suitcase and pulled out three academic-looking papers, none of which looked especially current. In fact, the paper on which two of them were printed was yellowed, and the text of the third, which smelled faintly of cigar smoke, was faded. But the titles fit the bill—two on reincarnation and one having something to do with precognition, whatever that was—and Mike was sure his clients would find them of interest.

"You did great," he said, passing her a thick stack of bills. "As agreed, all in cash, and you'll find there's a little bonus in there as well. That's for managing to walk out with these papers. I'm going to get out at the office, but Jack here will drop you anywhere you like."

Bethany smiled, put the cash in her purse, and thanked him for the work. "Any time, Mike."

"Count on it, darling."

Auburn was a complete bust. There were a couple of interesting old historic houses there—the Seward and Tubman places—but no sign whatsoever of the Doubledays. They found the plaque commemorating the Western Exchange Hotel but looked all around without finding any trace of the family bookstore. No one in town seemed to know anything that was of any use. They could not find a single place to put the maps to the test. And then, to top it all off, Hef developed a hacky cough and a fever. So rather than having a productive research trip and a relaxing day of tourism, they climbed back into the family SUV and headed home to Cooperstown.

The Trading Deadline

CI parked himself at the small conference table and placed a folder on the polished wood top. "Good morning, boss."

"Hell, CI. I thought you got lost or decided to take a vacation. Where the devil have you been?"

"I was busy finding things. You know that can take some time."

"Yeah, I know. And I'm sorry." This was something CI had seldom heard his employer say when in any of his posts, US Congressman, US Senator, or now as Commissioner of Baseball. "It's been a long day. I had a meeting with a group of agents this morning, and as always, they were just a bunch of arrogant assholes. Takes one to know one, I suppose."

This degree of self-deprecation is truly rare, thought CI. *It must have been a pretty intense meeting.*

"Well, let me brighten your day," CI said aloud. "Wait until you see what I, ah, found."

"Oh? Do we have it, you think? Let me see what you've got there." The Commissioner pulled the folder CI had placed on the table toward him, opened it, and glanced at the single-page document it protected. He paused for a long moment after reading it, pondering the possibilities that had just opened before him.

"I think I see what this is, but the only name here is Doubleday himself. Who are these other people? And who or what the heck is a Purple Mother?"

Point Loma Calif.
Dec. 19/04

Beloved Purple Mother,

Elizabeth has at last prevailed upon me to reconsider my initial reaction to your vision.

While I am not convinced that sport alone will propel our shared views to their rightful status at the apex of American society, I do share that goal. And as a devoted follower, I accept my responsibility to advance the Universal Brotherhood. Who am I to question a true revelation?

We all know that General Doubleday, a distinguished war hero, demonstrated through his leadership in New York that he too was devoted to our common search for truth, something he expressed personally to M.H.B. As both a patriot and a man of rectitude, he might well prove the icon around whom a broadening of our influence throughout society could be advanced. I think, therefore, that your vision has cast light on an intrinsic reality, and that the revealed path will have some chance of success. At the very least, it will broaden awareness of our movement and place us in a positive light. Only good can come from that.

This will take some time to arrange. But know that I will commence to plan it immediately, and I will make sure of the desired outcome insofar as I am able. In the meantime, please proceed to draft the requisite missives and prepare Mr. G. for his role. I agree that Akron will be the most propitious venue for the reasons you suggested. I will arrange with Mr. K. for the prompt publication of the letter of proof, and will signal you two weeks before I give S. his assignment, which should allow ample time for positioning Mr. G.

May our objective triumph, and our movement ascend the heights.

As always, you have blessed us by providing this serene truth-seeking community of ours. Elizabeth and I both recognize the good fortune that has brought us here.

With warmest regards,
A.G.S.

"Boss, I think that's the beauty of it. I spent some time with Jimmy before I went on my 'search.'" This last word he accompanied with air quotes. "Wanted to know what sort of thing I might be looking for. He told me that if the documents I found named names, if they were really specific, that would be really easy for people to check out and maybe even delegitimize. You know, other records, movement archives, which I assume they must have somewhere, people and places, all that. So I was looking for something, ideally, that was at once suggestive yet ambiguous. He said that would let people read into it whatever they wanted. And, of course, we could frame the documents in a way that would help them come to the proper interpretation. So that's what I went out looking for.

"I dug into everything we had on Spalding. What seemed important was that, after his first wife died, he married Elizabeth Churchill, who, like I think I told you before, had been his lover for years. Now Elizabeth was deep into this Theosophy thing. She was even a personal aide to Madame Helene Blavatsky, the Russian weirdo who founded the movement. And by the way, her followers typically just referred to her as M.H.B., just like in this letter. And this new wife, she was apparently pretty persuasive. Around 1900, a woman named Katherine Tingley took over the movement and started building a kind of philosophical retreat community out near San Diego, place called Point Loma. Named it Lomaland, and it was pretty extensive for the times—lots of stark white buildings with a combined Greek and Egyptian look, lots of domes and globes. Everybody apparently called her Purple Mother, or just Purple. Well, Spalding's wife was a member of Purple's inner circle and the director of the movement's worldwide system of Sunday schools. Purple told Elizabeth that if she moved out to California, she could be the Theosophy Society's first musical director, so she prevailed on Spalding to move out there to live. Once he did, he immersed himself in the movement in a big way. He was into books, and he had a large collection of works dealing with Theosophy, but his real impact was that he proposed building a road out to this colony from downtown San Diego, pushed it through, oversaw the construction, and even paid for part of it out of his own pocket. That made Lomaland very accessible, and it also would have put him in close and constant contact with Tingley.

"Oh, and one more thing. It's pretty clear that Elizabeth would have known Abner Doubleday or, at the very least, known a lot about him. She was a member of the New York Theosophy Society, and he was a recent past president of that chapter. She was also working there for a guy named William Quan Judge, who was a former colleague of Doubleday's and was sort of the bridge, though I wouldn't say willingly so, between Blavatsky and Tingley.

"So, to answer your question, we don't know who A.G.S. was for sure, but it sure sounds like Spalding. We don't know who Purple Mother was for sure, but it sure sounds like Tingley. Now, Mr. G. might possibly be Abner Graves, who, at the very least, played a mysterious role in the events that actually transpired. And I think I mentioned that book I read that was getting at that sort of thing, too. S., well, that could have been Spalding's man, Sullivan, I suppose. He did serve as Secretary of the Mills Commission once it was set up, and he was the one who sent around requests for information to the newspapers. Oh, and then there's Mr. K. Remember that Graves's letter claiming to have been there when Doubleday invented the game was published in the *Akron Beacon Journal*. Charles Landon Knight bought that paper in 1903 when it was pretty down and out, and he was looking to build circulation, maybe even desperate. Could have been him, I guess. Who's to say?

"So, here's the way I think we might lay this thing out. Doubleday is this war hero who retires to New Jersey, where he gets deep into this bizarre Theosophy movement. Reincarnation, lots of occult stuff. He gets in so deep, in fact, that he becomes president of the local chapter there in New York, where he would meet all sorts of people. He dies in 1893.

"Then there's Albert Spalding. Big baseball guy, knows everything and everybody in the game. He publishes an annual guide that lots of people read. His buddy, and a guy who's followed the game for years, Henry Chadwick, edits the guide. But one year he goes way off the reservation and claims that baseball is not an American sport so much as an English one. Now you have to remember that this is less than a century after the Brits burned the White House in the War of 1812, and Americans don't yet have a love of everything British like they have today. Quite the reverse. Plus, this is right when the country was starting to feel its oats in world affairs. Spanish-American War. Teddy Roosevelt. So Spalding, who's had this running conversation with Chadwick for years, gets all pissy and decides he needs to prove Chadwick is wrong. But how to do it? He tries writing a piece in the *Guide*, but Chadwick just doubles down.

"In the midst of all this, Spalding has married his second wife, Elizabeth, who's hooked him up with Tingley, like I said, and he's moved out to the colony near San Diego. And Tingley fills his head with all of her dreams of gaining power and influence in national and world affairs. Now, I'm spit-balling here. But you need to understand that this Theosophy movement, well, it had a lot of prominent adherents. Today maybe we'd call it nutty, but that was a different time. I mean, they had writers like L. Frank Baum, the guy who wrote *The Wizard of Oz*, and Yeats, the poet, and Lewis Carroll, and Edgar Rice Burroughs of *Tarzan* fame, and Arthur Conan Doyle. Jack London, E.M. Forster, James Joyce, D.H. Lawrence, T.S. Eliot, Henry Miller, Maxim Gorky, Tolstoy, and more. And Oscar Wilde—no surprise there. Edison was a member, and Wallace, the other guy besides Darwin who had a theory of natural selection, and Luther Burbank, the seed guy, and Carl Jung, the psychiatrist. And the painters were really into it as well—Gauguin and Kandinsky and Klee and Mondrian. Even Gutzon Borglum, the Rushmore sculptor, was a Theosophist, and also Maria Montessori. And Mahler and Sibelius. In politics, Henry Wallace, who eventually became our own VP, was into this along with Nehru and some others. Hell, Gandhi himself said Blavatsky had shown him the light. And Edgar Cayce, the mind reader. And that's just people who were alive back then. According to some sources, you can add Vonnegut and Jackson Pollock and Gloria Steinem and Albert Einstein and Jane Goodall and Elvis, oh, and of course, Shirley MacLaine. The point is, back in the day, this was not a fringe movement. It was instead one with substantial and rising cultural influence, and some political influence abroad, that they might well have wanted to increase here at home. So that was a possible motive for making a play, and it wasn't as off the wall like we might think today."

The Commissioner sat in absolute silence during this little soliloquy, something he was not accustomed to doing.

CI continued. "Okay, so Spalding decides to form a commission to prove his point, and who does he choose to run it? Albert Mills, a guy he's done business with before and a guy who has given a lot of money to . . . the Theosophy movement. But it gets better. Mills is a military veteran, and he apparently met Doubleday himself in New York at some

Grand Army of the Republic event, and the two became friends. Mills was actually the senior officer in the honor guard at Doubleday's burial in Arlington. And Spalding fills the rest of the commission with old baseball cronies and business partners, including James Sullivan, whom he puts in charge of actually operating the thing.

"Then it gets a bit speculative again. They look around for a newspaper that will help them out, and they settle on the paper in Akron, Ohio, not exactly the center of the known world of journalism. But the fellow who runs the paper there has just bought it, and he's desperate for advertising and visibility. That's Charles Knight, whose sons went on to build the Knight-Ridder empire, but this is back at the very humble beginnings. Now, I didn't find any evidence that Knight was a Theosophist or was corrupt, but so what. People today hate the media, and they'll jump to the right conclusion.

"Now, the way this plays out is that an itinerant of sorts, our friend Mr. Graves, happens to be in Akron when Sullivan happens to advertise in the Akron paper of all places for proof of the American origins of baseball. And Graves writes a letter to the paper claiming that he was present in Cooperstown the day Doubleday invented the game. Knight publishes the letter the very next day, which, in an era when things moved slowly and type was set one piece at a time, sounds like a setup. And in fact, there's some indication, or at least a suspicion, that Graves had spent some time in Southern California just before he wandered over to Akron. Graves also sends a second letter, to Spalding himself, and that gets published in some Theosophy newsletter in very short order. And right away, Theosophy claims credit for creating the National Pastime. Now, Boss, you want some whipped cream on your sundae?"

"You have my full attention."

"This," he said, holding up a piece of paper with some sort of logo on it, "is the official emblem of Theosophy to this very day. And yes, that's a swastika and a snake, along with a bunch of other weird symbols and that slogan along the bottom—'There is no religion higher than Truth.' Oh, they'll tell you each of these things has some deep religious or philosophical significance, and truth be told, there is a case for that. I looked into this thing a bit. This snake that looks like it's swallowing its tale? That's apparently some universal symbol for regeneration or immortality. Who knew? And the thing that looks like a Jewish star has something to do with creation and the struggle between the forces of good and evil. The stick-figure thing in the middle is some old Egyptian symbol for resurrection, and the swastika is supposed to represent natural energy. That squiggle that looks like a math symbol at the top is some sacred word in Sanskrit, something to do with the source of all existence. I mean, these people are really deep. But if you hold this up in front of most people today, the only things they'll remember are the Nazis and the first half of that slogan, 'There is no religion. . . .'"

With that, CI sat back and waited.

"CI, you have outdone yourself. Not only implicit proof of a conspiracy, but of a conspiracy that may have seemed natural in its time, but that could, that *would*, be seen today as contrary to the national interest. A power grab in the guise of national pride, all by a bunch of antireligious Nazis. Best of all, it's not us saying it. It's people reading that into it themselves. This is brilliant. But how could a letter like this be lost for so long? Wherever did you find it?"

"You know, it was the darndest coincidence. I was taking a day off, and I stopped by a flea market. And I came across this old picture frame some guy had held onto while he was cleaning out an old house. I don't remember his name, and he had so many old frames for sale he probably wouldn't remember this one. There was this old letter in it that must have meant something to the old man whose house it had been—William Smith, his name was, apparently known to all as Old Will—but the guy selling it couldn't make any sense of it, so he was just selling the frame. When I looked at the letter, I just couldn't believe my luck. It turned out to be exactly what Jimmy had told me to be looking for. Even though it was browned from age, you could still make it out. And if you look real close, there's an old, faded watermark with some initials that look to me like AGS, though it's a little hard to be sure. Honestly, I couldn't believe my luck. One of those amazing coincidences." CI was smiling broadly as he said this.

"And, CI, just who was this Old Will Smith?"

"Commissioner, who would you like him to be?"

"Okay, Super Sleuth," Liz teased as she sat, legs curled, on the sofa. "What's next?"

"Something a little closer to home, my dear. Cooperstown. That was apparently Doubleday's next stop in life, albeit briefly. It looks like maybe as he got into his late teens, his father was getting him ready for West Point. Ulysses, Abner's father, was in Congress then. So he was an orderly, educated, influential kind of guy. And apparently he shipped his son here to Cooperstown, where a fellow named Major Huff was starting a school. It was called the Cooperstown Classical and Military Academy. The consensus seems to be that the school started up in 1839, when Abner was already at West Point, and it wasn't around long, and that's where all of the confusion arose. But this Major Huff looks like he might have been something of a promoter. In fact, there was some question about whether he was ever actually in the military or just took the title. Guess it was hard to check on such things back then, or people simply took them at face value.

"But it did get me thinking. What if you were a bit of an operator, like this guy Huff may have been. And you wanted to start a school, say, like a prep school today. You know, doing just what Ulysses might have wanted for Abner—getting young men ready to attend West Point, which wasn't all that far away. Now, Ulysses was in Congress, so getting Abner into the Point would have been pretty much a certainty, which anybody would have known. So maybe Huff decides he can burnish his credentials and start getting a reputation for his school before it's fully ready to go. Basically, the same thing the Hall of Fame guys did a hundred years later, not that they were flimflammers, but just getting the pre-opening publicity and a head start on recruiting. At the Hall, they started inducting players three years before they opened the doors. That's when Cobb and Mathewson and Ruth and Wagner and Johnson got in—what they call their first class. Applying that same idea, if you were cranking up a new military academy, might you not set yourself up informally ahead of time and recruit a few students like Mr. Doubleday, a congressman's son, to get started? I can't say that happened, but as spotty as the records are from back then, I can't rule it out either."

"Okay. So you're grasping at straws. At least we don't have to travel anywhere to check on this one. Do you know where in town this school was supposedly located?"

"Actually, I do. Some place called Apple Hill. Ever heard of it?"

"Apple Hill? Are you kidding?"

"Should I be?"

"Apple Hill is where the Clarks built one of their first mansions. I don't think you've met any of the Clarks, but you know who they are, right? Started the Hall of Fame, funded all the museums. They're far and away the first family of Cooperstown, even today."

"Yeah. I know all of that. Did you forget it's all in my book? Heck, do you even remember my book? As in that's how we met?"

They shared a laugh, and Adam knew for sure she'd been pulling his leg.

"Apple Hill is where they built Fernleigh Manor. This was way back around the time of the Civil War. I know exactly where it is. It's right off River Street at the east end of town. Looks out over the river just a couple of hundred yards or so below the lake. It's a gorgeous piece of land. Kind of a shame nobody lives there, but they do keep the place up. And you know the best part?"

"What's that?"

"The company that maintains the landscaping at Fernleigh happens to be A. Holt Greenstick Landscaping of Cooperstown."

"By which, you mean, we do?"

"Indeed we do. You remember when we were trying to figure out what all of those keys were to, I told you that the family had some long-term clients from the very beginning back in the 1930s? Well, Fernleigh was one of those. Don't know why I didn't think of it when we were making the list. Probably because it was all but abandoned and no one was supposed to go in there. But yeah, us. Do you know *where* on Apple Hill this school building was?" she asked.

"Alas, no idea. Aside from the house, how many buildings are up there?"

"Approximately zero. I imagine when the Clarks built the manor house in the 1860s, they would have cleared out any derelict old buildings that cluttered the land. For all we know, there's a hundred-and-fifty-year-old oak tree standing on that spot today."

"Can we take a look in the morning?"

"I don't see why not. But unless Abner Doubleday was a guest at the manor house sometime after it was built and had digging rights, I can't think of a single landmark that he would have used."

They slept on that thought and, after an hour spent wandering the grounds of the old manor house the following morning, were led reluctantly, but expectedly, to the obvious conclusion. The map would do no good without a starting point, and there wasn't one of those apparent.

"Let's go back to the office and grab some lunch," Liz suggested.

"You know," said Adam, once they were settled, "we did make one key assumption here. We assumed that if Major Huff was getting an early start on his school, he was doing it from the same location where he later opened it. I suppose he could have been doing it from almost anywhere else in town—a hotel, a rooming house, an old barn, or who knows where. Unless there's some record of that I haven't found, we could spend the rest of our lives pacing off this map from every doorway in town and still not find anything."

"Time to move on?"

"It's a shame it couldn't be this easy and convenient. But yeah. Time to move on."

"Where's the next stop?"

"Well, if we were going chronologically, we'd start tracking his military career. West Point, which seems highly dubious, and I think we can forget about his various wartime postings. So probably San Francisco."

At this prospect, Liz brightened noticeably. "We have to go to San Francisco?" she said. "Damn!"

"Settle down over there. Settle down. I said that was if we were going chronologically. But there are some other places much closer to home where he lived later in life. He did live in New York City for a while. That's where he was president of the Theosophical Society. But if you think about what we are actually looking for, a collection of the guy's life's treasures, it seems to me that's the kind of thing, like a legacy of sorts, that you'd do pretty late in life, maybe when you were contemplating your final days. And at that point in his life, Doubleday was actually living in New Jersey, in a place called Mendham."

"Where is that?"

"It's only about thirty miles west of the City, out past Morristown somewhere. This weekend, why don't we go into town and stay in the apartment, and we can drive out from there. Shouldn't take more than an hour or so."

"Sounds good to me. But now, go home. I have work to do, and somebody in this family has got to earn a living."

"Okay. I guess I *could* stop at the bank on the way by and deposit this check I have been carrying around for the last several days." That got a laugh.

"See you at home around six," she said. "Love you."

"Give me Kiper."

"I'm sorry," said the unsympathetic voice on the other end of the line. "*Mister* Kiper is in conference at the moment. May I—" She never had the chance to finish the offer.

"Bull. You tell Kiper it's Mike Chaney on the line, and I don't feel like waiting. He'll take the call."

The Bach cantata went on almost to the point where Mike would have preferred waiting for a call back.

"Michael. How nice to hear from you. How can I be of service?" Kiper was the forensic accountant Mike had hired to chase down the source of Dickens's funding.

"EJ, I just got this . . . would you really call this a report? It reads in total and sum: *Professor Dickens's work is funded on a contractual basis by LanyMech Industries. Because this arrangement is contractual, as opposed to philanthropic, and may include certain trade secrets, the university is unable to release further information.* What the fuck is that? You expect me to *pay* for that?"

"Actually, Michael, I do not. It required all of one telephone call to some assistant vice president in the university research office. And if you will look at the second page, which is to say, the accompanying invoice, you will see that I did not bill you for the report."

"And you think *this* is what I hired you for? What or who the hell is LanyMech Industries?"

"Actually, I am able to answer that one. It used to be called Lany Mechanical and Industrial Services. Some corporate brand wizard got hold of the name, and it became LanyMech. They are major manufacturers of parts for commercial ventilation systems. And to anticipate your question, you told me the guy was an engineer, so this made sense. He's probably doing some kind of grunt-work system redesign they didn't want to waste their internal resources on, be my guess."

"EJ, let me be real clear. I don't pay you to guess. No, this guy is not doing heating and air conditioning systems or whatever. He's into something a lot deeper than that, and this LanyMech is probably just a cover. So here's what I want you to do: Some fucking forensic accounting! I want to know everything about LanyMech. If their CEO pisses out of the left side of his dick and never the right, I want to know about it, got that?"

"Michael, I get it."

"And more important, I want to know who owns this LanyMech, and who owns *that*, and who owns *that*, as far back as it goes. And I want to know what they all do and who they do it with and for. I want to know who's on the boards of these companies, and who owns most of the stock if they're public, and who the partners are if they're private. Do I make myself clear?"

"Crystal clear, Michael. Crystal clear."

"Do it. You have two days."

"Two—" The phone went dead in Kiper's hand. "Shit."

"Tony, Ryan, Sherrie, get in here!"

EJ Kiper & Associates, LLC, would be pulling a couple of all-nighters.

Adam and Liz made the Saturday morning drive to the City, with Hef napping serenely in his car seat in the back. They pulled into the garage in Adam's old building, grabbed a luggage cart, unloaded their suitcases, unbuckled their son, and headed upstairs.

It had been a few weeks since Adam, who had occasional business in town, had last been in the apartment, and much longer for Liz, who seldom was. After unlatching both deadbolts and walking into the musty front hallway, they both looked around and came to the same conclusion.

"We need to look for a bigger place if we're going to keep an apartment in the City." Liz was the one to speak, and Adam simply nodded.

"Guess I am not a bachelor anymore," was the best he could muster.

Liz made a quick trip out for provisions while Adam tended to Hef and began consulting online maps for the best way out to Mendham. He also started checking for any information on Doubleday's whereabouts when he lived there, and this time he was in luck. Abner and Mary Doubleday, he learned, had lived the general's final years right in the center of town. The house was torn down in the 1930s, but its location was known to have been in the side yard of the house that now stood at 13 Hilltop Road. Adam was able to locate that on the map and decided that should be their stepping-off point.

So, when Sunday morning dawned, the Wallace family piled back into their car, headed uptown, made the left onto Ninety-Sixth Street, then headed north on the West Side Highway to the GW Bridge. Once across, they followed a couple of interstates to Morristown, then wound their way to New Jersey 24. From there, it should have been easy: Jersey 24 became Main Street in Mendham, and Hilltop was the cross street right in the center of town. Alas, Adam had not counted on there being a Mendham *Township* centered right on the same road, which led to some brief confusion until he realized that what they were looking for was Mendham *Borough*. Still, it was not that long before they found themselves parked and standing in front of a well-maintained, gabled, white two-story surrounded by a wrought iron fence. The remnant of an old front walk off to their left marked the probable once-upon-a-time entrance to the Doubleday house, and under the canopy of trees behind the fence, someone had thoughtfully placed a historic marker.

Beside the text was a familiar photograph of the general. Best of all, the house itself faced almost due east.

Adam's excitement was palpable. This was the first truly promising location he had scouted, and he could not wait to pull out the enlarged copy of the map he had brought along.

"There's no way to know exactly where that old house was located," he said to Liz. "But I'd be willing to bet that the first part of the map, that first five paces to the east, would have taken you from the front door or the front stoop to either the street or whatever walking path was there at the time. Let's try picking up on the sidewalk where that old front walk is and see where that takes us."

Turning north, back toward Main Street, Adam marked off 211 paces while Liz trundled behind, pushing Hef in his travel stroller. Adam tried to maintain a constant gait as he passed an antique store and an

IT company of some sort and something called the Pastime Club, but nevertheless, he felt himself growing more and more excited as it became clear that the count would end almost precisely at the intersection ahead. Just as he was about to make the next turn to his left, he looked up and noticed a sign. In fancy lettering, it read:

> *Borough of Mendham*
> *Phoenix House*
> *Administrative*
> *Engineering*
> *& Planning Board*

Phoenix House, he thought. *Phoenix House! That's what that bird is on both of the maps. It's a Phoenix!*

"Liz!" he exclaimed. "Do you see what I see?"

Liz, too, having caught up, was staring with a mixture of excitement and wonder at the sign and at the office building on the corner, obviously a converted old house. It had a long front porch facing Main Street, topped by a balcony stretching its full length. "Oh my God," was about all she could muster. "Is this for real?"

"Well, let's make sure." Adam proceeded to walk fifteen paces to the west, along Main Street, which put him directly at the end of a stone stair leading to the front door. Another fifteen paces, this time to the south, took him up the stairs and right to the entrance of the building. Pressing his luck, Adam tried the door. Then he remembered that it was Sunday, and no public offices would likely be open today.

The thought of coming this close and then having to drive back to Manhattan empty-handed was depressing, and if they did not have young Hef along, they might have considered spending the night in a local hotel, even without a change of clothes. But that was not to be. Liz remembered passing an Italian restaurant not far away down Main Street, and they stopped there for a quick lunch before heading back to the apartment to do whatever research they could on that building and to make plans for their return.

<hr />

"Mr. Shirokan? Good morning. This is Mike Chaney, the investigator you hired."

"Of course. Mr. Chaney. I wondered when I might hear from you."

"Sir, I'm planning on sending along a written report if you want me to. But I thought you might appreciate a less formal summary of our findings before you make that decision. Hence this call. Should I proceed?"

"Yes, very good. Please do. What did you find?"

"Perhaps not surprisingly, we found that your Professor Dickens is a very private fellow. In fact, he is a little bit too private, if you know what I mean. His published work, as you already knew, bears no relationship with the interests of your organization or with the collections he has been acquiring. And his office—and really, it is a complex of office and other spaces—is inaccessible to outsiders. That accounts in large measure for the length of time it has taken us to develop a profile.

"Professor Dickens lives alone on the second floor of a brownstone in the West eighties. The house is a small-scale condominium, and he owns his apartment. The apartment itself has a main seating area, an updated kitchen, a master suite, and a second bedroom he uses as an office. In that office, he keeps mainly personal records and very few items relating to the university. He appears to have an earned income of $280,000 per year, all of it from the university via salary. He also has an investment portfolio, but no dominant single holding and no holdings in non-public companies, insofar as we know."

"How did you—"

Mike did not give him a chance to finish the question. "He is a man of simple tastes and not especially gregarious. In fact, one might describe his manner as cautious. He is, however, a creature of habit. He travels to work and home by the same route daily, begins and ends work on something of a routine schedule, eats his meals at a set time, always in one or the other of two on-campus locations.

"His workspace is most unusual. It is located within the engineering school, which is a secure building with a guarded entrance lobby. The floor on which it is located is not listed in the building directory and can be reached by only one of the three elevators in the building—and then only with the use of a specially-coded key card. The space is labeled 'Applied Human Potentiality' and includes at least one personal office and a document storage area that may be extensive. He may also have a laboratory space in the adjacent building that houses the Biology Department.

"The professor is either very disorganized in his office or overwhelmed by work. The space is filled to bursting with file boxes and stacks of papers. Many of these appear to deal with topics unrelated to engineering, specifically such matters as reincarnation and something called precognition. We have obtained a small number of examples of these which I will forward to you. We are unable to estimate just how representative these samples may be of the full range of materials in the office.

"Partly because of that disconnect, we have conducted an extensive inquiry into the sources of the professor's funding. Perhaps the most salient point is that it does not come from grants from government, foundations, or any other sources. If it did, we would be able to find and report on certain information that such entities are required to report publicly. But the university has confirmed that Professor Dickens receives his support via one or more private contracts between the university and an outside entity called LanyMech. These contracts include nondisclosure language and apparently also reference trade secrets, so they refused to provide any further information.

"We looked into LanyMech, which is the current name for an old-line industrial company called Lany Mechanical. They design things like commercial ventilation systems. Good cover for an engineer, I guess, but again, not related in any way to what is in his office. So we traced the ownership of LanyMech, which turns out to be a subsidiary of a subsidiary of a subsidiary until you run out of US-based companies and start bouncing around the Caymans and beyond. So it's obviously a cover. We could push that further if you like, but because that would involve international travel and probably some, ah, marginally ethical expenses, well, I thought I'd better see if you wanted us to keep going on that. The only coincidence we came across in all of that was that a Paul C. Mannington was on the boards of directors of a couple of the upstream companies. It's possible that's Paul Chi Mannington, the software billionaire. And that could mean something, but the fact is, when people set up these kinds of corporate strings, they will often either recruit a big name like that for credibility or even use a name like that without authorization on the assumption nobody will ever notice. Or they might just find somebody who, by chance, has the same name—in this case the same given name and middle initial—and pay them a fee to allow its use. If you like, we could try to reach out to the real Mannington, but those billionaires can be pretty elusive. And that is about what I have for you."

"Well, that's quite a report. And on reflection, you are probably right. I do not want to know how you obtained your information, and at this time, I don't think we'll require a written report. As to your questions, I think that, at least for now, we should stop here. If you'll be good enough to messenger over those papers you mentioned and, separately, to mail me an invoice, I will make sure that we settle up promptly."

"Will do. You should have the papers in an unmarked envelope by close of business. And thank you."

"Oh, no, Mr. Chaney. It is I who thank you. My colleagues will be very interested in what you have told me. Excellent work. Do have a pleasant day."

The more he read about Mendham, and specifically about Phoenix House, the more convinced Adam became that he and Liz had solved the puzzle presented by the map. Right around the turn of the twentieth century, a number of wealthy families from New York City and its environs had been building country manors and estates for themselves out in the New Jersey countryside as far as Morristown and toward Mendham. The trend didn't reach the town itself, but many of the residents either hired out as servants in the estates or established themselves as merchants and suppliers to that clientele. That trend was just getting underway when Doubleday died in 1893. The "borough" hadn't been established until about a decade later—something to do with plumbing, he gathered. There were lots of nice houses in the town now, but they went back only forty years or so. The commercial strip they'd driven through on the way into town had wiped out any history that might remain along Main Street to the east, but fortunately, the Doubleday homesite lay just within the start of a small historic district that had been preserved.

From what Adam read, Abner and Mary Doubleday had visited Mendham as early as 1873, when he had retired from the Army, and they returned for the duration not long afterward. While they were building their own home on what is now Hilltop Road, which was nothing more than a dirt strip back then, they lived in a nearby boarding house that had once served as a seminary for young ladies but had been converted to guest lodgings in 1820 by its new owner, William Phoenix. Dubbed Phoenix House, it was operated by his three daughters for the half-century from William's death in 1857 until 1907. In other words, Adam realized, Doubleday had actually lived for a time at Phoenix House and would surely have known everything there was to know about the building itself. Then he discovered a 1907 postcard photo of the building that showed the dirt road beside it, down which the Doubledays had resided, one that even hinted at including the front of their house in the distance.

Phoenix House, Mendham, N. J.

Adam knew he had to get inside Phoenix House as soon as he could. He halfway dreamed his way through the rest of the history but did learn that the property had been purchased from the Phoenix family in 1919 by a retired state senator, who then deeded it over to the Borough of Mendham, which began housing some of its offices there in 1938. One point that caught Adam's eye was that Phoenix House had been renovated and restored around 2017. That, he realized, might prove highly problematic.

Liz had been thinking she might enjoy a day of window shopping over on the East Side, but when Adam shared what he had learned about Phoenix House, she gave up any interest in Gucci and Jimmy Chu. Not that she would have been a buyer, but even the sport lost its appeal. The thrill of the hunt took over.

So first thing on Monday morning, they headed out once again, thankful that once on the GW Bridge, they were going against the morning commute. Still, it was a slower drive out to Mendham, and they arrived closer to midday than they would have liked. This time, they pulled right into the municipal parking lot beside Phoenix House, walked around to the front of the building, and went up the stone stairs and inside.

Rather than a reception area, they found themselves in an entry hall on the main floor furnished with an oriental rug and antiques—rocking chairs, a grandfather clock, and a table full of municipal brochures

118

and information sheets. There were offices to their right, and through a doorway on the left a sort of living room-dining room that seemed to have been, if not preserved, at least replicated. Here, too, oriental rugs and tasteful antiques prevailed. A pair of fireplaces topped by historical portraits completed the effect.

"Not your typical town hall," Liz observed.

"No kidding," was the best Adam could muster.

Climbing the stairs directly ahead of them, they found a second cluster of offices on the second floor. With no other apparent options, they selected one office at random and entered. A young woman behind a countertop looked up and asked how she could be of assistance.

"This will sound really strange," said Adam, who had given some thought as to how best to begin his search of the building. "But we are working on a biography of Abner Doubleday, and we know he once lived in this building. We were wondering if there's anyone here now who might be able to tell us what the building was like back then."

"Really?" replied the young woman. "Abner Doubleday lived here?"

"Yes, he and his wife, while they were building their house around the corner."

"Wow. Well, goodness . . . The only person I can think of who might know anything about that would be George downstairs in 102b. I don't know George's last name, but he's, like, kind of old and always talking about how the building used to be—you know they renovated a few years ago, and I didn't work here then, but I guess it was pretty bad—and all that. You might try him."

"Thanks very much," said Liz. They retreated downstairs and, after some further inquiries, did find George, who turned out to be George Taylor, an accountant in the finance office, which was not, as it turned out, in Room 102b. "Old" George looked to be in his late forties. All a matter of perspective, they guessed.

"Yes," he said, "it is true that the Doubledays stayed here for a while back when it was a guest house. That was maybe thirty years or more before the county took it over. Place was going to hell back then, and I guess they fixed it up to a point, though that was during the Depression. And then there was never any money to do much more and it started to get really run down. Finally they put together some grants a few years ago, back in the teens, and really fixed it back up. It's a nice place to work now!"

"George," interrupted Adam, "what we'd really like to do is see any parts of the building that might not have been touched in all of that and might still be the way they were back in Doubleday's times. I don't know, the basement, maybe, or if there's an attic?"

"Well, the basement, that's all mechanical stuff, and every bit of that was replaced when they fixed the place up. There's an attic of some sort, all the way at the top of the stairs. Never been up there myself. Hold on a minute; let me make a call.

"Richie? It's George upstairs. Listen, I have a couple of people, say they're writing a book, and they want to look around up in the attic to see if there's any remnants left over from before the county owned the building. Can you let them up there?" He paused. "That would be great. I might tag along myself since I've never been up there. See you in two. Thanks."

Then, to Adam and Liz, "We're good. Richie is the custodian. He'll meet us at the attic stairs in just a minute."

Liz, who had been tending to Hef all this time, asked if George would mind if she stayed put while they investigated the attic. George said he didn't mind at all, then grabbed a Nerf football off of his desk, which he handed to Hef.

"You just play with this for a while, young fellow. Your dad and I won't be long." Then, he turned to Liz and said, knowingly, "Three grandsons."

Adam and George disappeared for about fifteen minutes, then returned empty-handed. Richie had shown them the way to the attic and opened the locked door for them, but he had also told Adam, correctly as it turned out, that when the building had been renovated back around 2017, the first thing that happened was that some crew had come in and taken out everything that had been stored in the attic, and after a hundred plus years, there was quite a lot of it, and then replaced the flooring and made some other repairs. Neither Richie nor George knew what company that had been. In practical terms, that meant that, even if he was right and Doubleday had stashed something in Phoenix House sometime before his death, it was almost surely lost to history. Even if he'd stashed it inside the walls, which seemed unlikely, it would be lost because, from the sound of it, even the walls had been opened up either because of mold or because of structural issues and replaced with modern drywall. So near, and yet so far.

It was George who lit the one remaining flame of hope. "Maybe," he said, "you could find out who the architects were and see if they held onto anything of value."

Adam brightened. He actually knew who the architects for the renovation had been. He'd seen them brag online about an award they'd received for the project. He pulled out his tablet and called up that page. Then he pulled out his cell phone.

"Ladies and Gentlemen . . ." The voice was that of Joseph Armstrong, president of the Circle. "I am calling to order this special meeting of the American Circle Board of Directors. Please take your seats." He paused for a moment to allow them to comply.

"The Chair recognizes Jeremy for the purpose of reporting on his inquiries into Professor Dickens."

"Thank you, Joe. Following up on our charge from the previous meeting, my subcommittee engaged the services of an investigative firm and tasked them with profiling Professor Dickens. You will note that I have not delivered to you a written report of that investigation. That remains an option, but when I describe for you the results of their investigation, and when you consider the investigative methods the firm may have employed, you, like me and the other members of the committee, may think it best not to require that."

Shirokan proceeded to summarize the report very much as Mike Chaney had presented it to him. There were a couple of questions afterward but very little discussion.

"Thank you, Jeremy. That was very thorough in the circumstances. Those in favor of accepting the committee's report as delivered, please signify in the customary manner." Every hand went up around the table.

"Vivian, I believe you were going to look into additional resources for our defense fund?"

"Yes, Joe. Over the weeks since our last session, I have been able to convince several of our wealthier members to increase their contributions by a total of . . . $53,000. That is a disappointing number, I know, but do recall that these individuals are already major donors to the movement. In addition," she added, sitting straight up in her chair, a sure sign that something interesting was coming, "I have raised approximately $245,000 in one-time gifts through direct appeals to some of my dearest *personal* friends."

At this, there was a collective sigh of relief around the table, and a spattering of applause.

"In listening to Jeremy, however," Vivian Vance-Victor continued, "I have come to the realization that we do not have, and may need to recruit, one principal mega-donor to sustain our efforts. In days past, as you know, Theosophy appealed to many of the brightest and wealthiest people in the land, and many were members or supporters. But this is a more cynical era, to say the least, and there are so many more interests appealing for support. Now I know the danger in this suggestion: If we are too dependent on one individual, we are somewhat at the will of whoever that is. Our movement had such battles in its early days. The split between Brother Judge and Sister Annie Bessant that led, eventually, to the powerful influence of Katherine Tingley comes to mind. Yet it must be said that, in our present circumstance, without resources at such a level as a major benefactor might provide, this challenge may overwhelm us."

Armstrong asked the obvious question. "Vivian, do you have someone in mind?"

"There, too, I believe Jeremy's presentation might prove instructive. What about someone like Paul Chi Mannington? If we could attract someone like that to support us—perhaps as a member, were he so persuaded, but in the alternative, simply as an act of philanthropy—we could meet the challenge presented by this Columbia professor and any other challenge that might come along. Presuming, of course, that we could dissuade Mr. Mannington from getting overly involved in the activities of the Circle."

"You know," Jeremy Shirokan inserted, "even if he declined an invitation to support us, it might be interesting to meet with him and observe his reactions. Remember that it is just remotely possible that he is, in fact, the Paul C. Mannington who sits on those two corporate boards Mr. Chaney uncovered. If so, we might even be able to convince him to pressure those companies somehow to constrain Professor Dickens, or even terminate his contracts. It never hurts to ask."

"Does anyone here know this Mannington fellow?" Armstrong asked.

No hands.

"Anyone think they might have some way indirectly to reach out to him?"

No hands.

Once again, it was Vivian Vance-Victor to the rescue. "I am probably the one who is best positioned to give this a try. Let me see if I can find an avenue to Mr. Mannington through one or another of my charities."

And with that, the meeting adjourned. Armstrong and the others realized that the question of strategy had yet to be addressed. But that was probably still premature.

Adam's call to the architecture firm that had done the design work on Phoenix House was not immediately productive. The firm, he was informed, was not in the practice of removing artifacts from historic buildings, and the man he spoke with seemed rather disturbed that Adam might have thought otherwise. He did, however, after some verbal bowing and scraping, provide the name of the company that had been assigned the task of pre-construction cleanup, Howard & Son Remaindering. The name of the firm did not appeal to Adam, who knew what remaindering was in the book world, at least back when most people actually held books in their hands rather than reading electronic versions. It was the work of the vultures who swept into publishers' warehouses, gathered up all the books whose time in the market had passed, and sold them by the pound to discounters and secondhand bookstores and others who then resold them for pennies and never compensated authors. He had seen one of his first books treated in just that way, and he still bore the psychological scars. But maybe it was different in the world of building renovations. In any event, he knew he must make the call.

"You have reached Howard and Son Remaindering. We are closed for two weeks for our annual vacation period. Your business is important to us, and we hope you will call back. Thank you."

Adam was beginning to understand how George Washington must have felt back in the winter of 1779-80, hunkered down for months in nearby Morristown with nothing to do but wait. It looked as if he, and perhaps Liz, would be coming back out here yet again, though the absence of a date in the voicemail message left him uncertain as to just when that might be.

Liz, too, was disappointed, but she was determined to make something of the day, so she pulled out her phone and googled antique dealers in the area. Adam was less than overjoyed at the thought of doing *that*, but she had been a sport to accompany him, and fair was fair. Liz settled on a dealer in Morristown who looked promising, and that at least had the benefit of being on their way back to the apartment.

Thomas Hendright Antiques turned out to be an inspired choice. The large shop was filled with fine furniture from years past as well as the requisite lamps, crystal, books, papers, old photographs. Better still, Hef was fast asleep in his travel stroller. Liz pushed him to the rear of the shop and asked the owner if she might park the stroller there while they looked around. He was a sweet older man, and he readily agreed. After all, but for the Wallace family, the shop was deserted.

"What brings you folks in today?" the man asked.

"We were just out in Mendham," answered Adam, who had joined the others, "trying to trace the steps of Abner Doubleday. You know, he used to live out there."

The owner smiled broadly. "So it's Doubleday that interests you?"

"Yes," replied Liz and Adam, almost in unison.

"Well, you happen to be speaking with the local Abner Doubleday historian, unofficially speaking, of course. Tom Hendright," he said, thrusting out his hand.

"We're Adam and Liz Fairchild," Liz offered in return.

"Baseball fans?" he queried.

"Actually," Adam made sure he answered first, "we live up in Cooperstown, so it's more of a local history thing with us, though obviously baseball's a big part of that. Doubleday went to school in Cooperstown for a year or so, and we're just sort of tracing his path after that. Good way to pick vacation spots, because he was all over—New York City, San Francisco, Texas, and of course, toward the end, out here."

"Well, I'm very happy to meet you folks. I was up your way years ago reading some of his papers up at the Hall of Fame, and I have chased some others down over the years. That's kind of my excuse for a vacation. Have you ever seen a picture of their house?" he asked.

"No. We found the spot where it used to be, but it's all just trees and landscaping now, and a big wrought iron fence."

"Well, have a look at this old newspaper from here in Morristown," he said, pulling a plastic document sleeve from a drawer in his desk. "The house was torn down sometime before about 1937, but they found this old photo somewhere. As you can see, it was a two-story frame affair with a kind of bay window upstairs. Nice landscaping and a little fence out front with a gate. I've been keeping an eye out for the original of this photo, but it's never come through the shop. I did read some of those letters the article talks about, back on that trip I took up your way."

A thought occurred to Adam. It was not part of his charge, but he thought Paul might be interested in the answer.

"Tom, let me ask you a really strange question. Do you have any reason to think that Doubleday might have known Armenian?"

"You mean the language, like from Armenia? That's somewhere over in Europe, isn't it?"

"That's the place. Any idea about that?"

"Now, I can't say that specifically. But you know, Abner was something of a linguist. He spoke Spanish, I guess because he fought in the war down in Mexico. And he might have known some Indian, sorry, Native American languages—Seminole, Apache. Same reason. I know, too, that when he was retired, he translated two French language books on magic and the occult—apparently he was into that stuff in a big way—into English. But I never came across anything about Armenian."

"Well, I'm not surprised, but it was worth a shot. If you—"

"Hold on," Tom said. "This might not be what you're looking for but . . . Just a minute. Let me hang my Closed Until clock on the door. . . ." He moved catlike through the crowded shop, posted his sign, and returned. "Come along through the back with me. I live just behind the store, and there's something I want to show you and have a look at myself."

They exited through the rear of the store, walked across a yard that was beautifully landscaped with rocks and flower gardens, and entered the back door of the house opposite.

"Like any antique dealer," Tom was saying, "there are some special things that come through my shop that I hold onto. You know, Abner and Mary Doubleday were ardent book collectors, and they also had lots of memorabilia, especially from his military service. Gettysburg and all. And when you collect things like that, you need to have someplace to put them. Have a look."

Adam and Liz were in a large parlor room, and along one entire wall were two bookcases and two glass-fronted cabinet units. The workmanship was quite good, from what they could tell.

"These pieces are from around 1880, and they all belonged to Abner and Mary. I've traced them all the way back, and they are quite certainly from the Doubleday estate."

"These are gorgeous," said Liz. "May we touch them?"

"You can do better, and that's the reason I've brought you over here. Adam, if you would just give me a hand with these books," he said, pointing to one of the bookcases, "and Liz, if you would very carefully remove my treasures from that cabinet, we can put all of this carefully on the table over there . . . Now, Adam, if you would just help me rotate these two pieces so that we can see the backs . . . They're actually not very heavy . . . There!"

Tom leaned in to have a good look at the label on the bookcase, which amounted to a small slip of paper that had been glued to the piece well over a century before.

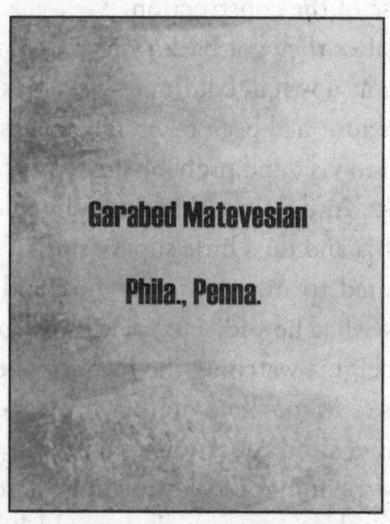

Garabed Matevesian

Phila., Penna.

"There it is. And yes, just as I thought. Do you see this label here?" he asked, making room for his guests to peer behind the bookcase. "This piece, and I think we'll find all of these beautiful pieces, were handmade by a craftsman named Garabed Matevesian. He was, we believe, the son of an Armenian bridge designer who came to this country during the Civil War. Matevesian worked in Philadelphia for most of his career. His family was among the very first Armenians in this part of the country, and maybe in the country overall. Can't say. But here's what's interesting.

"You know that Abner and Mary moved out to Mendham in the 1870s, right? What you might not know is that they rented rooms at a place called the Phoenix House, kind of a cross between a hotel and a boardinghouse right in the center of town there. Maybe you saw it. It's just a bunch of borough offices these days. Anyway, they rented there for quite a while as they were having their own house built right nearby. Mendham wasn't a very big place back then. And Mary, well, both of them really, they liked nice things, and as far as furniture went, why, Philadelphia was where you went to find the finest. According to some old letters I saw on one of my trips, the Doubledays traveled down to Philadelphia to arrange to have furniture made for their house when it was ready. Would have taken months of lead time back then, but they had that time because of the construction.

"Now, not long after they got back to Mendham, Mary heard that a favorite one of her aunts down in Baltimore—she was a Baltimore Hewitt, you know—well, her aunt had been taken ill and was asking for Mary. So Mary took herself off to visit and probably help care for her aunt. She was gone for several weeks. And during that time, she told Abner he ought to go over to Philadelphia and do a little supervising of the furniture maker. I think she just wanted to make sure her husband was occupied with something. So that's what he did. He spent most of that time she was away down in Philadelphia watching the furniture being made—which I know from his letters to Mary—and doing whatever else appealed to him.

"Now, I can't answer your question straight out, because I just don't know. But if he was spending weeks watching these here pieces of furniture being made, and you can see that would have been a slow and laborious process, and given his proclivity for languages, he might have just been talking with Mr. Matevesian. And given that Mr. Matevesian's English might not have been that great, well, maybe they traded lessons or something. I never saw anything Abner ever wrote down in Armenian, not ever. Or Spanish, for that matter. But he sure might have developed an ear for it.

"I remember I had a French teacher once who told us that you know you've mastered a language when you actually start to dream in it. Being in this business, I do have occasion to use my French, and I can *parlez-vous* it just fine, and yes, I have dreamed in French once or twice. But I can't write it worth a darn. Maybe he was the same way. Of course, we'll never know."

———

"Commissioner, how nice to hear from you." The call had come in just as Roger Coppersmith, Chief Operating Officer of the Hall of Fame, was finishing his morning coffee. "To what do I owe the pleasure?"

"Roger, I was wondering if I might ask a favor."

"Of course. As long as it's in my power to grant it."

"I'd like to arrange a special event up at your place. I want to invite about twenty reporters up there—principal baseball writers mainly, on my dime, of course—and set up a little news briefing in your auditorium. I have some important news I want to deliver, and I want to be sure it gets their attention. We'll put them on a couple of luxury buses and drive up from the City, drive them back so they have plenty of time to rehash what they heard."

"That sounds important. Might I ask what the big announcement is? You're not stepping down, I hope."

"No, not that," the Commissioner laughed as he replied, thinking to himself, *nice try, buddy.* "And I really can't say what it is right now. But I will tell you that it has something to do with the Hall, in a way, which is one reason I'd really like to do it up there. Can we make that happen? You are, of course, welcome to sit in. In fact, I hope you will."

"Certainly. Can we have a couple of weeks or so to prepare? We'll need to make sure we find a day when the facility is not already booked."

"Sure, sure. I'll have someone from my staff give you a call in the next day or so with our possible dates, preferred arrangements, logistics, and the like."

"I'll wait for the call, and in the meantime, I'll get someone to look over our calendar and tell me what's possible."

"Excellent. Thank you, Rog. I knew I could count on you." And he ended the call. Time to start building momentum and creating a little buzz on a few sports desks.

———

Adam had silenced his phone and placed it in his pocket while he was doing some writing, so it was a vibration and not a ring that attracted his attention. He pulled it out and checked the screen. The number looked vaguely familiar, so he answered.

"Adam Wallace."

"Adam, it's Paul Mannington. Did I catch you at a good time?"

"Paul. Sure. I mean, absolutely. What can I do for you?"

"It's been a while now since we visited, and I was getting curious as to whether you were making any progress. How's the search going?"

"Funny you should ask that. I just got home day before yesterday from some related travel, and I was trying to decide whether I needed to give you some sort of interim update."

"And . . . ?"

"And it's a classic good news/bad news situation, at least so far. But there is some serious good news. We figured out where the map is based, and we followed it."

"We?"

"Oh, sorry. I got my wife, Liz, involved in the search. Two heads better than one sort of thing, and she actually is quite good at piecing things together. I think you said that was okay."

"Yes, that's fine, as long as we all understand the terms."

"That's not a problem. She's completely on board."

"Good. And you were saying you found a fit for the map?"

"We did. We spent several days visiting some key locations in Doubleday's life. We figured one of those might be the starting point. We started from the beginning—Ballston Spa, where he was born; Auburn, New York, where he grew up; and here in Cooperstown, where he supposedly invented the game while he was in school. They were all dead ends. Then we decided to start at the other end. We went down to Mendham, New Jersey, where he retired and eventually died. We were able to locate the spot where the house he built there used to be, and when we used that as a starting point for the map, it led us directly to a place called Phoenix House, which is now the municipal office building there. But the house itself was built by the Phoenix family back around 1820 or so, and between 1857 and 1907, it was operated as a hotel or a boardinghouse. When Abner and his wife moved out there to build their retirement house, they stayed for several months at Phoenix House. And you know those drawings of birds on the maps?"

"Phoenixes!" Paul had jumped ahead.

"Exactly. So we went inside and talked with some folks in the building, and we even got to look around in the attic. They've had offices in there since 1938. But there was nothing there that related in any way to Doubleday, or, for that matter, to anything or anybody before about 2017. That's when the building was completely cleared out and renovated. And that's where we get to the bad news, at least so far.

"I talked to someone at the architecture firm that designed the renovation and remodeling to see if they might have held onto some old artifacts from the building. That was a dead end. In fact, they got a little huffy that I would even ask such a thing. But I was able to get the name of the company they brought in to do the cleanout before the demo and construction started. It's a small local company, and I tried to contact them, but they are closed for vacation. Guess they all go at once. I'll follow up with them in a few days and see if it's worth going back down there."

"It sounds like you are being very thorough, Adam. That's exactly why I wanted you on this project."

"Paul, wait. I haven't actually gotten to the good part yet. And here's where we both have Liz to thank. On the way back from Mendham, she decided we should stop at a big antique shop in Morristown, which is like the next town over. And it turned out that the proprietor was New Jersey's biggest Abner Doubleday wonk. Guy spends his vacations chasing down Doubleday's old correspondence and who knows what else. Well, we got talking about Doubleday, so I asked him in passing if he knew whether Doubleday had ever studied Armenian. I know that was not part of my task, but I figured, what the heck. At first, he said he had no reason to think so. But then, all of a sudden, he says he wants to close the shop and take us to his house to see something.

"So we go into this guy's house, and he starts clearing off some old bookcases and cabinets, and he says these actually belonged to Abner and Mary Doubleday. I guess they had a lot of books and memorabilia. So we look at the back of a couple of these, and there's this label from the maker in Philadelphia, and it's pretty clearly an Armenian name. So then this guy tells us he's seen correspondence between Abner and Mary suggesting that Abner spent several weeks down in Philadelphia supervising the making of the furniture. I looked later, and there were almost no Armenians in the US back then, but there were a few. And apparently this furniture maker was one of them.

"Of course, it doesn't prove that Doubleday learned Armenian while he was there in Philadelphia, sitting all day with this craftsman, but it sure might have been possible. He was into languages."

There was silence while Paul processed this information.

"Paul? Are you there?"

"Sorry. I was just taking in what you said. That's an amazing bit of detective work, Adam. And it might be the answer to one of the biggest questions. Good work!"

"Paul, before you go, I have one question. I think it's a tremendous longshot that we'll find the box Doubleday supposedly hid away. It's too long ago, and that building has been through no telling how many changes since then. But on the off chance that we should somehow come across that, or a way to find it, when we talk with the remaindering contractor, well, how would you like us to handle that?"

<hr />

"Mr. Mannington, it's so good of you to see me while you are in town." Vivian Vance-Victor had followed through on her plan, and the approach had borne fruit. She was seated in one of Mannington's offices, this one in Midtown Manhattan. "Francesca Valle sends her regards."

"How is Franki?"

"I just saw her last month. We sit on several boards together. I don't know if you were aware of her surgery, but she came through it well and she's mostly recovered now."

"I was not aware of that. I hope it was nothing serious, and it sounds like it had a good outcome." He paused for a moment. "Now, please tell me what I can do for you. And please call me Paul."

"Thank you, Paul. I'm Viv. And as to your question . . . One of the boards on which I sit is that of the American Theosophy Circle."

Paul maintained his poker face but was curious as to just where this conversation was going.

"I don't know if you are familiar with Theosophy, but it's been around for many years, and there are national and local organizations all around the world. Our members are philosophers and scientists and thinkers in general who share a common belief in peace and love and the other grand human values and believe that our potential as human beings is far from being fully realized. You could say we share some beliefs with Buddhism and some of the other Eastern religions that are alien to Western belief systems. We believe that these ideas need not be taken on faith but that they can be tested and demonstrated and more fully appreciated.

"In any event, our Circle maintains an extensive library of books and articles and correspondence and other writing pertinent to our beliefs, a collection we have historically built either by bequest, usually from the estates of deceased members, or by acquisition, for which we have a modest budget."

Paul could now see the path this conversation was to take. In fact, he could no longer keep count of the number of times he'd had the very same conversation as it related to one worthy cause or another.

"Things had gone along in this way for many years. But recently, we have encountered a problem. There is a professor at Columbia University, a Professor Dickens, I believe, who has been purchasing these collections both privately and at public auction at prices that are far beyond our means."

This was not what Paul had expected, and he raised his guard from what he thought of as DEFCON Five to DEFCON Four, or perhaps Three and a Half.

Vivian continued. "At the very least, this is depriving us of our heritage. But more threatening still is the fact that we do not know this professor's intent. Over the years, Theosophists have been falsely and unfairly accused of many antisocial views. Today we are little known, and that has proven an effective deterrent. We are not a threat to anyone, and no one perceives us as such. However, depending on what may or may not be in these various collections of documents the professor has been gathering up—and I emphasize that we have no way of knowing what that might be—there might be something in there that he, or his sponsor, could put to some evil purpose." DEFCON Three, for sure.

"We have tried to find out who or what is behind Professor Dickens, and we have hit something of a wall. He seems to be working in secret, protected by a barrier of contract language and shell companies. Goodness, there were even a couple of these that listed a board member named Paul C. Mannington, so they are even trying to suggest your own involvement."

Vivian watched Paul intently as she relayed this news. For his part, Paul continued to show nothing, even as he mentally slipped into DEFCON Two.

"Now we know," she pursued the point, "that people who form these kinds of offshore arrangements often use names or find shills with names similar to famous people in an effort to appear legitimate, and I can assure you we are confident that is the case here. So please don't think otherwise. But in learning about that, we thought of you in a different way. We thought that perhaps we might persuade you to come to our rescue by seeing the merit of our cause and providing us with the financial wherewithal to discourage and hopefully dispose of this well-endowed professor."

Back to DEFCON Three, but Vivian was presenting him with a most engaging dilemma.

"And just what level of wherewithal are we talking about here?" Paul asked.

"Honestly, it is difficult to be sure. These collections become available only irregularly and vary from one another in extent, composition, and value. All we really need to do is to find and exceed Professor Dickens's upper limit. If we are able to do that two or three times, we rather expect he will simply go away. We might be talking a maximum of one or two million dollars here, perhaps less."

"And in return?" Paul laid the question on the table. "What might I expect in return? That sounds crass, but we are not talking here about curing cancer or sick kids. We're talking about bailing out a fairly obscure, and from what you say, sometimes controversial . . . what . . . school of philosophy? Religion? Fringe group? Cult?"

"Paul, I can assure you we are neither fringe thinkers nor cultists. Many of our views are widely shared in other parts of the world, if not here. And while it may be that we are a religious movement in some key ways, we are also open-minded about such matters and engaged in serious scientific inquiry. But I take your point, and I can agree that our need carries less emotional appeal than many others. And yet, we are trying to preserve the record of a movement that stands for freedom and for maximizing human potential. I am sure you must receive many appeals from people like me. If it's psychic gratification you are looking for, perhaps you will find it there. Or perhaps, as you come to know us, you might even come to share some of our values. As a spiritual matter, we would welcome you as we welcome all. But as a practical matter, we are simply asking for your help in preserving our heritage."

DEFCON Four.

"Viv, let me give this matter some thought. In truth, the amount that you're asking for is not consequential to me. You probably know that. But I do try to be very careful in making these decisions, and I like to have a chance to perform some due diligence. Please give me some time to consider your request. I do appreciate your coming in. And please give my best to Franki and tell her I'm glad to know she is feeling better."

Vivian Vance-Victor left Mannington's office having gleaned little new intelligence, but at the same time hopeful that she had been sufficiently persuasive. Only time would tell.

———

The Commissioner simply did not trust his clerical staff to undertake such a delicate task. He had inherited most of them from his predecessor, and he harbored suspicions that some number of them had divided loyalties—or worse. A leak at this point would spoil his plans. So as usual, he turned to CI, the one person he genuinely trusted.

"CI, I want you to make the arrangements for the trip up to Cooperstown. If there is some genuine scut work, you can pass that off to the crew out there. But make sure there is nothing anybody could leak or even sabotage. I don't trust those drones at all. Anything that matters, you take care of that yourself."

"Okay, boss. Got it. What, exactly, do you want me to set up?"

The Commissioner laid out his plan to bus the selected reporters back and forth from the offices in Chelsea and gave CI a list of the two dozen names he'd settled on as offering the best collective combination of gullibility, self-importance, and actual influence. Put some meat in the pot and throw those three traits together to stew for a couple of hours on the ride back, and he was pretty sure he'd get just the kind of coverage he wanted.

"Open bar on the bus?" asked CI.

"Only on the way back. And make it top shelf. We want them to feel special for having been chosen, special for the exclusive access they just had, and warm and fuzzy, and maybe a little fuzzy-headed, on the way home. And let's arrange a nice big lunch just before the news conference, too. Slow 'em down a little, muddle their heads."

"Decided what you're going to tell them?"

"I have. Here's some material to work with." He handed a packet to his aide. "We'll want to put together a press kit that includes the text of my remarks, maybe a page or two of FAQs, some backgrounders on these people and this religious cult, a graphic with those connections you made behind the Doubleday selection, for sure a big glossy printout of that Theosophy emblem, and, of course, a copy of the Spalding letter you dug up. That's the really important part of the work I need from you. I'm going to give them a conspiracy so deep and dark they'll need a flashlight to find the way out. And I'm going to give them an enemy that people can join with us in tearing down. Baseball will reclaim a moral high ground it lost to the damned Black Sox a hundred-some years ago, and the commissioner will be a white knight slaying the dragon. If we do this right, people will forget all about the last few years."

CI was skimming through the packet of working materials he'd just received. "Don't you need to be a little careful here, boss? I mean, if this really is a religious group and if they're still around, couldn't some of this be considered, you know, hate speech? Like here, where you say—"

"CI, I'm surprised at you. You know I'd never engage in anything like that," the Commissioner interjected with a broad smile. "Oh, I might cozy up to the line now and then, but I'm always very careful. And you be the same when you put that press packet together, you hear me? But thank you for looking out for me. Now just go and have yourself some fun."

CI knew exactly what had just occurred, knew that he was now potential cannon fodder in the event of real trouble. It was a fact of life working for the man, one they mutually understood, and one he willingly accepted. It had always worked out so far.

All he said was, "Yes, sir. I'm on it."

<hr />

Adam could not remember the last time he had spent so much time in New Jersey, and yet, here he was, once again, headed into the Garden State. Liz had needed to spend some time in her office, so he was on his own. And he had made an executive decision: Rather than head east, pick up I-87, and skirt the City to the west, he would invest what was only an extra half hour or so, avoid the population centers, and wend his way down to Port Jervis and Milford, cross the Delaware—twice, as it turned out—and come in from the rural north. It turned out to be both a relaxed drive and a pleasant one. *Maybe*, he thought, *the Garden State grows more than parkways, people, and rusted industrial buildings.*

The day before, and for at least the third time, Adam had phoned Howard & Son Remaindering, and at last the call was answered. Vacation was over! When he asked if he might speak with Mr. Howard, the woman on the other end of the line had laughed and then told him that Howard was actually the first name of the firm's founder but that now the company was basically, as she put it, just "and son." Howard of the unknown last name had passed away a few months earlier. She transferred the call to his son, Andy, who readily agreed to meet with Adam the following afternoon.

It took him about three and a half hours to reach Mendham, and another five minutes or so to reach the western edge of the borough and locate the world headquarters of Howard & Son Remaindering, which turned out to be a small brick office building of indeterminate origin, an extensive yard filled with salvaged lumber, brick, stone, and other building materials, and in the distance a row of three Quonset huts. The furthest one away looked like it probably dated to the Second World War. The two nearer huts looked not new by any means but newer.

Adam parked in front of the office building, opened the door and entered. Inside, he found, to his right, a woman behind a desk piled high with all manner of papers, and to his left, a man behind a desk covered with a cacophony of small objects—old trophies, a couple of clocks, a variety of those executive toys you might find on the desk of a bored insurance agent, some bric-a-brac Adam could not even identify, and, in the front center of it all, a large nameplate that read, simply, "Andy." Adam took his cue from this.

"You must be Andy," he said with a smile. Reaching out his hand, he continued, "Adam Wallace. We spoke on the phone yesterday."

"Oh, hey, yeah. I remember. Nice to meet you. You were coming down from . . . Cooperstown? Long way to come for junk. What can I do for you?"

"I'm not totally sure," said Adam, "but I am hoping you can help me out a lot. Back a few years ago, the borough here did a big remodel on their offices in the Phoenix House, and I understand from the architects who worked on that project that your company was the first on the site . . . that you went in to clean it up and do the demo work. And from what I saw outside, you might have done some salvage there as well. Does that ring a bell?"

"Ring a bell? That was the biggest job we had that year. Dad and I spent a couple of months over there. That's like an eternity in this business."

"Oh, I meant to offer my condolences on your father's passing. Your . . . assistant over there mentioned it when I called. That must have been hard, especially since the two of you worked together."

"Yes, it was. Hard on Doris there as well. She was Dad's sister."

Doris looked up with a small smile, and Adam nodded in her direction.

"I'm getting used to it, but it's like there's a hole I can't fill, you know. Not just personally, I mean, but here, too. Over the years we had sort of worked out a division of labor. I was the big-picture guy, the one who knocked down the walls. Dad was the smalls guy. He was the one who went into these old buildings first, when we had one, and pulled out all the junk people had accumulated. You know, the old tools and machines, and clothes, and books, and plates, and silverware, and, well, just about anything you can think of. It's amazing to me the kinds of things people just set aside when they're done with them and never give a second thought to. Then they die or move away, and maybe another generation or two of people who never cleaned the old stuff out add their own then die or move away, until eventually there's enough stuff in there that a ceiling collapses from the weight on the floor above. Or the maintenance gets deferred forever. And by the time we get there, half or more of uncovering the underlying structure is just getting to the parts of the actual building we need to knock down. He had the patience for that part of the work, and I never did. I'm having to learn it. Sorry. That was a rant, I guess. You were asking something about the Phoenix House project."

"I was. I know that's a house with a long history, and I got interested in exploring that history a bit through exactly what you're talking about, some of the old objects that might have been stashed in a cellar or an attic and long forgotten. I'm a writer, and I'm interested in resurrecting things like that and telling a story through them. Phoenix House looked like a prime candidate for that, until, that is, I came out here and discovered that it had been stripped out and renovated so recently. I looked in the nooks and crannies that are still there, but, well, you guys obviously did a great job of clearing them out. What I was hoping, though, is that you might still have some of that stuff, whatever it was. Or did you mostly just clear it out and chuck it in a dumpster?"

"Adam, you could almost say that we are the dumpster. We do clear out a lot of stuff that we can't repurpose, and we recycle what we can and dispose of the rest. We try to be good citizens with the refuse. But as you could see if you looked at our yard, we hold onto any building materials and such that we can, and we resell that, sometimes in bulk and sometimes retail to people who come in looking for one thing or another. That's where we make our real money."

"Interesting. But I was actually thinking less of architectural salvage than of old objects, the kind you were talking about a moment ago. You know . . . hurricane lamps or old commercial lighting or signs or furniture or old boxes and the like. Maybe stuff you'd sell off to antique dealers or put out at a flea market. Do you gather up any of that kind of thing?"

At that, Doris, who would have heard every word spoken in the small office even if she had not been listening in—which, to be sure, she had been doing—burst out laughing, and Andy quickly joined in the joke. Only Adam was left with a quizzical expression.

"Adam, you have no idea . . . ," Andy gasped for breath, "how funny that question is. You remember I told you my dad was the guy who cleared out the smalls? Well, he cleared them out of all those old buildings, all right, but then he held onto them for dear life. Almost every blessed one. Maybe God knows why. I surely don't. I guess today you'd call him a hoarder. You probably didn't notice, but way at the back of the yard, there are four old Quonset huts." Adam had apparently missed one in his earlier count. "And every one of those old buildings is full up with stuff Dad pulled out of buildings over the years. He just kept adding stuff and adding stuff, and he never would sell anything. I mean, we could have made a lot of money on some of that stuff. So he'd bring this old junk in and just stash it in a hut back there. And when one hut would get filled up, why, he'd just buy him another. And then he'd fill that one up. By the time I grew up and got into the business with him, he was starting on his third hut.

"That was bad enough, but then he decided he needed to organize what he started calling his 'collection,' so he started moving things from one hut to another. But as he got older, he started to lose track and he'd start over moving things again without rhyme or reason. The result is that we have four buildings full of whatnots back there, and no idea what's there, or where 'there' actually is. I'm thinking about hiring some kids next summer to start clearing it out. But I keep putting that off for the simple reason I wouldn't want to throw away things that might have some value we could recover. But enough of my problems. I probably just created one for you. Or at least, I didn't solve yours for you."

"Well, I'm not so sure of that. Do you remember if your father might have stored some things he pulled out of Phoenix House out in one of those sheds?"

"Oh, I'm positive of it. He was really pleased with himself after that job. Told me he'd found some antique furniture in the attic of that place, and some old pictures, like from the Civil War, a fancy old puzzle box of some kind, somebody's old mineral collection. I mean, he just went on. So yeah, there's things out back somewhere."

"You mentioned a puzzle box. What was that?"

"I really don't know. That was what he called it. Fancy old wood box, I think, and you had to move parts of the box to get into it. You know, like solving a puzzle. I guess that's what they used to do instead of using a lock and key. He kept saying he was going to solve the puzzle and probably find gold bullion inside. But then we got onto another project and another, and he forgot all about it. That's the way he was."

"Andy, I know this is probably a strange request. But I would really like to search through whatever treasures you have stored out back. See if I can somehow find those things that came out of Phoenix House. That box, for example, sounds absolutely fascinating. Just the sort of thing I'd be looking to write a story from. Or I might come across some objects from a different place altogether and get some spark of an idea. I'd be happy to pay you for the opportunity to spend a couple of days or so just poking around out there."

"Tell you what, Adam. You wouldn't be bothering anybody being back there, but I got to tell you it's a total jumble. I can't even promise you could fight your way in. I haven't been in those buildings myself for . . . well, way before Dad died. Maybe before Phoenix House, even. You'll probably want to change your clothes. And you got to promise not to sue us if something falls on you or you get hurt. Doris is my witness. But you can go back there and look around for free on the condition that if you find anything you want to hold onto, you bring it back here and we agree on a price. And I warn you, I'm a hard bargainer, especially if I know you want something I'm selling."

"Andy, you have a deal. I'm going to go find a hotel somewhere nearby and, like you say, change my clothes. I'll probably try to get in a couple of hours this afternoon, then start fresh again in the morning. Do you know, are there lights in those old huts?"

"Good question. No electricity at all, so you'll want a good flashlight. But there are windows along all the walls. I'm sure they're dusty, but there might be some light. The huts are padlocked, but Doris can give you the keys. And if you need to use the facilities, well, just come on back up here.

We're usually here between about seven and six." Andy went on to suggest a local chain hotel, a recommendation that was seconded by his aunt.

"I really appreciate this. Really." And with that, Adam made his way back to his car and headed off to secure a room.

Vivian Vance-Victor had met with Paul Mannington on short notice, but that didn't mean her report to the Circle board was promptly rendered. The timing was such that she had left Mannington's office with little time to spare before the limo service was set to pick her up from her apartment and deliver her to the VIP departure area at Kennedy Airport. From there, she was off on a long-planned tour of European spa destinations. One was carefully chosen for its world-renowned facials, one for its mud baths, one for its mineral springs, and one for its soothing massages. Two weeks of such treatment, and then it was two full days after her return before she finally remembered the need to contact Joe Armstrong and share her impressions. And that was all she had at this point—no commitments, no conclusions of any kind, just impressions.

"Joe," she said, opening the conversation. "I'm sorry to have been out of touch for so long, but I was, in fact, able to arrange an appointment with that fellow, Mr. Mannington." She made no reference to the timing of the appointment or of this call—a small concession to vanity. "I found him to be a rather reserved fellow but pleasant enough. Now, I did try to probe him just a little bit about those shell companies we discovered, just to see if he gave any sign of recognition, and I must say there was no sign that he is in any way involved. Perhaps not surprisingly, he didn't seem to know anything at all about our movement. So I explained to him about our problem with this professor, and he seemed sympathetic but noncommittal. When I asked him for funding, he asked why he should take an interest, and that's a question we all know how to answer. He asked how much support we might need, and I threw around a figure of one or two million dollars. Of course, he didn't bat an eye at that. I wondered if I had made a mistake and should have asked for more.

"In any event, at the end he said he would take our request under advisement, perhaps do some due diligence, and get back to me. Honestly,

I don't know if we'll ever hear from the man. But there's a chance. I did explain to him the urgency and righteousness of our situation."

"Vivian, it sounds as if you gave it your best shot. I must say, I'm impressed simply by the fact that you were able to get in to see someone at that level. You never cease to amaze me, my dear."

"Joseph, you're so sweet to say that. I will let you know the moment I hear anything."

***

Adam returned to the salvage yard, picked up the keys from Doris, and worked his way back to the Quonset huts. From what Andy had told him, he decided to begin with the hut he judged to be the most recently added, which seemed to be the hut he had not originally noticed. It was located directly behind and perpendicular to the three parallel units. He was encouraged to see that the padlock on this hut looked newer than the other three.

Choosing the one somewhat shiny key of the four he'd been handed, he opened the lock and opened the door. The inside was dimly lit, mostly from the windows along the side of the hut furthest from the other three. This was as good as it was going to get for illumination, and Adam was glad he had brought along a large LED flashlight. He flicked it on.

Adam's first thought as he studied the mass of items before him was that if this was the newest and least crowded of the Quonset huts, the village had been due to grow again when Andy's father had passed away. There were aisles, and there were piles. Whether it was the puzzle box Andy had told of or some other box, it was clear that finding Abner Doubleday's treasure trove would not be easy. And of course, there was no guarantee it was here at all. Even if Howard had collected and saved every item he found in the attic at Phoenix House, Adam could not forget that nearly half a century had passed between Doubleday's death and the transfer of the house to municipal ownership, and going on another ninety years since then. What were the odds that any single thing had remained in the house through all of that time?

But likely or not, here he was, and it was time to get down and dirty. Adam knew he'd need a system of some sort. He had no idea how

Howard had chosen to fill the space—side to side? back to front? front to back? selective placement by some criterion? pure random whimsy?—so he decided that he would start at the front, push down each long aisle about five or six feet, and once he'd done that, go back to the first aisle and move in another few paces. He might get halfway through this building by close of business, when he had to turn in the keys. And he didn't want to think about how long it might take him to work his way through all four huts.

The time passed quickly, and Adam was continually amazed at the array of castoffs that Howard had managed to pull from the buildings he cleared. There were many pieces of furniture, most of it undistinguished, but some probably very nice when it was cleaned up. There were boxed and unboxed old toys and dolls, wooden-handled tools, and old mechanical devices like hand-cranked calculating machines and fruit presses. There were safes, some of them sitting open, some sealed shut. There were boxes, bottles, rolls of craft paper, old signs. Over all of these items lay a coating of thick dust that stirred every time Adam touched or moved anything. And there was a lot of moving, because these were not trinkets that neatly lined display shelves but miscellaneous objects of differing weight and scale that had been tossed on top of one another and abandoned. Here and there were some signs of the efforts Howard had made to move and organize things, but the overall impression was that he had been overwhelmed by the task and had not truly pursued it.

In its way, that was actually good news for Adam, because it made his search more like an archeological dig, where the objective is to pull away successive layers and, in the process, move backward in time, than it was a random search with no useful sedimentary record of any kind. It meant that if he could just get himself back to the correct period, only a very few years ago, his chances of finding the puzzle box and everything else that came out of Phoenix House were pretty good.

On the first afternoon, he was able to progress about ten feet into the hut down all three of the main aisles. He could tell that the company had cleared out at least one gas station, at least one bank, and what appeared to be some sort of retail operation, perhaps a small department store, as well as an unknowable number of old houses. He made a mental note to ask Andy in the morning whether that afforded any specific estimate of where he was in the history of remaindering. For now, though, after the long drive and the intensity of the dig, he was exhausted. He dropped the keys with Doris just before six, headed back to his hotel room, ordered a pizza and a large cola, chatted with Liz briefly while he waited, then ate, stripped, showered, and fell into bed. The next thing he knew, it was morning, and the seven o'clock sun was streaming in through his east-facing window.

<hr />

CI popped his head into the Commissioner's office.

"Boss, have you got a few minutes?"

"Yeah. Of course. What is it you need? How are you coming on that press packet and the logistics?"

"That's what I wanted to talk to you about. The logistics are coming along fine. We had to push it back a bit because the Hall has some big events coming up and they need some downtime in the interim. But it's okay, because it gets us out of the doldrums and into the prime media scheduling, with high-vis sporting events across the board, so the audience will be especially keen then. I didn't check with you on that because we couldn't change it anyway without making a fuss, and I do think it will work to our advantage. It also gives us a couple more weeks to prime the pump."

The Commissioner remained silent, but CI did not judge him to be angry.

He continued. "We've got the buses all lined up. We decided to use party-type buses, because they're all fitted out with bars and plush-looking seating along the windows rather than in rows. It'll be a little odd going up, but I think the journos will appreciate it on the way back. The buses have Wi-Fi and plenty of outlets in case any of the passengers actually want to write and file during the ride. One thought was to put a couple of retired players or league execs on each bus who'd be available for interviews, especially going up."

"Nix on that part," the Commissioner quickly replied. "I want there to be one, and only one, story that day, and I want to control that story as completely as possible. I don't want a bunch of has-beens and gasbags sucking up the oxygen."

"Got it. Lunch is all set once they get to the Hall. We're having it catered, and we're planning a big, heavy meal right before the press conference. That should get the blood flowing to their bellies, and maybe make for fewer and simpler questions. And decaf coffee only, even though we'll use black carafes as well as orange ones."

At that, the Commissioner let out a hearty laugh. "CI, you still have the ability to amaze me. I love it. Now, how are the press materials coming?"

"That's why I came in today." He lifted up a fancy folder filled with papers. "I'll leave this with you to look over. You can see that we are playing around with art for the cover of the folder—old photo of Doubleday, another of Spalding, and this one with the symbol they use for that Theosophy business. Just putting that on the cover of the folder could get a bunch of overfed, drunk sportswriters, not the sharpest tacks in the box to begin with, thinking all sorts of conspiratorial thoughts."

"Excellent, but be sure you get some old pictures of Mills and Graves on there as well. And Tinker or Tingler or whatever her name was. And full names for everybody. Make it look like they're all spinning around that logo."

"We can do that. There's a draft release in there, and a draft of your statement that you'll want to spend some time looking over. Then we have the Spalding letter and the backgrounders. There's one on Spalding and the Mills Commission, one on all the people through history who have said that was a bullshit theory, and one on Theosophy that ends with a quote from Thorn's book. We thought we'd use the one where he speculates that Tingley, Sullivan, Graves, Mills, Knight, and both Spaldings might have set the whole thing up. The guy sort of makes your case for you, and he's got credibility. Everybody knows he was good at his job. Then you can just say you're acknowledging and officially endorsing his suspicions, and you've found new evidence to back them up. It'll make it look like you are making nice, still friends and all that. And then you can work off that to build out the rest of the conspiracy theory any old way you like, and then flash the Spalding letter as the ultimate proof. That, at least, is how I've got it laid out at this point."

"I'll take a hard look, but it sounds to me as if you've got a good handle on this. Those are all great ideas. Man, this gets my juices flowing. It's just like the old days in politics."

"On the other hand," CI deadpanned, "it's always good to grow as a person."

They both had a good laugh, and the aide returned to his own office, leaving the draft materials on the Commissioner's desk.

Adam washed up and dressed quickly, eager to get the day started. He grabbed a cup of bad coffee and a stale doughnut from the breakfast buffet at the hotel, which he consumed during the short drive back to Howard & Son. The office was open, as promised, and Doris was waiting for him, the key perched atop the "Out Box" on her desk. She quipped that if she had had a "Way Out Box," she'd have put it there instead. Adam laughed, grabbed the key, and headed off to another day of moving, digging, sliding, testing, and blowing billows of dust off piles of remnants.

Or perhaps not. He couldn't believe his luck. It wasn't more than ten minutes after he started working his way down the left-hand aisle when he came upon several old desk chairs bearing ancient glued labels indicating their ownership by the Borough of Mendham. Behind them were two old oak desks with similar labels. Atop the desks were half a dozen bulky old typewriters with inventory labels and a box filled with rotary dial telephones, each with two banks of push buttons for direct connections. These were all labeled Administrator, Finance, Assessor, Legal, and so forth—all clearly indicating the various borough offices. These had to be the items Howard had pulled out of Phoenix House. But they stretched further than Adam could reach, so he backtracked to the front of the hut, then went down the center aisle and worked his way to the same point. What he found there were not the castoffs of numberless bureaucrats but chairs and other items that looked like furnishings from an old house. He could see that these more residential leftovers dominated in the first three or four feet off the aisle, then seemed to merge with the office equipment stacked toward the other side. And sure enough, there toward the middle of the row, resting on top of yet another old oak desk, he saw a wooden box. Could this really be it? Needless to say, the box was out of reach, so Adam began moving chairs, a table—he would have moved Heaven and Earth if necessary—until he was finally able to reach the box. He stretched out and tried to lift it, but it was simply too heavy for him. So he spent another several minutes clearing a path that would put him close enough to clasp the box firmly in both hands.

Adam set the box down on the floor and carefully replaced all of the things he had pushed away or moved aside, at least enough so that the aisle was reestablished. Then he lifted his prize and headed for the light of the doorway to the hut. He found a chair and a table in the accumulated detritus, dusted them off as best he could, set the box upon the table, and sat himself down.

Adam blew off the layered dust, careful to sit back, away from the resulting cloud, and began to examine his prize, which was perhaps sixteen or eighteen inches long, a foot deep or more, and eight or ten inches in height. The first thing he noticed was the quality of the box, its materials, and its construction. It was solid wood, finely formed, and even after so many years of heat and cold and light and darkness and who knew what else, it was in every aspect tight and intact, and with a little polishing, probably quite beautiful. The next thing he noticed, and the thing that got his heart rate accelerating, was the parquetry on the top of the box, which formed the initials "AD." Above the initials were two finely formed mosaic stars. General Abner Doubleday? Could this really be it?

The remainder of the top of the box was covered with fine carvings of birds, animals, and various other natural forms, and these extended down the two longer sides. On the remaining two sides were scenes of ancient warfare, complete with chariots and archers in medieval garb. This was all probably part and parcel of theosophical history and belief, he guessed. Here and there were other bits of inset parquetry. The box was heavy—he guessed it might weigh as much as ten pounds—and when he tipped it on edge so he could view the underside, he could both hear and feel the contents shifting. The bottom side was nicely finished but seemed otherwise unremarkable.

When he went to open the box, Adam realized that old Howard must have been right. He could see no hinges nor any lock, and he could find no seam where the top met the bottom. It was seemingly a solid block of wood, albeit with a hollow interior. A puzzle box, indeed.

Adam had heard of puzzle boxes before, but he'd never seen one first-hand. He knew that such boxes were opened by following a fixed sequence of movements in which one part's change of position created a way to move the next part, one after another, until the final piece of the puzzle was solved and the box could be opened. It sounded easy enough, but in looking at this particular box, he couldn't even see anything that moved to start the sequence. He poked and prodded but without much success.

Adam decided this would be a good time to call Paul Mannington and bring him up to speed. Paul would probably know how best to proceed. He entered the number he'd been given and was once again surprised by the alacrity with which it was answered. *Jeez*, he thought to himself. *I can call one of the richest men in the world, and he takes my calls!*

"Adam, is that you? How's it going?"

"Paul, hi. Man, you're not going to believe this. I am sitting here holding what I firmly believe is Abner Doubleday's box."

"Are you serious?"

"Well and truly. Here, just a sec, and I'll snap a picture and send it to you." He switched to the camera app on his phone and took a photo of the top and one side of the box, which he dispatched to Paul's phone number.

"You should have it in a moment."

"Already here. Wow. So tell me about it."

Adam described how he had located the box in the middle of a pile of old furniture and other things that were clearly from Phoenix House. He went on to emphasize the parquetry letters "A" and "D" and the stars on the top, as well as the various other details of appearance, size, weight, and condition.

"Can you tell if there's anything inside? Have you opened it?"

"Yes to the first, no to the second," Adam responded. "There is clearly some stuff moving around inside. But as for getting into it, the box itself is one of those Chinese or Turkish puzzle boxes, the kind where you have to move around some number of wooden pieces in a particular sequence to unlock it. It's so dusty right now, I can't even find anything that half-way wants to move. That's when I decided I'd better call you. I don't want to mess it up, and I figured maybe you know how to work these things."

"No clues or hints? Maybe like a paper glued to the bottom with instructions? An owner's manual?" Now Paul was reaching, and he knew it. Adam's response made the point clear.

"Okay," he continued. "Adam, here's what I'd like you to do. This box is very clearly the property of the salvage company there. And while we could have you just offer them a couple of hundred dollars for it, which I'm sure they'd take, I don't like to do business that way. Kind of feels like cheating.

"So I'd like you to take the box over to the fellow who owns the place. Tell him you think it's from Phoenix House and it's probably pretty old. Tell him it might have some value, depending on what's inside. Say the man you are working for—and don't say who that is—would like to meet with him up there in Mendham, at your hotel room, at noon tomorrow, to clean up and open the box if he can, and then to work out a mutually acceptable arrangement for your guy selling it to him. But tell him—and really emphasize this—that it is crucial that he not dust the box off or make any effort to open it between now and then. If he does that, there'll be no deal, ever. Can you do that?"

"Absolutely. I take it you'll be flying in. We're maybe fifty miles west of Newark, but maybe there's something closer."

"Actually, Newark is good. Bigger airports are better places when you don't want to attract too much attention. Plus, anyone who sees me or the plane will just assume I have business across the river. We park there all the time. You'll send along the details on the hotel?"

"Yeah, but I warn you. You are not going to be impressed. Although I just might be able to lay in a few bags of chips and cookies from the vending machine down the hall, and there's always the minibar. Now on the plus side, you'll see for sure that I'm not being extravagant with the expense money."

Paul let out a hearty laugh. "I'll see you at your hotel around eleven tomorrow, and we'll take a few minutes to talk strategy. In the meantime, send me some more photos of the box, all the way around, some close-ups of the carving, whatever you can do. Bye." And he was gone.

After taking a few more close-ups and dispatching them to Paul, Adam stood up, lifted the box, exited the Quonset hut, careful to close the padlock behind him, and headed to the office for a little chat with Andy. *This*, he mused, thinking ahead to tomorrow, *will be fun.*

———⊰⊱———

Adam phoned Liz that evening to fill her in on the latest developments and to let her know he'd be away another day or two.

"And the guy, what's his name—Andy—he agreed to that?" she asked after Adam had explained Paul's proposed course of action, at least as far as he knew it, which included only about the next twenty hours or so.

"Yeah. I mean, he thought it was pretty odd. Said he would be happy to just sell me the box and I could be on my way. But I told him my boss wasn't sure whether he wanted it or not without seeing it in person, but if he did, he would pay Andy more just for the courtesy of doing the deal this way. Of course, I never told him who my boss was. And I have to say, I'm looking forward to that, if Paul decides to let him know. You know, it is kind of curious. If the guy is willing to sell it for a couple of hundred bucks and consider himself lucky, or even clever, well that's literally chump change for Mannington. He could do that deal in his sleep, then have all the time in the world to find out what he had bought. There's certainly no real need for him to fly in from wherever he is and go through some sort of negotiation with Andy. There have to be some other moving pieces here that we simply don't know about. That's the only way any of this makes sense."

"Think you'll ever find out what they are? Assuming, of course, that this really is the Doubleday box."

"Hard to say, hon. It probably depends on just what sort of book it is he wants me to write. And that, for the moment, is entirely his decision."

———⊰⊱———

Paul Mannington flew into Newark Liberty, easing into the approach queue among the arriving flights of Alaska Air, American, Jet Blue,

United, and a couple of international carriers. His Gulfstream almost looked lost on the taxiway amid the array of commercial aircraft. But he found his way to the Signature Flight general aviation FBO facility and parked. His preferred low-vis ride, a Toyota Highlander, was ready nearby, and he quickly worked his way out of the airport and onto I-78, then west to Exit 48, which put him directly onto New Jersey 24. That, in turn, took him directly to the center of Mendham and right past Phoenix House. At that point it got a little more complicated, but he had Adam's hotel on his GPS and had no trouble finding it. With some of these systems, you never could be sure. But the sign ahead told him there were no problems this time. In total, the drive took him less than an hour, which made him a little early for his meeting with Adam. *Well*, he thought to himself, *that's Adam's problem. I just hope he's dressed.*

He was.

Paul had reviewed the additional photos Adam had sent him yesterday, but he wanted to hear again the eyewitness description of the box. He had also had a chance to study the carvings and inlay on the box and had some thoughts as to how he might try to open it. He had come across a few of these puzzle boxes over the years simply because they were favorite toys of his Silicon Valley friends, who delighted in demonstrating their brilliance but then always gave away the secrets of how they had solved the puzzles. Paul had observed that the smallest, simplest boxes could be the most challenging—a two-part box that was held tightly closed by opposing rare-earth magnets came to mind—while some of the more pretentious, seemingly more complicated puzzles were more easily solved. In the present instance, though, he thought he might have an unusual advantage. He just might have the key.

Paul then explained to Adam how he wanted the conversation to go and where he hoped it would lead. Noting Adam's expression of surprise, he said that if this was the box they sought, he would explain everything to Adam in due course. But if it was, in fact, the prize, he had some work he needed to do before that could happen.

"Trust me, Adam. This will be a book everyone will want to read."

At that point there was a knock on the door, and Adam rose to open it for Andy, who held the box in his hands. From the layer of dust, Adam was confident that the box had been neither cleaned nor disturbed. "Andy, come on in. I'd like you to meet—"

"Paul Chi Mannington?" It was Andy, and not Adam, who spoke the name. Paul had grown a trim beard since Adam had last seen him but had otherwise not done anything to disguise his identity. Still, he may not have expected to be recognized quite so easily. He reached out to shake Andy's hand. Andy passed the box to Adam so that he could return the gesture.

"It's a pleasure to meet you, Andy. I guess the beard's not much of a disguise."

"I'm a little embarrassed to admit it," Andy said, "especially being in the business I am, but I read *GQ*, and they just had a piece on how you were—"

"Growing out a beard. I knew that would come back to haunt me."

Smiles all around as Adam handed the precious cargo over to Paul and everyone took a seat.

"Adam, did you get those microfiber cloths I asked you to?" Adam nodded his head in the affirmative, grabbed a nearby container, and passed it to Paul, who spent the next several minutes dusting and wiping down the exterior of the box. He took particular care to clear any dust out of the intricate carvings, which emerged, to his great pleasure, as having been very finely done.

Paul quietly examined the box all around and smiled a soft smile of satisfaction. He was pretty sure he knew how to open this one. While Adam and Andy looked on in rising admiration, Paul began identifying and moving bits and blocks of wood. On the top of the box were two serpents facing away from one another, one to the left, one to the right. Paul played for a moment with the left-facing serpent, pressing here and there until he felt something very subtly give way. He slid the serpent outward until it extended an inch or so beyond the edge of the box. Looking closely at the newly revealed space, he noticed a small wooden tab nestled at the bottom, almost flush with the main area of the top. He pressed this tab inward and simultaneously put outward pressure on the second serpent, which responded by sliding a similar distance to its mate, but in the opposite direction. From deep inside the box came a small click.

Suddenly, Adam realized what he was seeing. He remembered the nonsense rhyme they had seen at the very bottom of the Armenian translation.

The snakes turned to the left, the snakes turned to the right, turtles walk, birds in flight. . . .

And Adam knew what Paul's next move would be. His hands felt delicately around the cluster of turtles to the right-hand side of the initials "AD" on the top, gently probing for any sign of give. He tried pressing in the center of the grouping, on each of the four cardinal directions, and in various combinations thereof. Next he tried tipping the box toward its left side, with no effect, and so on around. It was when he tipped the box toward himself that they could all faintly hear a slide mechanism inside the top give way, and when he set the box down, the turtles took a dive, sinking inward of their own volition. Paul then turned to the next element, the birds in flight—in this case, two bald eagles soaring above a tree. These were on the side of the top opposite the turtles, and try as he might, he was unable to move them in any direction. He even pulled out a magnifying glass to have a look and could not detect the slightest seam. Finally, whether in frustration or in a moment of inspiration, he rapped sharply on the birds with his knuckle and was rewarded with the sound within of something dropping on a surface.

Seemingly satisfied, Paul turned next to the flying arrows. There were, as Adam had noted, two scenes of conflict, one featuring chariots and the other medieval knights, located on opposing sides of the box. Unnoticed beneath all of the dust, now cleared away, were four separate arrows, two toward the edge of either side. Paul began again his routine of feeling gently for any seams or give. The clue this time was a little ambiguous. How many arrows flew? In what sequence? In what direction?

Adam and Andy watched, almost mesmerized, as Paul played with this arrow and that, this sequence and that. Then he just stopped and closed his eyes as if trying to remember the exact language of the rhyme, which he might have brought with him but was not prepared to reveal in Andy's presence. Then, as before, his lips formed into that wry little smile. Using his thumbs and middle fingers for maximum stretch, he pressed inward on all four arrows at the same time, moving those on the chariot side upward and those on the knightly side downward, all in unison. Again, the mechanism responded. Three of the arrows moved the now customary distance beyond their respective edges, while the fourth, the one to the right of the knights, moved an inch or so further. Examining closely the space cleared by this last arrow, Paul uttered a single word. "Eureka." He tilted the box toward the longer slot and out dropped an old and fairly delicate-looking skeleton key.

"Now," he said to no one in particular, "we just need to find your lock." Adam and Paul shared the same thought. *Where is the crown that is to be raised?* A thorough examination of the carvings yielded nothing. For all the variety and all the complexity of the woodworking, there did not appear to be anything resembling a crown. No pointed bands. No bejeweled headdresses. Nothing at all that looked particularly regal. It was clear to Paul, and separately to Adam, who had not let on to Andy that he understood the game that was playing out before them, that this last challenge might be the most difficult. Finally, his impatience getting the better of him, Paul decided to lift the box up and have another look at the bottom. It would be just like a puzzle-maker to lead his mark away from the solution with every move. Rather than lift or tilt from the bottom, though, Paul went to lift the box by spreading his fingers and grasping two opposing corners of the top, and when he did, the topmost inch or so of the box pulled away from the rest, supported by an inner structure of secondary wood. The crown in question, it turned out, was not one meant to reside on a royal head but simply the top portion of the box. The separation revealed a metal lock on one of the longer sides, a lock that had waited a century and a half to be reunited with her mate in holy matrimony. The key went in, the lock turned. Paul pulled open the lid, and three pairs of eyes leaned in to have a look at the contents.

———

At that moment, the only person who seemed uninvolved in the events that were spinning with increased rapidity was Liz Wallace.

James Charles Dickens, Professor of Engineering, had just stumbled across some information that would add to the mystery as it unfolded, though he was as yet unaware of the connection.

The Commissioner of Baseball had just signed off on the draft of the statement he planned to offer at the news conference in Cooperstown some two weeks hence, and on the accompanying press packet.

Jim Prevost, known to the Commissioner as CI and the man's most trusted aide and confidant for many years, had just arranged for an authenticator friend who would not ask too many questions to endorse the legitimacy of the Spalding letter he had "discovered" at the flea market.

The staff at the Hall of Fame, just a couple of blocks across town from Liz's office, were beginning to discuss the logistics of the Commissioner's press event and selecting the catering team for the planned luncheon.

The directors of the American Theosophy Circle were holding their regularly scheduled meeting, which included a discussion in camera of ways they might limit the activities of the aforementioned Professor of Engineering.

Even Max Tomhoff and his staff at Marbury House were busy, in their case, preparing for their next major event—an auction of Civil War artifacts to be held in less than a week.

But for her part, Liz was settling Hef into his roll-about for a nice walk around town on this lovely day, careful to take along her cell phone in case Adam called with news and with word of his plans to return home. Like the song said, just another day in paradise.

<hr />

Andy walked out of the room in something of a daze and carried the box down to his truck. It had taken Paul just five or six minutes to reverse the puzzle sequence and re-lock the box after he had returned its contents to the chamber within.

Part of his sense of being disconnected from reality was the simple fact that he had actually met and conversed with Paul Chi Mannington. He had to think there were not many guys in the architectural salvage business who could say that. And, in fact, he had sworn that he would not, either.

But it was the rest, the agreement they had reached, that really set his mind to spinning. Paul had returned the box to its original state, sans the dust, and handed it back to Andy as the rightful owner. He had given

Andy the name of an auction house in New York City and said that to-morrow he should call, ask for the acquisitions director, some guy named Frederick, and say that he had a puzzle box that he believed had been the property of a Civil War hero, Abner Doubleday, and that he would like to put the box up for auction with a reserve of fifty thousand dollars. Paul assured him that the auction house would accept the proffered box and further assured him that it would sell for not less than the reserve. Fifty thousand dollars! His head was filled with a jumble of competing things he could do with that much money.

Rosters Expand

While Adam checked out of the hotel and headed north toward home, calling Liz along the way, Paul Mannington's work was just beginning. He made two calls from his car as he drove toward the City, one to Frederick Marchant, Acquisitions Director at the auction house, and one to Dickie. Paul knew all of the principal executives at Marbury House because, as a major purchaser of fine art, he had been a guest at several of their VIP social events. And he already knew of the upcoming Civil War and militaria auction from the House's seasonal brochure and catalog, of which he always received an advance copy. He told Frederick that he should anticipate Andy's call in the morning and be helpful, even to the extent of inserting the object in question into that particular forthcoming auction, albeit without notice or advertising. He assured the man that there would be at least one buyer at the reserve Andy would set. His call to Dickie was brief and to the point. They should meet at Paul's Manhattan office in two hours.

And now, here they were, the two old friends, sitting in a pair of comfortable chairs, sipping a remarkable old Bordeaux that only someone like Paul could afford. Paul opened the substantive part of the conversation.

"Dickie, let me start by telling you that we found the box. I'll have it for you in about a week, and I think you'll find it very interesting, but we're not keeping it. I'll come back to that later. The salient point for now is that the composite translation of those two documents in Armenian, along with the maps, took us straight to the box—well, not straight. That Wallace fellow did a terrific job of locating the map in a real place, following it, and tracking down the prize. I must say, I was impressed. Also, you remember those nonsense phrases, that little rhyme at the end that made no sense? That turned out to be the instruction set for opening the box. It's a puzzle box—are you familiar with those?—and there are some inlays and ornate carvings on the outside that match up with the rhyme. Inside was an old piece of paper where Doubleday had written down something very close to the translation. Even signed and dated it . . . November something, 1877."

Suddenly, a puzzle of his own clicked into place in Dickens's head. "That wouldn't be November 28, would it?" he asked.

Paul looked at him with a quizzical expression. "Matter of fact," he said, "now that I think of it, it was the twenty-eighth. How did you know?"

"Just a guess, maybe. But while you were out gallivanting all over the wilds of New Jersey and wherever else, one of us has kept his nose to the grindstone going through all those documents. And I came across something interesting on the Armenian front, though it didn't fit into any pattern until now. There was this guy, George Ivanovitch Gurdjieff. Now, he wasn't a Theosophist, but he was some sort of mystic or spiritualist, so he had some ideas that were similar to some of the theosophical beliefs. Reincarnation is a good example. I came across this journal article that suggested he and our old friend Madame Blavatsky had led sort of parallel lives, both traveling around, both pushing the envelope of logic. The author even suggested that Gurdjieff had studied Blavatsky and her group and tried to use their terminology and her image to gather his own following."

"Okay," Paul interjected, "so she has a successful movement and there were guys like this Gurjy, or whatever his name was, who were doing knockoffs. What's your point?"

"My point is that George Ivanovitch Gurdjieff was Armenian, and although there are conflicting reports about when he was born, his passport listed the date as November 28, 1877. So here you have an Armenian spiritualist pseudo-Theosophist who was born on the same day, as you tell me, that Abner Doubleday wrote his note, of which we have two potentially independent transcriptions in Armenian. I couldn't tell you what that means, but I can tell you it is starting to freak me out."

"Wow," said Paul, almost under his breath. "That's going to take some processing . . . Okay, maybe it's time that we have a little discussion of what all of this might be . . . Here are some hypotheses.

"H1. The whole thing is a coincidence—the overlapping Armenian texts, the correspondence to the note in the box, the maps that just happened to lead to a place the box used to be, and the rest. I don't know about you, but to me it seems like we are beginning to see exponential odds against H1. I don't think this is a coincidence.

"So then there's H2. Abner Doubleday, for whatever reason—maybe just as a practical joke on Madame Blavatsky—and we have to remember that he knew her and was president of the Theosophists in New York City for a time—Doubleday set the whole thing in motion. He planted the box, got that furniture maker in Philadelphia or somebody else to translate his note into Armenian and sent a couple of versions off to friends in different places to be planted, and the rest. Possible. But if he did that in 1877, which might or might not be when he actually did it, I mean, the guy lived another sixteen years, and he never said a word. Either he had a very deep, dark sense of humor, or H2 doesn't work all that well.

"Now, H3 would be that somebody else, for whatever reason, did all of that stuff, not as a practical joke, necessarily, but maybe as a con. Could have been that Gurjy fellow—"

"Gurdjieff," Dickens corrected.

"Okay, Gurdjieff. You said he was trying to mimic Blavatsky and some of the Theosophist beliefs. Maybe this was an elaborate scheme to do that, and in the process, to shine a light on himself as a powerful spiritualist of some kind. The use of Armenian, which I think you said he was, would seem to support that as a possibility, and I suppose Doubleday might have been a highly visible target within the movement, second-tier compared to the head lady, but that might be an advantage in running a con like that. But it's hard to see how he would have been able to plant that box where it was or have any idea of what to put inside, let alone pull that off. And, of course, it could also be something contemporary, somebody playing out a hoax today in real-time. Between hindsight, the ease of travel, and the internet, it could actually be pretty easy to do these days, so we can't rule that out.

"I suppose a corollary to that, let's call it Corollary 1, is that at his birth, Gurdjieff gets this vibe from Doubleday and later translates the vibe into Armenian and by some mechanism causes it to be copied by these two kids in England and Ohio. That seems a stretch, but I suppose we can't rule out some sort of intermediary processing of the text, so let's put that on a low shelf for now.

"Or . . . and let's call this Corollary 2, maybe it was some Theosophist who was setting the whole thing up as a kind of phony proof of concept— a set of seemingly unrelated events and finds that collectively proved some belief of the people in that movement. Somehow, the argument would be, information or some other kind of essence traveled around the world. As I think about it, remember that phrase in the Doubleday note where he talked about the map and how he never actually drew it? That could have been meant as a hook. If you got to the box using those directions, and you were able to open it using the lines at the end of the note, why, this must be the real thing. Reincarnation, or mind-reading, or communicating with spirits, or whatever they were pushing at the time, well, it has just been proven.

"One fellow who comes to mind in this scenario would be Albert Spalding, a fellow Theosophist and one who would know just what to put into the box to support the myth he was about to spin. Somebody like that might have had something to gain from all this, and he would have been working after Doubleday's death, so he couldn't have been questioned. I don't know about you, Dickie, but I don't feel like I can rule that one out at this point. But then you get back to the core of the thing. Spalding surely had to know at some point that people weren't buying his story about the origins of baseball, which raises the question: if it was him, why didn't he spring the trap and show everyone the proof? So that's not a bulletproof explanation, either.

"Last but not least," Paul continued, "there is H4. Everything is just as it seems. Abner Doubleday put together a box of goodies, wrote his note, then upon his death somehow psychically transferred its contents, in Armenian, to people being born that same day in two separate places, people he did not know and with whom he'd never communicated. And let's not forget that, according to the notes from those two collectors or whoever gathered those notes, both of those people had marks on their bodies or infirmities that corresponded to Doubleday's own war wounds. And the other thing I keep coming back to is that apparently, in all of his many papers and his correspondence throughout his life, Doubleday never once made any mention of having designed this game. Yet that claim is front and center in the box. Wait until you see what's in there. Was he setting up Spalding to make the claim? We can't say no, but the box is dated 1877, almost twenty years before Spalding set up his commission, and at that point, I don't think Spalding was even part of the Theosophy movement. I think that came later. So that seems to be a stretch.

"Of course, the whole idea of H4 is a stretch, isn't it? It seems to depend in its entirety on some form of telepathy or psychic connection or something. On the one hand, that is totally bizarre. It is just really difficult to give such a thing much credence."

"And yet, on the other hand," the professor asserted, picking up his friend's train of thought and guiding it into the station, "that might well be the one big thing we have been searching for in all of this. Because if this is what happened here—and I agree with you that, bizarre as it is, it is emerging as a candidate interpretation of the data—if this is what happened, then it happened through some process that is more likely to be general and recurring than it is to be unique to Doubleday and these two kids. And if it's general and recurring, there must be some underlying mechanism that can be discovered. . . ."

"And," Paul picked back up, "if it can be discovered, perhaps it can be reverse-engineered, duplicated, and deployed under controlled circumstances. It would be a true breakthrough technology. And that is exactly why we set up this project in the first place. Let's hold off on final judgment, at least until we have a chance to authenticate what's in the box. I know what we'll need, and I can set that up in advance, so it should happen very quickly once we have the box. Assuming that result points toward H4 here, let's redirect the entire project. I will want you to stop the kind of global search for potential mechanisms we've been doing and focus on finding evidence on the underlying nature of this one. I can't say there are not even more possibilities somewhere in those materials you've been collecting, but this is a highly promising lead, promising enough that I think this is where we should go. That work for you?"

"Paul, I want to see what was in that box, and I want to wait until we can check to see if it's bona fide, which I think is what you have in mind. But if the stars line up, then I am all for going in this direction. Just think of the reverse-engineering challenge alone. It actually sounds like fun, and it's the sort of thing that really could have practical applications all over the place. Hey. It could be the next electronic transactions algorithm!"

"Ouch!" said Paul, and they had a good laugh.

———————

Max Tomhoff looked out over the room with his customary discerning eye. He saw several of his regulars who had a penchant for buying Civil War relics and firearms, as well as a few other familiar faces. The room was about three-quarters filled today, a sign that however many truly nice things they might have on the auction block, this sale lacked a zinger. No single object was of sufficient import or potential value to bring in the big money and the buzz. Aside from that woman auction blogger who always seemed to hang around, he did not recognize anyone from the media. Just another weekday auction.

Max did his best to stifle a yawn. After all, it was Max Time, and that simply wouldn't do.

From the Confederate cannon said to have been dragged across the hills to Gettysburg, then abandoned in the retreat, to the usual array of swords from both sides, and thence through the last collection of uniform coats, caps, canteens, and belt buckles, the sale wound on toward its conclusion.

"The final item in today's sale is not in your catalog, though it has been on display in the showroom for the last several days. We apologize for this limited notice, but the seller in this instance was quite anxious to effect a sale, and the House has chosen to accommodate his request. This item is a puzzle box, finely carved and extensively inlaid, and is believed to have once belonged to General Abner Doubleday, who, I am informed, fired the first Union shot in defense of Fort Sumter at the beginning of the Civil War and also fought at South Mountain, Antietam, and Gettysburg. General Doubleday had an extensive military career in the years before the war as well. This box and its unknown contents, which can be heard moving around inside when it is shaken, were salvaged from a building in which the general and his wife once boarded. You'll note the initials 'AD' inlaid on the top."

This mystery box somehow managed to grab the attention of the room, and several prospective bidders showed signs of interest.

"The seller," Max continued, "has placed a reserve on the box of $50,000."

The room seemed instantly to deflate, like a tire that had encountered the point of a spike. Max could read the faces like a book.

"Do I hear $50,000?"

A lone bidder at the back of the room, a bearded man in a nondescript baseball cap who looked vaguely familiar to Max, raised his paddle. He looked just a little like Paul Chi Mannington, the software billionaire. But he was probably just imagining the resemblance. Frederick had told him of Mannington's call, which was followed up the next day by a visit from some mechanic out in Central Jersey. But Frederick's take was that Mannington was himself the seller and was simply using an intermediary to permit him anonymity. Why would Mannington sell the box and also bid to buy it? Must be someone else.

All of that flashed through Max's brain in the time it took to raise his hand and recognize the bid. It vanished with equal alacrity.

"The gentleman in the rear has bid $50,000." Many heads turned to see who would make such a bid, but as they did, the bearded man looked down at his lap, apparently lost in reading the auction catalog.

Max tried to get the bid up, first in increments of ten thousand dollars, then five, then one, and finally asked for bidders at $50,500. There were none.

"The bid is $50,000. $50,000 going once . . . $50,000 going twice . . . Fair warning . . . *Sold* to bidder number 372 for $50,000.

"Ladies and gentlemen, this concludes today's auction. We ask that all successful bidders who have yet to do so conclude their business with one of our clerks at the tables in the rear. Our next major sale will be in three weeks, when we will be auctioning off three paintings attributed to the School of Rembrandt, one Klimt, and a large number of other fine works. We hope to see you there. Thank you."

His work done, Max left the podium.

———✧———

"Vivian, hello. It's Paul Mannington. How are you?"

"Paul, how nice to hear from you."

"I apologize for taking so long to get back to you after our meeting. But I assure you, I have not forgotten what we discussed. In fact, I have been working the problem for several weeks."

"Oh?"

"Yes, I reached out to that Columbia professor, Dickens, and I had a long talk with him. I hope you don't mind. We went off in several directions, but most importantly, he asked me to assure you and your society there that he harbors no ill will whatsoever toward you or your beliefs. To the contrary, he finds certain aspects of those beliefs fascinating, and one reason he has been purchasing the collections that you referenced is his intense desire to study them more closely."

"I suppose he knows he could do that simply by joining our Circle or visiting our library," she interjected.

"Well, yes, I suppose he does. But I did not get the impression that his interest was, ah, spiritual, might be the word. I think he just sees it as a sort of intellectual puzzle to be pieced together."

"As do we."

"Yes. But my point is that I don't think Dickens will be coming after you with charges of necromancy or anti-Semitism or the other things you mentioned as having occurred in the history of your movement. I did not get the impression he is thinking in those terms at all. Which should, at the least, relieve some of the pressure on you and your fellow directors.

"Now, I did take your point about an outsider acquiring collections of writings that might be material to your group's legacy. And when I raised that with the professor, he seemed taken aback as if he'd never thought about the matter in those terms. And I took that as an opportunity to see if I might somehow broker a peace treaty of sorts between your folks and him.

"What I have in mind, if it is satisfactory to you, would be an arrangement in which Dickens would continue his purchases—honestly, I don't think he'd be open to ceasing them altogether—but in which your Circle, as you call it, need not bid against him. Rather, he would agree to donate to you those of the materials he acquires in which he does not harbor a particular interest, which appears to be the bulk of the material from what he was saying, as soon as he has had an opportunity to review them and make a determination. The remaining items he would agree to pass on to your group when and as his specific interest ends. The benefit to you would be that much of the material you have regarded as lost to the society would be found once again, while the benefit to Dickens would be the lower cost of acquisition once the principal opposing bidder leaves the field. And if you take the long view, Professor Dickens and whoever is supporting him—you had mentioned some mysterious chain of shell companies, as I recall—well, in effect, they will be buying these things for you.

"Now, he was generally amenable to this arrangement, subject to the approval of those funders, whom he did not name, with the condition that he would be granted full and unfettered access to the extensive collection that you told me earlier is already in your library as well as any new materials you might acquire going forward. He seemed to think he could make this happen on his end.

"If that sort of arrangement is acceptable, and if you were to desire, I would be willing to take on some sort of intermediary or mediator role until things seem to be on a mutually acceptable track. Professor Dickens has no objection to that and, in fact, saw it as a positive thing. But I would only do that for a limited time and only with the full approval of your leadership. The last thing I need to do is get involved in a pissing contest—forgive my language—over this sort of philosophical contretemps."

"Paul Chi Mannington," Vivian responded once Paul had set out his proposal, "you are a wonder. Where we saw a conflict we could only hope to avoid, you have found a resolution that seems to be in everyone's interests. I can't commit the board or the Circle without checking with my colleagues. But I will present this proposal with my strongest personal endorsement, and I am all but certain others will see it as I do."

"Very well. I have no horse in this race, but perhaps that has helped. Just let me know if you'd like me to pursue this with Dickens and whether you will want me to stay involved. And by the way, although I will not be making a financial gift or underwriting your acquisitions process as you had requested, I do have a small gift for the Circle, which I'll pass along in a few days."

"Paul, again, thank you. I'm sure you'll hear from me very soon."

The meeting convened in Paul's conference room the morning following the auction. He and Dickie had had a long conversation the evening before about how to handle the box and its contents. Their true interest, they concluded, was confined to the fact of the box's discovery, the note inside that roughly matched the two documents in Armenian, and at least one of the entries in the journal. Once authenticated and tested for any latent messages or other markings they might contain, the originals could be copied to meet their needs. That set of conclusions locked Paul's intended plan into place.

It was agreed, which is to say, Paul decreed, that Dickens would not attend the next day's meeting, which had been scheduled several days earlier in anticipation of the purchase of the box. In his dealings with the Theosophy Circle, Paul saw an advantage in maintaining the fiction of his separation from the professor. With that exception, those settled around the two-inch-thick, double live-edge, figured bubinga table included some of the nation's most respected experts in radiometric dating techniques, forensic fiber analysis, chemical analysis of inks, ultraviolet and infrared deciphering of faded inks, handwriting analysis, authentication of autographs and writing samples, nineteenth-century arms and militaria, American furniture of the nineteenth century, antique jewelry, and the philosophy of religion, as well as three prominent historians, one each specializing in the Civil War, in New York State in the nineteenth century, and in baseball and other sports.

"Ladies and gentlemen, I want to thank you all for participating in this project. I know some of you are here by choice and others because I have prevailed upon your institutions or employers, all of which I have supported generously over the years, to dispatch you to this meeting. Either way, I hope by the end of this meeting, you will share my excitement for the project we are all about to undertake. The time frame is very short, which may create some pressure on your work, but that brevity means you'll all be returning to your customary activities very soon— hopefully within a week or less. All of you will be well compensated for your participation, and all of the expenses of this project will be fully covered.

"Some of you may judge our purpose here to be trivial, and in some limited sense, it may be. But I assure you that, in my view, and for reasons that will remain unstated, this task is very important indeed. Each of you has signed a two-part nondisclosure agreement covering this work. The first part pertains to today's meeting, which you are not free to discuss with any person at any time under any circumstances without my prior written approval. It includes any reference to this meeting, per se, or to any of the topics we shall discuss, as well as the identification of any other participant. To be clear, these requirements are more stringent than the Chatham House Rule that frequently governs such gatherings. I want you to understand that I take this agreement most seriously, so if there is anyone here who is not prepared to honor it, this would be the time to leave. As to the second part, pertaining to the work that you yourself perform, most, if not all, of you will be released from this agreement shortly after we conclude our task, and in those cases, you will not only be free to discuss your work and its results with colleagues or the public but encouraged to do so. Is there anyone who chooses not to participate under these terms?"

No hands were raised, nor was any other sign given. Paul clearly had the rapt attention of the group.

"In that event, since you all come from such disparate fields of expertise, let us take just a moment to go around the table so that each of you can tell us your name, your affiliation, and your area of specialization. I'll begin. My name is Paul Chi Mannington. I am the founder, chairman, and CEO of Chi Square Industries. And for purposes of today's meeting, my expertise is making sure that all of you get paid."

That last line broke the ice, and a more relaxed group went around in a clockwise fashion, each set of credentials seemingly more impressive than the last.

"Some of you," Paul resumed, "will be thinking that this is a rather odd collection of specialties to bring to bear on a single undertaking. Once you see the task at hand, however, I think you will begin to understand." With that, he placed a decorative wooden box on the table.

"This is what's called a puzzle box. Perhaps some of you are familiar with the genre. Essentially, the box is designed so that certain moving parts interlock to keep it closed. When those parts are moved in a particular sequence and manner, the box opens and its secrets are revealed. I purchased this box at auction yesterday, but given the advance arrangements made for your attendance today, it will not surprise you to know that I knew sometime earlier both the method for opening this particular box and what would be found inside."

As he spoke, Paul proceeded to move the bits and pieces around and to open the box.

"I have reason to believe that this box belonged to a man named Abner Doubleday. You can see his initials, 'AD,' here on the top." He tilted the top, now separated, so all could see. "Since some of you may not be familiar with Mr. Doubleday, I'll be distributing a biographical sketch at the end of the meeting. The long and short is that he was an Army officer who rose to the rank of major general. Hence the two stars you can see here just above his initials. He served in the Civil War and other conflicts. And about ten years after his death, he was credited with having invented the game of baseball. That latter claim has been long and widely discounted.

"Professor Farber," he added, turning to the furniture expert, "at the conclusion of today's meeting, I will be handing the box itself to you for analysis of the woods and the construction.

"Inside the box are several objects. The first is this single-page letter, obviously intended for whoever should first find the box and decode the puzzle."

I write these words in the expectation that they will be read in the future.

In this box are found the four elements of truth. These are intellect, love, valor, and competition.

I include my personal journal, which can be understood only through intellect, a necklace of gold belonging to my darling Mary, the hilt of my sword from the battle at Gettysburg, and the leather ball used in the first regulated contest of base ball.

If you were guided to this box and its contents, know that the path existed only in my consciousness, was never set out on paper, and could only be conveyed to and through one who, through his very life, recreates my own.

By these precepts have I lived.

Abner Doubleday
Ret Major Gen, U.S.A.
Mendham, N.J.
November 28th, 1877

"The letter was found in this envelope." Paul placed a well-aged envelope on the table. "We were able to retain most of the wax seal when we pried the envelope open.

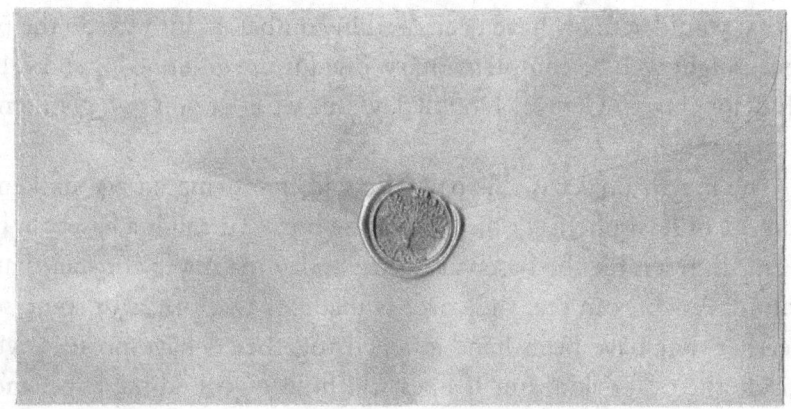

"My interest here is not the content of the letter, per se, which is primarily a listing of the remaining items in the box, except as it relates to its correspondence with the style of the day and with other exemplars of Doubleday's writing. In other words, does it appear to have been written at the time implied, which I judge to have been sometime between 1873 and 1893, perhaps as indicated in 1877, and does it fit with Doubleday's style? Several of you will have a shot at solving that one. We should also determine whether the paper and ink used on this document were period appropriate. That will involve several more of you and probably some collaboration, given the constraints of time. Let my staff know what your needs are in that regard and we'll get them addressed.

"The second object in the box," he continued, holding up the item in question, "is this gold necklace said in the covering note to have belonged to Doubleday's wife, Mary. This one will go to you, Ms. James, with the same question. But in this case, the time period might be much longer, so please broaden your analysis back to 1852, the year of their marriage.

"The third object," Paul went on while lifting it from the box, "is this hilt from a sword which, according to the covering note, was used by Doubleday at Gettysburg. Now this is potentially controversial, as Mr. Devon here, our armaments specialist, and Professor Carbon, our Civil War historian, will attest, because there is a complete Doubleday sword, together with various accouterments, on display at the Luce Center of the New York Historical Society Museum. To me, that sword, which incorporates brass, gilt, and silver, appears to be more ornamental than one that would actually have been used in combat, as his was. So the two objects might well be complementary, one for use and one for show, but both belonging to General Doubleday. But we'll let you two gentlemen sort that one out.

"The fourth object is this ball," he said, removing an age-darkened and more or less spherical object from the box. "I'd call it a baseball, but it seems to resemble the baseballs in use today mainly in the fact that it is round. As you can see, the cover is made of two pieces of some sort of leather that have been hand-stitched together. I have no idea what is inside the outer skin, but it does still hold its roundish shape, more or less. I have several questions about this object, and they will involve several of you. For one, is this ball similar to those in use back around the 1830s for any of the various types of games that were being played with balls and sticks or bats. I know there was a game called town ball, and another called barn ball, and rounders, and two old cat, and, of course, cricket. So the first question is where this ball fits into that framework. Now, I just specified a period of the 1830s, but that, too, is an empirical question. How old is this object? There is organic matter here, which ought to lend itself to Carbon-14 or some other form of radiometric dating. If you don't have access to the updated IntCal20 calibration curve, we'll make sure to arrange that for you. The type of stitching might also yield some clues. In addition, I would like to know if there is any writing or marking on the ball that is no longer visible to the naked eye. UV and IR testing ought to answer that one for us. And if there is, I will want Messrs. Frankel and Cartwright here to have a look at any handwriting or autograph that might be revealed. In sum, I want to know as much as possible about this particular object in all of its aspects.

"Finally, there is this diary or journal." Paul removed from the box a leather-bound volume of handmade but lined paper, perhaps an inch thick. He placed the book on the conference table for everyone in attendance to see. An extended flap of the leather served to protect the unbound edges of the pages, and the book was held closed by a thin leather strap that had been sewn to the end of the flap. After a moment, he opened the book to the first page, where someone had printed in bold strokes the numerals "1837."

"This gives every indication of being Abner Doubleday's diary from the year 1837, when he would have been in his late teens. I want this analyzed by all the methods we have available for period dating, and I want the handwriting analyzed in comparison with known exemplars, just as with that initial document. Then I want you, Professor Constanz, to look through carefully for any indication of how the content squares, or fails to square, with the history of the state during the year in question, along, of course, with any prior years that might be referenced. There are, for example, some biographical references here to other persons where there are sure to be available public records against which to check. I'm sure you know the drill.

"In sum, ladies and gentlemen, I want to know, with confidence and in writing five days from now, whether or not this box and all of its contents are genuine articles. Could this be Abner Doubleday's puzzle box; did he write the cover note and the diary, and if so, did he write them at different times in his life; is there any evidence of writing by a third party in the documents or on the leather ball; are the sword hilt and the necklace and the baseball, more likely than not, exactly what they are purported to be? Is this a genuine article?

"One last thing. If and as you reach a point where you think a collaboration with one or more people around this table is necessary or might be possible, please contact us and we'll make that happen. That includes indicating ways you might be able to contribute that I have not anticipated. Now, I know that we've covered a great deal of ground in the last couple of hours. Are there any questions before I distribute these materials to get you started?"

There were a few questions raised, more of them logistical in nature than substantive. Once those had been addressed to everyone's satisfaction, and once he had introduced an aide who would be responsible for coordinating their activities, Paul adjourned the meeting, and the assembled experts rushed to begin their appointed tasks. The Paul Chi Manningtons of the world had a way of making things happen.

"Paul called," Adam told Liz when she came home for a quick lunch and a few minutes of playing with Hef. The boy's confidence in his mobility was increasing daily, and he was beginning to express himself in meaningful words and phrases. Liz didn't like to miss the fun for too long at a time.

"He wants me to come down to the City at the end of the week to talk about the book. He said he'd have some new information for me about the stuff in the Doubleday box but that he'd decided he wants me to do something he'll actually publish, and there are some documents and things he now wants me to have access to. It all sounded a little mysterious, but then, what's been normal about this whole deal?

"Anyway, if I'm going to be down there for the weekend, I thought maybe we could all go. Maybe even use the time to scout out one or two bigger apartments since my lease on the old one only has a couple of months to run before I have to re-up. I mean, look at this little guy. That place is only going to get smaller."

"That's a good idea," Liz replied. "When I get back to the office, I'll take a look at what I have Friday and Monday, and we can decide this evening."

Wild Card Game

The pair of party buses pulled out of Chelsea on time—eight o'clock sharp—and headed up the Joe DiMaggio Highway, still known to most locals as the West Side Highway, then onto the Henry Hudson Parkway toward Cooperstown. Amazingly, given the hour, every one of the twenty-one sportswriters on the invitation list had shown up. All of the major papers—the ones that remained—were represented, as were the broadcast and cable sports networks, the primary websites that specialized in sporting news, and a couple of prominent bloggers. They divided themselves by friendships, media clusters, or whatever other criteria appealed to them, having in common only a look that said none of the assembled multitude was accustomed to seeing the sun at this particular angle, which is to say, in the eastern sky. The coffee urns that the Commissioner had thoughtfully provided on both buses—all, as per CI's plan, filled with decaf, regardless of their markings—were quickly drained, and the sugar highs from the accompanying supply of Krispy Kreme doughnuts may have been the only thing keeping certain travelers awake by the time the buses reached Albany and turned west.

That was just fine with the Commissioner, of course, who had no interest in an alert press corps being present for his event, only a prominent one. And, with the unwitting assistance of the Hall of Fame staff, he had planned carefully to preserve his advantage. The pre-conference luncheon buffet was big on meats, potatoes, and rich desserts and light on salads and greens. Then, as one o'clock approached, the attendees were herded into an adjacent room for the main event.

"Lady and gentlemen," the Commissioner began, noting the *Times* representative as the exception to the rule and earning a glower from her and a chuckle from the others present, "I have invited you up to Cooperstown today because I want to right a great wrong that has for too long been a part of organized baseball."

The Commissioner went on to set out the long history of the Doubleday myth, which he relabeled the Doubleday Deception, and of the many challenges to its viability. He went over the early history of the game and the establishment of the Mills Commission to assert its uniquely American roots. Then he turned to the critiques of the myth as they had been presented, beginning with Henry Chadwick and continuing through John Thorn and other contemporary critics.

"For far too long, he said, baseball has turned a blind eye to these contradictions, even as the Hall of Fame, where we meet today, which was an early and substantial beneficiary of the Doubleday/Cooperstown scenario—as I'm sure our good friend Roger Coppersmith here would attest—even as the Hall of Fame and many prominent students of the game have come to reinterpret that history. We've helped to keep it going in team names, stadium names, on historical markers in several states, in the stories we tell to our children. As an American institution, we are complicit, knowingly complicit, in perpetrating this misguided story.

"Now, we have all come to believe that Albert Spalding had only the most noble of purposes in perpetrating this, I will use the word, this fraud. He was anxious to have the world accept baseball as a wholly American invention at a time when the country's standing in the world was very different from what it is today. He saw this as a way to bolster the country's reputation and also the confidence and sense of national pride of Americans themselves. That is the interpretation of events we have all come, at least implicitly, to accept.

"But I am here today to tell you of my belief that this is a false narrative, one that covers up a deception that had an altogether different and far more sinister purpose. In fact, one might well call it a conspiracy . . . what I have come to think of, for reasons that will become apparent, as the Great A.G. Conspiracy. It concerns a fringe religious movement called Theosophy and a number of its adherents who, I have come to believe, were engaged in a systematic attempt to achieve power over the American public, its social and cultural institutions, and its core beliefs, if not also its political institutions. New evidence has come to light that points directly to this conclusion. This was a pseudo-religious cult on the very threshold of capturing the American psyche.

"Albert Goodwill Spalding was, in his later years, a highly influential member of the Theosophical Society, whose values and beliefs you will find summarized in one of the inserts in the briefing books you found on your seats. I will just say that they are not in the mainstream. On the cover of your briefing book, you'll find a reprint of their official logo, which, as you can see, includes such elements as a swastika and a snake consuming itself, as well as a credo that directly attacks our belief in a Supreme Being.

"As it happens, Abner Doubleday was also a leader of this movement, having served for a time as the president of the New York chapter of the Society. All of this has been noted by historians, notably by Mr. Thorn, who, in his 2011 history of the early days of the game, went on to speculate about the significance of that connection. But those who have speculated along these lines have not been in full possession of the facts. I have brought you here today, to this shrine to our national game, in order to share those facts with you."

At this point, the Commissioner signaled to an aide and a document was projected onto the large screen behind him and off to his right.

"A member of my staff has brought to my attention this letter, which we have had authenticated. A copy of this is also included in your packets. The letter is definitely written by Mr. Spalding in his own hand. It is addressed, as you can see, to someone he called Purple Mother. We cannot be certain, but I can tell you that Purple Mother was the preferred appellation of a woman named Katherine Tingley, a prominent leader of the Theosophy movement, who established a colony of sorts at Point Loma near San Diego in about 1900. Albert Spalding and his wife, Elizabeth, referenced in the opening sentence, were among the earliest residents in that colony. Elizabeth was a close aide to Ms. Tingley, and Albert himself played a substantial role in the colony's development. You'll find details of his involvement in your packet. As you will see in the next paragraph,

Spalding had adopted the goal of, in his words, 'propelling our shared views to their rightful place at the apex of American society.' In other words, Spalding's identification of Doubleday, a fellow Theosophist, as creator of the National Pastime, was intended not to elevate baseball, or even Doubleday himself, but rather to elevate Theosophy to pre-eminent status in America. The third paragraph makes this linkage explicit.

"But it is the fourth paragraph of this letter that sets forth the specifics of the conspiracy. In this paragraph, three individuals are identified only by their last initials. It cannot be coincidental that these correspond with those of three key players in the known history: Albert Graves, AKA Mr. G., whose letter to the Mills Commission expressly placed Doubleday's name on the table by stating that he had witnessed the famous first game; Charles L. Knight, AKA Mr. K., publisher of the *Akron Beacon-Journal*, where the Graves letter was published in an oddly expedited manner;— By the way, are any of you from Knight-Ridder papers? No? Probably just as well.—and Ted Sullivan, AKA S., who was a business partner of Spalding and had already told the *Cincinnati Enquirer* that baseball was 'the product of American genius and temperament,' especially compared to rounders, which he characterized as 'primitive and plebian.' Not much doubt where he stood.

"The only major participant in the whole conspiracy who was not mentioned in the letter was Abraham Gilbert Mills, a former president of the National League, who Spalding named to chair the commission that would determine the origins of the game. Mills, however, was himself a financial supporter of the Theosophy movement. And perhaps coincidentally, if you believe in such things, when Doubleday died in 1893, his funeral cortege was accompanied by a military honor guard from the Grand Army of the Republic. That honor guard was commanded by then Colonel Abraham G. Mills, who, it seems, had himself known Doubleday as a friend for perhaps two decades. As for Graves, there is no evidence that he was a Theosophist, so far as I know. But there is some indication that he was in the San Diego area shortly before he traveled on to Akron, where Mr. Knight published his letter just one day after publishing Sullivan's notice that the Mills Commission was looking for information on the American origins of the game. Remember, this was in 1905 when things didn't move nearly as quickly as they do today.

"Lastly, I would direct your attention to Spalding's singular statement toward the end of the letter. 'May our objective triumph.'

"So what we have with this letter, which has never been seen publicly before today, is the outline of what I believe to be a conspiracy by this religious cult of Theosophy involving four men with strong or possible ties to the movement, one of them long dead at the time, and the others named Albert G. Spalding, Abraham G. Mills, and Abner Graves. Now again, if you believe in coincidences, the fact that these three men shared the same initials, A.G., might qualify. But in the world of a group devoted to spiritualism and the occult and all manner of strange beliefs, well, I'm not so sure that wasn't part of their plan. And that's why I call this the Great A. G. Conspiracy.

"And here's the smoking gun. In 1905, two full years *before* the Mills Commission published its claim that Doubleday had invented baseball, a magazine called *New Century Path*, published at Point Loma by the Theosophical Society, carried an article that quoted from the Graves letter, which had then only recently been published in Akron and was not generally known, as proving that Doubleday, and I quote, 'this stanch Theosophist, well-known Army officer and author, that the national game of Base Ball owes not only its *name*, but also in large degree its development from a simpler sport; or indeed, according to some writers, its *very invention*.' End of quote. Spalding had to have placed that article, and then, once it was published, he forwarded it to Sullivan for the Commission as further evidence of Doubleday's role, a view to which he then gave his personal endorsement. The whole thing, in my view, was a deliberate setup intended to serve baseball, perhaps, but more fundamentally, intended to enhance the authority of Theosophy in national life. I'm an old politician, as all of you know, and I know power grabs when I see them. This conspiracy was nothing short of the first step in an attempt to gain control over our national identity and perhaps even our government. We cannot know how General Doubleday himself would have reacted to the acts taken in his name, but I have to believe he would have been a patriot first and would never have tolerated such an action during his lifetime. He was by all accounts an honorable man, and all I can say is, thank goodness he was not alive to see it. All of this is spelled out in great detail in the press packet we have for each of you.

"And that brings me to my fundamental purpose today. Baseball is the American National Pastime, the quintessential American game. We don't need an elaborate fraud to make that so, and I don't believe we ever did. And we most especially do not need to remain captive, even if only as a remote pseudo-memory, to some heinous power grab by a bunch of religious zealots who sought to advance their own cause at the expense of our sport. So I'm here to rip off the bandage, so to speak, and to level with the American people about the history of the game. No more wink and a nod lies. In this day and age, people have got to be able to rely on the honesty and integrity of the game and of those who lead and represent it, and this is my effort to contribute to that objective. This is the beginning of a new era in our sport. I hope that's what your readers, listeners, and viewers will learn from you tomorrow and in the days ahead.

"And now I'll take your questions before we load up the buses and head back to the City. And by the way, there is ample Wi-Fi service available on both buses if you choose to file on the way home, and we've also provided a bit of liquid refreshment for the trip."

The press buses pulled out of Cooperstown shortly after 3:30 that afternoon and headed back toward what, for some, passed as civilization. Most of those on board were tired, too tired to write, and figured they would file later that evening or even tomorrow. Take some time, maybe even review the materials in the binder. *Besides*, they thought, *the Commissioner has provided these delightful beverages for us. We ought not to offend him by declining his hospitality.* The liquor, after all, was top shelf, and even the plastic cups were pseudo-elegant. And the arrangement of the seating along the sides and rear of the buses rather than in rows added to the camaraderie, precisely as their host had hoped.

Being journos, the group on one bus began a round of what they called Name That Headline—guessing how various news outlets might write up the story they were covering.

A sportscaster, an ex-jock whose face was known to millions, got the ball rolling. "*New York Daily News:* Commish to Doubleday: Drop Dead! Again!!"

"Good one," shouted a print colleague. "How about: *New York Times*: Baseball Commissioner Decries Religious Cult, Cites Impact on Cultural Institutions."

"Wait, wait," offered a third voice. "*Los Angeles Times*: Southland Residents Had Possible Role in Early History of Baseball."

"You guys are leaving out the broadcast side," argued a fourth. "Fox Sports: Commissioner Sees Conspiracy; Yankees Lose in Ten."

"No," came the rejoinder. "You got that backward. It should be, Yankees Lose in Ten; Commissioner Sees Conspiracy."

From another, "*Washington Post*: Abnergate: Former Senator Alleges Dangerous Baseball Conspiracy, Wrongdoing; Bezos Not Implicated."

Then there was, "*Kansas City Star*: Twister Hits Baseball, Doubleday Flattened."

"Hey! *Dallas Morning News*: Baseball Invented Year after Texas Gains Independence."

"You guys are leaving out SportsCenter!" shouted ESPN.

"Nobody watches you anymore!" came the response from down the bench, followed by general laughter.

The boys on the second bus were considerably less rowdy, though no less willing to partake of the available refreshments. The only exception was the *Times* reporter—not a boy at all, of course—who was tapping away at her keyboard. She had read through the entire press packet and, in particular, had studied the newly discovered Spalding letter. It wasn't quite "Baseball Decries Religious Cult, Cites Impact on Cultural Institutions," but at least one correspondent was treating today's press conference as a serious event and was planning on filing a long piece in time for the next morning's editions.

<hr />

Careful readers of *The Times* that next morning hit the Trifecta without ever visiting an OTB office, but few probably realized it.

Those who turned to the sports section found this article, accompanied by a photograph of the newly discovered Albert Spalding letter. The article did begin on the front page of the section, as the Commissioner might have hoped, but only at the bottom left, and after just two paragraphs, it jumped to the middle of the seventh page.

Baseball Commissioner Notes Historic "A.G. Conspiracy": Promises to Clean Up Game's Image

By Claire Voya Nance

Cooperstown. At an unusual news conference yesterday in this base-ball-centered town, the Commissioner of Baseball revealed that Albert Spalding and other adherents of Theosophy, a religious movement of the nineteenth and early twentieth centuries, had conspired to gain influence over American society through the claim that Abner Doubleday, also an adherent of Theosophy, had invented the game. The proof is found in a newly discovered letter from Mr. Spalding to Katherine Tingley, a central figure in the movement. The letter sets forth the objectives, strategy and tactics of the elaborate conspiracy, which was to be achieved through the formation of a commission to name Mr. Doubleday, by then deceased, as inventor of the game, to secure baseball's place as the central icon of American culture, then to reveal Mr. Doubleday's Theosophical beliefs as a driving force and a positive path for Americans to follow. The apparent expectation, and objective, was to leverage the nation's love of baseball to establish Theosophy as the leading cultural force in early twentieth-century America, an alternative to the prevailing nationalism and imperialism sym-bolized by Teddy Roosevelt and his Bully Pulpit.

Mr. Spalding was a former player himself who also held management positions within the game. He was, as well, the founder of a sporting goods line that continues to the present day, and was an influential member of a Theosophist colony in Southern California that was led by Ms. Tingley. Spalding's second wife, Elizabeth, who had recruited him to the movement after their marriage, was a principal aide to Ms. Tingley.

From the letter, it is unclear whether it was Ms. Tingley or Mr. Spalding who first conceived of the idea for the conspiracy. What is clear, however, is Mr. Spalding's role as its prime mover. Also mentioned in the letter are Ted Sullivan, a Spalding business associate who served as sec-retary of the commission and who, in that role, advertised for proof of the origins of the game, and Abner Graves, an itinerant of sorts, who was, it is suggested, pre-positioned to respond to that advertisement with a letter claiming to have been present when Mr. Doubleday created his invention. The Graves letter was published by Charles L. Knight, another possible co-conspirator, in his Akron, Ohio, newspaper and was subsequently ac-cepted by the commission as proof of concept. *The Times* reached out to Knight-Ridder Newspapers, which descended many years later from Mr. Knight's *Beacon Journal* in Akron, for comment, but by press time, none was forthcoming.

Not mentioned in the letter, but himself a contributor to the Theosophy movement, was Abraham G. Mills, another business associate of Mr. Spalding, who appointed him to chair what became generally known as the Mills Commission. Perhaps coincidentally, while in the military, Mills had commanded the honorary unit that accompanied Mr. Doubleday's casket during his funeral parade a dozen years earlier.

The Commissioner made much of the fact that Mr. Spalding, Mr. Mills, and Mr. Graves all shared a pair of initials—A.G.—as did Arthur Gorman, another member of the Mills Commission. He suggested that this seeming coincidence might have held special meaning for the Theosophists themselves, given what he characterized as their beliefs in such things as the occult, reincarnation, clairvoyance, spiritualism and mind reading.

In his prepared remarks, the Commissioner stated that "[i]n this day and age, people have got to be able to rely on the honesty and integrity of the game and of those who lead and represent it, and this is my effort to contribute to that objective. This is the beginning of a new era in our sport."

Those who turned to the Business section and continued to the occasional section on Philanthropy, which came shortly before the financial tables, found this article, which drew primarily on a news release issued the previous day.

Philanthropist Donates Artifacts

New York (From Wire Service Accounts)—Noted philanthropist and software billionaire Paul Chi Mannington yesterday announced a series of gifts following his purchase at auction of a decorative box believed to have belonged to Abner Doubleday, a Civil War general and the reputed inventor of baseball. Mannington had acquired the box through an auction purchase earlier in the week.

The box itself, which he described as a richly carved and inlaid "puzzle box," he will donate to the New York chapter of the American Theosophical Circle. Mr. Mannington indicated that his research had definitively shown the box to have belonged to Mr. Doubleday and that Mr. Doubleday himself was an adherent of Theosophy, having served as a leader of the movement in New York during his later years.

A puzzle box is a box that is held closed by a series of wooden levers and other mechanisms which, when moved in a particular sequence, yield access to the contents. It is clear that Mr. Mannington himself was able to solve the puzzle, but in his statement, he did not reveal its secrets.

Perhaps the most significant item Mr. Mannington says he found inside the box when opened was a diary kept by the young Abner Doubleday in the year 1837. There have long been doubts regarding the origin myth of baseball and Mr. Doubleday's role in it. The story has been that the game was invented by him in the village of Cooperstown, New York, in 1839, at a time when Mr. Doubleday was actually enrolled as a cadet at West Point. A strong argument against this myth is that Mr. Doubleday himself, a prolific writer and correspondent, never made any mention in any previously known document of having invented baseball. The diary Mr. Mannington has discovered is dated two years earlier, which places it before his enrollment at the Academy. One entry in particular may change the accepted history of the game. It suggests not only that Mr. Doubleday might well have set forth a new set of rules but that none less than James Fenimore Cooper, for whose family the village was named, might have been present at the time.

This remarkable diary entry appears to be substantiated by the second object pulled from the box, a round leather ball referenced by Mr. Doubleday in his diary as having been the ball used for that first game of baseball employing his rules. The diary claims that Mr. Cooper declared Mr. Doubleday's rules to be the newest and best of their kind and promised to write them down and promulgate them himself. The diary further claims that Mr. Cooper, an established celebrity, autographed the ball itself, perhaps as a favor to Mr. Doubleday.

Mr. Mannington stated that he had commissioned intense evaluations of the diary and the baseball, including analysis of the paper and ink, the age of the ball, and the period appropriateness of both. These studies uniformly concluded that these materials were authentic in every regard.

The baseball was then subjected to tests employing ultraviolet and infrared light frequencies. These tests were able to detect writing on the ball that precisely corresponded with the claims on the relevant page of the diary. Handwriting and autograph experts were then commissioned to examine that writing, and both confirmed that it matched known exemplars of that of James Fenimore Cooper.

Mr. Manning has indicated that he will donate the diary and the baseball to the National Baseball Hall of Fame and Museum in Cooperstown. That, he said, "is where these crucial artifacts belong."

Also found inside the box was the hilt of a sword that Mr. Doubleday is said to have wielded at the Battle of Gettysburg, where he played a role in the fighting around Cemetery Ridge. Markings on the hilt, Mr. Mannington said, confirm its provenance. This item he plans to donate to the Smithsonian Museum of American History.

Finally, Mr. Mannington is donating a golden necklace found inside the box and believed to have belonged to Mr. Doubleday's wife, Mary, to the New Jersey State Historical Society. The couple lived their final two decades together in the town of Mendham.

The experts consulted by Mr. Mannington in authenticating and otherwise analyzing the objects he is donating came from a cross-section of the nation's leading universities, science centers, and technology companies.

The Times story cut off here for want of space. Had it included the entirety of the information in the wire service reports, there would have followed a list of experts whose names resonated with leaders in all of the referenced fields. Their conclusions, it could be said, particularly since each one reinforced the others, were entirely beyond reproach.

The article in *The Times* included a photograph of one page from the Doubleday diary that had been referenced but not incorporated in the wire coverage but which Paul's office sent along on request.

Page from diary of Abner Doubleday, 1837. Photo courtesy of Paul Chi Mannington.
[AUTHOR'S NOTE: A transcription of this journal entry is included in the end notes for the convenience of the Reader.]

The third leg of *The Times* Trifecta that morning would have been easy to miss. Unsigned, it was buried among an array of other metro-area news in the New York section.

Arrest in Queens

The Federal Bureau of Investigation announced that it has broken up what it described as a one-man forgery ring with the arrest in Queens last week of Anthony G. Castorell, known in certain underworld circles as "Tony Wallpaper." A highly placed source at the Department of Justice, who was not authorized to speak on the record, told *The Times* that Mr. Castorell had been on the FBI's radar for many years. He was known to forge many types of documents, including passports, law enforcement and security credentials, financial instruments, counterfeit historical documents and more. His work was so fine that these forgeries could easily pass undetected, even by experts, and he was so prolific that the Bureau had believed for many years that these items were being produced and distributed by a ring of five or six perpetrators.

According to the FBI, Mr. Castorell owned the Queens duplex in which he was arrested in last week's raid, living in one of the units and using the other as a print shop and laboratory for mixing inks and other purposes. He also had a professional-quality photo studio and darkroom on an upper floor.

Agents were surprised to discover that Mr. Castorell had maintained a detailed record of his clients and of the jobs he performed for them. The FBI has sent these materials to its laboratories at Quantico, Va., for analysis. It is expected that these records will lead to the discovery of security breaches and other crimes, which will, in turn, produce a cascading number of arrests.

Also found in the duplex, according to the Justice Department source, were mockups, drafts and remnants of a number of Mr. Castorell's most recent projects, among them passports for two persons on the FBI's Ten Most Wanted List, paperwork granting clearance to enter a secure storage warehouse at John F. Kennedy International Airport, a bearer bond purportedly issued by the government of Argentina, and letters purportedly written by Abraham Lincoln, General Douglas MacArthur, Albert Spalding, and other prominent figures. These and other recovered materials have also been forwarded to Quantico.

The Bureau's news release indicated that the announcement of Mr. Castorell's arrest was delayed to avoid alerting other potential targets of the investigation. However, the United States Attorney's Office for the Southern District of New York declined to comment on whether he would be offered a plea bargain in exchange for his testimony against some of his clients.

Paul and Dickens met early that morning at the latter's Columbia office to make plans. Paul, who had entered the building using a disguise and a false persona that Dickens had pre-cleared, took the lead, turning first to the proposed exchange of materials with the Theosophy Circle.

"They have no idea what we have, so we are quite free to choose the materials we'll—sorry, you'll—share with them. What I'd like you to do is go through the published materials in the other room first, and if there are duplicates—I'm guessing there are a lot—hold onto the best copies and any that have marginal or other annotations and pass the rest along to them. I'll help you arrange that. Then see if there aren't some loose files that are transparently not of interest to us and bundle those up as well. I know there's a risk there that we'll overlook something, but given the volume of materials you've collected, that risk probably exists anyway, and this will give you a reason to put eyes on everything again. The lesson of your remembering the British Armenian note is that there's value in doing that. See how much you can accomplish in the next couple of weeks, then we'll get back to our main business. Can that work?"

"Yeah, sure, I can do that. There's a lot of stuff we can cull, especially in the published books, and I'd add the newspaper, newsletter, and journal articles. Whether it's what you have in mind or not, we are likely to bury them in paper."

"That's okay. It shows good faith, and we'll want to establish that so that once we have a better idea of what we are looking for, we can get you into their library at some point to see if there are functional little gems hidden that they themselves would not appreciate.

"I'm also going to give them the puzzle box, but on a long-term loan, I think, rather than as an outright gift. I had the team look at that from every angle; even had them X-ray it to see if there were any latent metal parts or additional hidden chambers. That all came out negative. But we can't entirely rule out that the box was somehow a part of the transmission process that led to the translations. Until we can, I want to keep a legal claim on the thing.

"Now, wait until you have a look at the rest of these reports. I'm not sure what they have to do with our larger project, but they sure are interesting. The cover note is clearly in Doubleday's handwriting, and it compares mainly with exemplars from the latter part of his life. I guess these things change over time. They were able to date the paper, which seems to have had some unique fiber characteristics, to 1877 or later. I think we can safely put a range on it then of 1877 to 1893, when Doubleday died, although if there was ever a case to doubt the end of that range, this might be it." They both smiled.

"The ink was something called powder ink made by E.S. Curtis. I guess that made it easy to store or move around. The ink expert sent along a couple of photos of the old bottles they used to sell the stuff in. Apparently you mixed it with water or some other liquid before you used it. Curtis started up around the 1840s, and they were still going fifty years later.

"A couple of the historians looked at the language in the note, and the philosophy professor considered it in the context of the theosophical beliefs of the day, and again, everything checked out. So we know pretty firmly that the note in the box was legit, although that doesn't tell us anything about the Armenian versions or how they came about. That's a place we are going to have to look at pretty intensively, because if we can't discount them as part of some elaborate hoax, that has to point toward where we'll find the underlying mechanism.

"Now, one of the things I had those experts do is subject the note to every test they could think of—chemical, luminescent, hi-res photography, whatever—to see if they could detect any sort of hidden markings or indentations, and they said they were certain there was nothing like that on the note. So, what I want to do is make some really good copies of that note for us to use, which ought to serve our purposes adequately, and I'm going to put the original back in the box when I give that to the Theosophy people later this week. I never mentioned the note in my press release. Let's see how long it takes them to find it; I imagine I'll hear from them when they do.

"Aside from authenticating it—and they did—I had one of my own people check out whether the metal in the hilt of the sword could have served as any sort of transmitter or radio beacon. That came back negative. And I don't think the sword or the necklace will give us any useful information, so I'm going to give those away without any conditions.

"As for the diary—that checked out as period appropriate, too. The handwriting guy said the writing was again consistent with Doubleday's known exemplars, although in this case, because it was the earliest example he knew of, he was extrapolating from the record. He suggested there might be some roughly contemporaneous examples in the historical files at West Point, and I told him to wait a week or so and then contact whoever maintains the old records up there and see what he could find. I don't know if they'll have anything going that far back, but it wouldn't surprise me, and I would guess they'd be happy to cooperate.

"The book itself was typical of some that were sold in higher-end printing shops and binderies at the time, and Doubleday's father was a prominent fellow and probably traveled a lot, so he could easily have had access. Probably gave it to Abner as a gift. There's at least some speculation here that it was an import from France. It was just a basic blank journal.

"It's not much to us, but the baseball historian got really excited about the diary. He said that the first thing of interest was the date—1837. I guess in the myth that's been around for so long, the assumption was that the game was invented up in Cooperstown in 1839, which is when some eyewitness claimed to have been there to see it. But Doubleday apparently wasn't in Cooperstown in 1839—he was at West Point, and the supposed witness was something like five years old in 1839. And all that, among other things, has been the basis on which almost everyone has now discounted the myth. But, judging from the date written on the first page, the diary places Doubleday in Cooperstown two years earlier, seemingly as a student at a kind of prep school that didn't open until the next year but that may have been going through what we'd call today a kind of soft open.

"The . . . well, let me show you this page. It's the one from June 26 that was in the paper this morning, and it's both remarkable and pretty compelling. It's the whole story of how the thing came about, and it makes total sense. You can just see an eighteen-year-old kid sitting down and writing this after what must have been the most thrilling day of his life. I mean, distant travel, a new school, an apparently classy new uniform, hobnobbing with arguably the leading writer of the day. The state historian says somewhere in here that James Fenimore Cooper's family were the Coopers in Cooperstown, and he had actually just moved back home from Europe shortly before that, so it all fits. And it just oozes off the page. It also sets up an explanation for the baseball. Of course, nobody has ever come up with any notes Cooper made from that day, or at least nobody I've talked with is aware of that. One of the experts did tell me, though, that Cooper once wrote a description of a ballgame in a novel called *Home as Found*, which, intriguingly enough, he published in 1838. Guess that's another bit of research for somebody, but not us. Too tangential. Cooper's papers are probably stored someplace, and some literary or baseball historian will probably pile through them now to see. Which brings us to the ball.

"You can see here," he said, turning to the final set of reports, "that the baseball is extraordinarily interesting. Let's start with the leather. Since it's organic, the team was able to use Carbon-14 dating, and with the new chronological data standards, that got them into the late 1830s, so very close. But then, somebody got the idea of taking a DNA sample to see if they could find a general match. Apparently, there are people in this world who keep records of cattle breeding going back to the 1600s. I never cease to be amazed at what people get interested in. Anyway, they were able to show that the leather came from a Hereford cow. And when they dug further to see if there even were Herefords in New York State back in the day, they found an interesting story. It seems that the first Herefords were imported into the US in 1817 by none other than Henry Clay, who put them on his farm in Kentucky and started a breeding program. In 1837 and 1838, he shipped about two dozen of the resulting cattle to a buyer in New York, but transportation being what it was at the time, two of the females died shortly after they arrived. One of our experts thinks the ball might have been pieced together from scraps left over when the hides were processed. Put the likelihood at around eighty percent. There's no record of whether the Coopers were the buyers of any of those cattle.

"The ball was about six inches across, though it had lost some of its shape, and it was hand-stitched. The first sewing machine wasn't invented until about ten years later. The thread was a type of cotton that was just becoming available around that time. It was apparently prized for its strength, which would make sense. There was a gap in the stitching at one point, and I authorized one of the experts to poke around inside with a remote camera system like the ones surgeons use for microsurgery. That result was kind of weird. There was a wrapping of yarn inside the cover, as you might expect, but inside that the core of the ball was partly made of . . . fish eyes. At least, that's what he said. Of course, they were pretty deteriorated after nearly two hundred years, but when we brought the baseball historian into it, he said that was a somewhat common practice. And of course, they were on a lake, so I guess if they actually made the ball at Cooperstown, they might have used whatever was at hand.

"But here's where it gets really interesting. You remember that the diary page said that James Fenimore Cooper had written a birthday message on the ball and then autographed it? We had the ball examined under all sorts of light frequencies, and damned if there wasn't evidence of some writing on it. The physics guys weren't able to reveal the whole thing—you can imagine what would have happened to the ink over all those years, and who can say whether Doubleday—remember, he was just a kid—might even have held it often, maybe to show it off, or rubbed it, or even played another game with it. No way to know. But they were able to bring up and photograph the words 'Happy Birthday' and the signature. Not surprisingly, there are lots of examples of Cooper's hand out there, and the autograph expert was able to confirm that he was actually the one who wrote the words and signed the ball."

"Wow," said Dickens, who had remained silent throughout Paul's review of the reports. "I have to say, I don't know anything about baseball, and honestly, I don't care a great deal. But the history here, well, that's just . . . I'm not even sure of the word. What are you going to do with the ball, and I guess the journal, too?"

"You know," Paul replied, "I've been thinking about that. Again, I don't think either of these objects has anything to do with our little project, and I do think they ought to be out there for people who care about baseball to look at. Plus, they fundamentally change the narrative of the history of the game. It makes you wonder whether that sporting goods guy, Spalding, who formed the commission, whether he knew about all this, maybe from Doubleday himself. I have no idea if they ever met, but they were both high-level Theosophists back in the day. So it could have happened. But if so, you have to wonder why Spalding didn't just have Doubleday stake his own claim while he was still alive. After that, even if he knew about this stuff, he probably couldn't have gotten hold of it. Who knows? And it's not one we'll ever resolve. Let somebody else take that one on.

"But to your question, it's like I said in that statement I put out, the one that was reported in *The Times* this morning. I'm just going to give both the ball and the diary to the Hall of Fame, along with copies of the relevant reports. They'll know what to do with them.

"Which gets me to one last thing, and it may be the most important of all. Those two notes in Armenian you found and passed along? I had a follow-up meeting with the people who did the original paper and ink analyses, and I gave them the originals of those two notes to work on again. I wanted to make sure of their results and get a bit more detail. The paper in both cases was rag-based, even though wood-pulp paper was available pretty widely at the time. But, if I heard you correctly, we have to remember that both pieces of paper came not from those children but from the Theosophists who were interviewing them. Those guys probably saw themselves as making a record, so it's understandable they would have opted for a high-quality paper. It wasn't visible to the naked eye, but under UV, the paper from Ohio had some kind of embossed bird pattern on it, which would have been commonplace at the time. Unfortunately, there was no record of who produced that particular paper. The paper in Manchester, on the other hand, had a badly faded watermark in the upper left that put it early in the twentieth century, so a good fit.

"The team used a new technique called thin-layer chromatography to analyze the ink from Ohio. I'm a tech kind of guy, but I confess I have no real idea what that involved. Then they compared the result against a library of known inks that one of the labs maintains, to see if there was a match. If there was, that would be a potential indicator of fraud. But the Ohio ink was unique, and the chemical analysis showed it to be a common sort used widely at that time. The English case was a little different. As these guys reminded me, there were no ballpoint pens in use in 1908. And the newfangled fountain pens of the era, which had replaced things like quills that you just dipped into the ink, were a challenge to use, especially for someone not used to them, like, say, a barely literate teenager. So whoever conducted that session had that girl use a pencil.

It was so dark it looked like ink, and until I saw their report, I thought it was, but it wasn't. Basically, they told me graphite was graphite, but the wood in pencils changed over time. Under magnification, they were able to identify tiny remnants of the wood from the pencil that was used, which they determined was something called Incense-cedar, which came from the Sierra Nevada mountains in California. That wood was first used for pencils right around 1900, and it very soon came to be exported as the new standard—even in places like Manchester. And that tells us that this note was written sometime after 1900, which fits, though it could have been much later."

"And let's not forget a couple of other things, Paul," Dickens interjected. "First, the two Armenian notes both had the rhyme at the bottom that let you open that puzzle box. But it's not on Doubleday's original note, and if it was, it would not have served any purpose. After all, you needed the key to get to that note in the first place. We can't rule out that he might have written that down separately, and then he, or someone else, sent copies to the two Theosophists who conducted the interviews with those two kids back in the day. But at this point, there's no evidence of that. And second, remember the rest of what they recorded. Both the boy and the girl had physical markings on their bodies and demonstrated manual weakness, which in both cases corresponded to wartime injuries suffered by Doubleday. Again, it could have been an elaborate hoax. But if it was, why was it never sprung?"

"Man, Dickie," said Paul. "I'd let both of those things slip my mind. I knew there was a reason I'm paying you the big bucks! Now, get to work on sorting all that stuff in the other room, because I want to refocus the Theosophy group away from the things we're still holding onto. Make them think they got the Full Monty. And then, let's get down to work. I'm starting to get excited about the potential here."

Adam Wallace was excited as well but for different reasons. He had begun the day as he did every day now, by sitting down with his iPad and reading the online edition of *The Times*, end to end. By the time he was through, he had visions of best-sellers swimming in his head. At least one

Times reader, it seems, *did* hit the day's Trifecta. *This*, he thought, *has to be what Paul wants to talk about this afternoon.* He hurried Liz along, and they headed for the City.

Adam had never been to Paul's office, and he found it every bit as impressive as he had expected. Mannington had the top two floors of one of the East Side's classiest office towers, and the space had been decorated with a contemporary flair tastefully executed. The reception area had none of the heavy wooden and leather trappings of those typical of major law firms he had visited over the years, yet it was elegant in its own way. He had little time to appreciate it, however, because it was not five minutes after he arrived that the receptionist approached and ushered him to Paul's corner office.

"Adam, nice to see you," Paul said, anxious to start the meeting. "Thanks for coming down to my little East Coast hideaway."

"If this is what you call hiding away," Adam replied, "I'd hate to see you when you're showing off! Although I did hear about that Bugatti from about five different people."

"Boys will have their toys," Paul said, smiling. "Listen, I wanted to talk with you about the book. As I said, I think I'd like you to go ahead and write it on the assumption that we'll go public. You saw the paper this morning?"

"I did."

"Well, you knew already what was in the box. I think the lesson of the rather elaborate authentication process we went through is that it's the real deal. All of it. I have a copy of the full set of reports that you can have today. I think you'll be pretty impressed. And if you want to interview some, or all, of the experts we used, and I would strongly encourage you to do that, I'll make sure they'll talk to you and be pretty open as well.

"You probably know a lot more than I do about how you tracked that box down, and you can be upfront about that, too. I'm also going to set you up with a professor up at Columbia, guy named Chuck Dickens. He's the one—and this is not generally known—who found the Armenian-language documents and had them translated. And, of course, he had those two maps. If you don't mind, I'd like to work with you a bit on just how you do the reveal on that material. There are some other things going on related to that, and I am still thinking through how much of that you need to know to tell the story. Obviously, I'm interested in all of this and I want to tell the story. But at the same time, I am still a businessman, and I have some other interests and responsibilities that may prove constraints. Can you work with me on that?"

"Sure," Adam responded, "I can do that, as long as it doesn't require me to lie. I draw a big, thick line there."

"Agreed. One other angle you might want to use, especially since you're living up in Cooperstown, and the diary and the baseball will be going up there to the Hall in the next few days, is to play up the baseball angle. If you think about it, these objects will change a lot of things in the way people see the history of the game. And it is obviously going to get complicated. Did you see that other article today? The one about the Commissioner and Albert Spalding, and how the Doubleday story was part of some anti-American conspiracy? Isn't it remarkable how that broke when it did? And you and I know, and the world will know shortly, that it's total bullshit. I don't see how the guy can survive as commissioner. Of course, that's of no particular concern to me, but if you were to weave that into your book somehow—and maybe a somewhat less pejorative take on Theosophy might be a possible way, given that's now out there the way it is—but some way, I think that might make a hell of a book."

"Paul, you're reading my mind. Especially . . . Did you see the article about the FBI arresting a mob forger out in Queens? Well, maybe mob. But a major forger in any event."

"No, I missed that. Same paper?"

"Yeah, it was in the metro section. If I read it right, that Spalding letter the Commissioner put out to prove his conspiracy? It looks like this guy might actually have forged it. At least he forged some Spalding letter; it was mentioned in the piece. The FBI's got some sort of evidence about it."

"Holy crap . . . Hell, why are you still sitting here? Go. Write!"

Paul gave Adam copies of the various reports and analyses on the box and its contents and a list of contact points for the several experts he had hired, and sent him on his way.

At the special meeting of the directors of the American Theosophy Circle, Joseph Armstrong and Vivian Vance-Victor led the discussion toward a favorable response to Paul Mannington's offer of assistance in arranging a truce with Professor Dickens up at Columbia.

"Why is he doing that?" asked Harvey Andrews, one of the less engaged directors, who had been traveling in Greece and Italy and had missed the earlier discussions. "Is he one of us?"

"No." Vivian took the lead in replying since she had the most direct knowledge of the situation. "When I met with him, I left that open as a possibility, but I didn't get any sense of his being interested. Frankly, since we were trying to solve a particular problem, and since someone with a similar name had shown up as a director of a couple of shell companies that were behind this professor, I was more interested in seeing if I could get a rise out of him in that context. But again, no. So I just moved on to asking for a purpose-built donation, and I think he was just being nice with his offer. It also meant he wasn't committing any real money to us. Now, I will admit, it is a little curious that he was so easily able to get that Dickens fellow to agree to an arrangement. But maybe that's just money talking, or fame. You know how greedy and self-promoting those academics can be."

"I do think it is nice," said Armstrong, once again asserting his authority over the conversation, "that he is apparently passing along the Abner Doubleday box." That box would end up sitting on Armstrong's personal desk for several years until his successor began playing with the locking mechanism. He would eventually discover that the puzzle box had something in common with the ones that hold Cracker Jacks—there was a prize inside. Paul had not seen fit to mention that and could not have been unhappy that it took that long to find his real gift to the Circle.

"Stephen," he said, turning to another member of the Board. "Could I ask you to recruit some help and draft a nice letter of appreciation to Mr. Mannington? Something suitable for release to the media and the public. If you'll get started, we can fill it out a little once we get a look at the box itself. But do be sure to make some reference to Doubleday's early role in the movement."

In Cooperstown, several executives of the Hall of Fame filtered into Roger Coppersmith's office as each arrived at work. The Board Chair was out of the country, but it would not be long before that call came in, and everyone, but especially Coppersmith, felt the need to be ready.

All eyes were turned to the Chief Operating Officer, and on every tongue was the same question.

"What the heck is going on here?"

"Let me see if I have this straight." It was Gene Seyforth, the general counsel, who took the lead. "When the Hall was created, we used the Doubleday story to rationalize locating the facility here in Cooperstown, and we opened shop in 1939, the hundredth anniversary of the supposed event. We have an old baseball on display that was somehow supposedly linked to Abner Graves, the guy who wrote the letter to the Mills Commission that credited Doubleday, although we've always been clear about the issues of provenance there. Over the years, everybody and his uncle basically disavowed the Doubleday story, and we did that ourselves, in a soft sort of way, during the seventy-fifth anniversary events years ago.

"So yesterday, the Commissioner of Baseball hauls a bunch of reporters up here for a news conference where he repeats what everybody at this point agrees on, that the Doubleday myth is just that. But he brings with him a newly discovered letter from Albert Spalding that, he says, proves what a couple of historians have already suggested, that the whole thing is a conspiracy by some religious cult to gain power. And he says the initials of three or four of the main characters, A.G., somehow makes the whole thing part of some Satanic ritual or whatever. So everybody goes home last night pretty much where they were in the morning, and the Commissioner must figure he has somehow redeemed the name of the game.

"Then we wake up this morning and we find out that some mobster in Queens forged the Spalding letter. Did everybody see that? If not, it's buried in the New York section of *The Times* somewhere. Says the FBI actually has documented proof. What it *doesn't* say is whether the Commissioner knew about that, or maybe even had it done. But it means that everything that happened yesterday is a roaring fucking embarrassment. Anderson?"

"I'm on it," Kim Anderson, the Hall's new communications director, hastened to reply. "I have my staff pulling some things together, and we'll get out a release or a statement by about noon. But—"

"Yes, but," Seyforth cut her off and resumed his narrative. "But the other news this morning is quite extraordinary in its own right, and yet of a piece with the other developments. Somehow, Paul Chi Mannington, of all people, has come up with a story of his own, and apparently a Doubleday diary and an autographed baseball, of all things, which he claims to have had fully analyzed and authenticated. And suddenly, Abner Doubleday and Cooperstown are right back in the game, although, if that's to be believed, we actually opened the doors on the hundred-and-*second* anniversary of the great event. And he's about to dump the whole steaming fuck-up of a mess into our laps. Does that pretty much capture it?"

"More than adequately, Gene," said Coppersmith. "More than adequately. I know you haven't had long to think about this, but aside from any other complications, do we have any obvious legal liability here? Maybe by hosting that news conference? Or anything else?"

"At first glance," Seyforth responded, "I don't see any. We simply provided the venue for the news conference, as we do for all kinds of other special events. And we have not made any claims about this of any kind. But it's a potential minefield. Kim, everything we do for the next few days needs to be in writing. Nothing off the cuff. And I don't think anything goes out without being passed by Legal first."

"I agree," Kim said. "But you have to know we are going to be getting press queries. In fact, the phone was already ringing when I came in this morning. What should we say?"

"Just tell them," said Coppersmith, "'we are as surprised as anyone by this strange sequence of events, and we are trying to make sense of them. We don't have any information that is not already public, and we're still waiting to hear from Mr. Mannington. We hope he can cast some light on all of this.' Let's try to buy at least a day while we sort this out. Gene, do you agree?"

"Yes, perfect. But Roger, I think you need to get on the phone and see if you can talk with Mannington. Somebody must know how to reach a guy like that. That release came out from his New York office. It might be you could just run on down there and have a chat. Anybody happen to know, by chance, if the guy's a member of the Hall?"

Kim Anderson spoke up. "That was the first thing we checked on. He signed up as a Benefactor just last month."

"I can confirm that," Coppersmith inserted. "He was in the building, and I had a chance to meet him very briefly."

"Last *month*?" asked the attorney. "Isn't that just a dandy coincidence of its own?"

"I guess so," said Kim, responding to what was probably just a rhetorical question. "But it does mean we have some contact points for him in the membership database."

"You almost wonder," speculated Coppersmith, "if he didn't do that just so we'd be able to reach out to him. Makes you wonder just how much he knew."

"And when he knew it," said Seyforth.

Casey, Mighty Casey

The only person, it seemed, who had not read *The Times* that morning was the Commissioner of Baseball. Yesterday had been a triumph, he had concluded, but he was feeling quite drained by the travel back and forth and the tension of the day. So he had slept in and then, realizing the time, rushed over to Chelsea.

When he finally did arrive at his office late in the morning, CI, who had been maintaining a vigil that could, at the very least, be described as anxious, rushed to intercept him.

"Boss, I've got to—" He never got the rest of the words out.

The Commissioner held up his hand. "Later," he said sharply.

CI knew better than to protest, though he knew, too, that if ever there was a time to challenge that raised hand and dismissive tone, this was it.

As the Commissioner moved toward his office, the young woman at the reception desk got his attention.

"Commissioner, there's a phone call. It's the attorney general on line two."

"Which attorney general?" he asked. In New York, as in many states, the chief legal officer was elected to the position, which required that he, or she, undertake a statewide campaign every few years. He had spent the last several weeks dodging calls from the current incumbent, whom he firmly believed was an asshole of the first merit, with oak leaf cluster. The scuttlebutt was that he had plans to run not for reelection the next time around but for governor, and that invariably meant fundraising. As a former senator himself, the Commissioner knew the game well. So he was surprised when he heard her response.

"Of the United States, sir."

That was better. Alonzo Garrigan. They'd first met back in the Commissioner's Senate days, when Garrigan had been nominated for the job and was making the rounds of the key senators, seeking to lock in their support. The Commissioner hadn't taken a liking to the man at first—the term pompous ass came quickly to mind—but as they talked, his view softened. By the end of the two hours, he had told Garrigan, and later the president, that he would support the nomination, and since then, they'd been on generally friendly terms. They'd even gone fishing together once or twice on some stream up in Vermont, where Garrigan had been governor years ago, and the Commissioner assumed this might be an invitation to do that again. He moved into his office, sat down at the desk, and picked up the phone.

"A.G.," he said, using the customary shorthand for the office, which, in this instance, doubled as the man's nickname, "how nice to hear from you. To what do I owe the honor?"

For his part, Alonzo Garrigan had never really liked the Commissioner, née Senator, but he had studiedly masked his contempt for a man he judged to be venal and corrupt. When you held a prominent position in the administration and were dependent in many ways on the goodwill of a small cluster of senior and highly influential members of the upper chamber, you played the game. But the man was not in Washington any longer and held no real power, and this was a call the attorney general was going to relish.

At some subconscious level, perhaps he resented the Commissioner's reported references yesterday to a so-called "A.G. Conspiracy." He knew that some old Senate hands, including the Commissioner, liked to call him "A.G. the A.G." behind his back, which often got shortened to simply "Ag-Ag," or even "A Gag," and that they didn't mean it nicely. It would take a shrink to sort that out. But he was so sufficiently put off at a conscious level by the way the Commissioner had named this little conspiracy he'd manufactured that he had begun looking for a suitable, if subtle, way to respond—something clever, something that would not have any blowback that might reduce what he was rapidly coming to see as the Commissioner's emerging legal troubles.

That's when he recalled the words of Alexander Graham Bell, inventor of the telephone—who, he knew, had routinely signed his personal correspondence "A.G. Bell"—when he first demonstrated the device by sending his aide to an adjoining room then delivering the first telephone message: "Mr. Watson, come here. I want to see you." Perfect opportunity for a little play on words, albeit one the Commissioner probably would not even notice.

So it was with a delicious sense of irony that United States Attorney General Alonzo Garrigan channeled old Alexander Graham Bell as he answered, with a slight variation, the question that had been posed.

"Mr. Commissioner, please come here. *You are wanted.*"

"I beg your pardon?"

"Have you not seen the papers today? Let's just say that that little show you put on yesterday has tied you directly into an ongoing FBI investigation, and we are drawing up some documents charging you as a party to a conspiracy to commit fraud. If you would prefer to surrender voluntarily—and the alternative is to have a couple of agents drag you out of your office in handcuffs, which I'd be glad to oblige if it's your wish—but if you'd prefer something a little, uh, less disruptive, then I suggest that you present yourself down here at my office in Main Justice in DC at noon tomorrow. I strongly suggest that you come accompanied by counsel, because I'm sure the agents would like to talk to you. Oh, and bring that factotum of yours, Prevost, along with you. We'll have his name on a warrant as well." And he hung up.

"CI!" the Commissioner bellowed. "Get your ass in here this instant!"

———

Hanging up the phone, the attorney general turned to the man sitting across from him at his desk, a friend of long standing and now a colleague in a small off-the-books venture in service to a game he had grown up loving, even if he lacked any talent for playing it.

"I rented view plus Uncle Hooch," said the man now also known as Legal Eagle.

"Oh battle unhappiest," came the response from a man known to some as Lot Lizard.

Revenge was indeed sweet.

"I've made up stuff that's turned out to be real, that's the spooky part."

—Tom Clancy, quoted in *The New York Times*, July 27, 1986

The Box Score

Acknowledgments

I apologize to readers for any geographical and architectural errors which may have found their way into the text. This book was written during the COVID-19 lockdown period, when it was not possible to travel to the locations referenced in the book, some of which were unfamiliar to me. I was able to use satellite views, virtual tours, photographs, and other materials published online to add considerable, and hopefully accurate, detail to these scenes. That was, however, easier to do with respect to exterior features such as building entrances, plazas, and map locations than with respect to certain building interiors. In particular, several scenes are set in three academic buildings and two food service facilities of Columbia University. I reached out to the university with several questions about the interior characteristics of these buildings but received no response. So I was unable to conform the details in question to the actual locations.

One place where I did find help was in the Borough of Mendham in New Jersey. I especially want to thank long-time Mendham resident Pat Serrano for educating me on the history of the Doubledays in Mendham and on the ins and outs of the borough today. Though she would not describe herself as a "local historian," her knowledge of the area was nearly encyclopedic, and her willingness to share it, even going out of her way to track down minor facts, was most valuable. In the 1990s, Pat was one of the moving forces behind the establishment of Doubleday Day in Mendham, with an assortment of baseball- and Civil-War-themed events; the placement of the commemorative marker in what was once the Doubledays' front yard; and the naming of a town baseball field after the general. She hopes for a renewal of the Doubleday Day celebration, last held in 1999, and so do I.

Thanks are also due to Sophia Rose Glassner, whose photos of the interior of the main level of Phoenix House in Mendham Borough provided the basis for the description thereof and the inspiration for the description of the upper level. Several of Ms. Glassner's photographs are included in the book.

In addition, I extend my appreciation to William Westhoven of the *Morristown Daily Record*, to James Lewis, Department Head of the North Jersey History and Genealogy Center, Morristown and Morris Township Library, and especially to Cynthia A. Muszala of that center, for their assistance as I sought, unsuccessfully, to track down a useable photograph of the Mendham residence of Abner and Mary Doubleday. Mendham and Morristown have both shown themselves to be places where folks will go out of their way to be helpful. Thanks as well to Drew Cuthbertson of IMAGN, the Gannett archiving subsidiary.

Thanks again to Lawrence Knorr of Sunbury Press for his commitment to baseball fiction, to Sarah Peachey, whose editorial skills make any story better, and to Crystal Devine, whose design skills do the same for any book.

Finally, I want to thank Marja Artamaa, International Secretary of the Theosophical Society, for her considerate responses to my inquiries.

Pleading Poetic License

The author is not one to let history get in the way of a good story. I am aware that historians of the game, such as Philip Block, Thomas Gilbert, William Ryczek, and John Thorn, among many, have long questioned the Doubleday myth and offered alternative hypotheses, even some centering on the Theosophical Society—an intellectual debt which I enthusiastically acknowledge; that the Hall of Fame has backed away from the story that served to frame its opening in the place and on the hundredth anniversary of the mythical seminal playing of the game; and that many others, going back as far as Henry Chadwick himself, have largely discounted the claim.

And yet, through it all, we have Doubleday Field in Cooperstown, where the annual Hall of Fame Game was played for nearly seventy years; Doubleday Field at West Point, in honor of an early graduate; and Doubleday Field in Mendham, New Jersey, where the retired general lived out his final years. The Little League and Babe Ruth Fields in his birthplace of Ballston Spa, New York, are named in his honor, as were the professional Auburn Doubledays of the Class A Short Season New York-Penn League, who played in the town where he grew up until they, like so many other long-established minor league teams, were victims of the brutal corporatist purge, AKA reorganization, of the minors imposed by Major League Baseball in 2021. (Even so, the appellation lives on with the Auburn entry in the Perfect Game Collegiate Baseball League.) So there's that.

In the end, of course, this is an acknowledged work of fiction.

Or is it?

Notes

Pg.	Note

xi   "When I was younger"—*Mark Twain's Autobiography*, Volume 1. New York: Harper & Brothers, 1924, p. 96.

6   "We are seekers"—This is a capsule summary of the views espoused by the New York Theosophical Society and found online July 27, 2020, at https://www.theosophy-ny.org.

8   "the thing about the Astros' cheat"—See Martino, passim.

9   "Then, he started really messing with the rules."—This list can be found in Griffiths.

10   "two different baseballs in play"—Bradford, William Davis, "Major League Baseball secretly used two different types of baseballs last season," *Business Insider*, November 2021, found online January 15, 2022, at https://www.businessinsider.com/mlb-used-two-different-balls-in-2021-2021-11.

10   "he goes all NBA on us"—The reference is to the close ties between the National Basketball Association and its players and the Chinese government. The baseball-related actions described here are reported in Beyrer.

14   "He had rules for his players"—See Ross, especially p. 38.

15   "There's even a letter"—The text of which was found online November 29, 2020 at https://deadspin.com/bud-selig-thinks-abner-doubleday-invented-baseball-of-5684393.

17   "stuck up there in The Mudd"—A reference to the Seeley W. Mudd Building, which houses the engineering school. The characterization of the building's design appeared in "Architecture View: A stylish New Building at Columbia," *The New York Times*, December 11, 1977, p. 139. Found online September 27, 2021, at https://www.nytimes.com/1977/12/11/archives/architecture-viewa-stylish-new-building-at-columbia-architecture.html.

18   "The engineering school honored"—Mr. Fu and his gift were the subjects of Karen W. Arenson, "Chinese Tycoon Gives Columbia $26 Million," *The New York Times*, October 1, 1997, found online August 2, 2020, at https://www.nytimes.com/1997/10/01/us/chinese-tycoon-gives-columbia-26-million.html.

25   "Doubleday was born"—The biographical sketch that follows is based on several sources, including Gumpert, Gumpert, and Anderson; "Abner Doubleday," found online, August 3, 2020, at www.newworldencyclopedia.org/p/index.php?

title=Abner_ Doubleday&oldid=1025987; and "Abner Doubleday," found on-line August 3, 2020, at www.fortwiki.com/Abner_Doubleday.

26 "an old advertisement from the local paper"—Found online August 3, 2020, in a summary of early bound volumes of the newspaper at https://www.allotsego.com/bound-volumes-january-30-2014/.

27 "after he retired and moved to New Jersey"—"Covering the Bases with Abner Doubleday."

27 "he joined the Theosophical Society"—For a summary of Doubleday's participa-tion in the Society, see the listing for "Abner Doubleday" on Theosophy Wiki, found online February 9, 2022, at https://theosophy.wiki/en/Abner_Doubleday. The date of 1877, which becomes significant in this story, is one of two possible dates associated with the beginning of his membership.

28 This and all of the subsequent documents in this book are fictitious and rendered by the author.

32 "the standard frequency characteristics in English"—See, for example, the data found online August 4, 2020, at http://pi.math.cornell.edu/~mec/2003-2004/cryptography/subs/frequencies.html.

33 "he was a hotshot pitcher"—Much of this biographical sketch is drawn from Levine's excellent treatment.

34 "They made the first"—These claims by Spalding were found online August 5, 2020, at https://www.spalding.com/about-spalding.html.

34 "That team won"—See McMahon.

34 "Spalding and Chadwick were friends"—Schiff, found online August 5, 2020, at https://sabr.org/bioproj/person/henry-chadwick/.

35 "by the time he died"—The point is made in https://en.wikipedia.org/ wiki/ A._G._Spalding, found online August 5, 2020.

35 "And in the meantime"—Miller, p. 50.

36 "And there might have been"—According to Phillip Block, at the very least, Spalding was quite familiar with Doubleday through the Theosophical Society.

40 "Remember that Spalding was once"—See Levine, passim, but especially pp. 113–114; and Hill.

41 "Well, so was Mills"—Basic biographical facts were found online, August 11, 2020, at https://en.wikipedia.org/wiki/Al_Reach; https://en.wikipedia.org/wiki/Arthur_Pue_Gorman; https://en.wikipedia.org/wiki/Abraham_G._Mills; https://en.wikipedia.org/wiki/Morgan_Bulkeley; https://en.wikipedia.org/wiki/James_Edward_Sullivan; https://en.wikipedia.org/wiki/George_Wright_(sportsman); and https://en.wikipedia.org/wiki/ Nicholas_Young_(executive).

41 "when Mills was"—Philip Block, pp. 32–33.

41 "Now, the story is"—Thorn, *Baseball in the Garden of Eden*, pp. 4–19.

42 "based largely on a pair"—Thorn, "The Letters of Abner Graves."

42 "It seems like Abner Graves"—Thorn, *Baseball*, pp. 275–276.

47 "That one seems to have been discounted"—See Gilbert, pp. 26, 46–47, et passim.

48 "the Mexicans at that point"—For an interesting account of this period, see Guinn.

50 "issue of the Esoteric School"—Ryan, Chapter 21.

51 "Or those of"—Otto.

84 The contents of this memo and of the two previously illustrated Armenian texts were rendered equivalent through an iterative process of cross-translation using a readily available software program. The author is not versed in the Armenian language and apologizes for any potential errors or inconsistencies among the documents.

88 "Born in 1819"—This biographical summary is drawn from that in the *New World Encyclopedia*, found online August 17, 2020, at https:// www.newworldencyclo pedia.org/entry/Abner_Doubleday.

96 "He was able to find"—This reference is buried in an article about a rival publishing firm, Derby & Miller, found online August 18, 2020, at http://cayuga museum.org/a-look-at-auburn-publisherswith-a-focus-on-the-firm-of-derby-miller/. James Derby had worked for Doubleday before opening his own store.

101 "a woman named Katherine Tingley"—Levine, pp. 125–126.

101 "he proposed building a road"—See Wikipedia on this point as found online, August 19, 2020, at https://en.wikipedia.org/ wiki/A._G._Spalding.

101 "It's pretty clear that"—Philip Block, p. 42.

102 "that book I read"—See Thorn, "The Letters of Abner Graves."

102 "Doubleday is this war hero"—In recent years, baseball historians have begun to fill in the pieces of just such a possible theosophical conspiracy as the one imagined here. See, for example, Philip Block, passim; Thorn, *Baseball in the Garden of Eden*, pp. 260-272, et passim; and Thorn, "The Letters...."

103 "a lot of prominent adherents"—There are several lists of prominent adherents, among them those found online November 30, 2020, at https://theosophy.wiki/ en/Category:Famous_people; https://www.listal.com/list/famous-theosophists; and http://www. katinkahesselink.net/his/influence-theosophy.html.

104 "the official emblem of Theosophy"—For an illustration of the emblem and a thorough discussion of its elements and their respective significance, the reader is encouraged to consult "The Emblem of the Theosophical Society," an official posting by the Theosophical Society of Australia, found online June 9, 2023, at https:// theosophicalsociety.org.au/statics/the-emblem-of-the-theosophical-society.

112 Photo of the Doubleday historical marker by Sophia Rose Glassner. Reproduced by permission.

113 Photo of Phoenix House today by Sophia Rose Glassner. Reproduced by permission.

117 "a nearby boarding house"—See https://www.njht.org/dca/njht/funded/site details/thephoenixhouse.html, found online August 20, 2020.

118 Photo of Phoenix House, circa 1907, by Frank McMurtry, Mendham, New Jersey. The dirt road to the left of the building is Hilltop Road, formerly known as Church Street. The Doubleday's house was part of the way down the block on the right, in the vicinity of the last visible house in this photograph. The photograph appears on a postcard in the possession of the author.

118 "One point that caught Adam's eye"—See https://morriscountynj.gov/2017/10/ freeholders-award-historic-marker-to-mendhamborough-for-phoenix-house-project/; and http://www.ctsarch.com/the-phoenix-house-mendham-nj; both found online August 20, 2020.

119 Photo of the entrance to Phoenix House today by Sophia Rose Glassner. Reproduced by permission.

125 "Well, have a look"—Douglas.

126 "he translated two"—See https://havechanged.blogspot.com/2017/12/madame-blatavsky-and-beginnings-of.html, found online August 27, 2020.

146 "the one where he speculates"—See Thorn, p. 276.

159 "I came across something interesting"—Petsche, passim.

168 "more stringent than the Chatham House Rule"—The Chatham House Rule, promulgated by its namesake organization in 1927 to encourage open debate on controversial issues, reads in salient part as follows: ". . . participants are free to use the information received, but neither the identity nor the affiliation of the speaker(s), nor that of any other participant, may be revealed." Found online October 1, 2021, at https://www.chathamhouse.org/about-us/ chatham-house-rule. With his statement, Paul was telling the group that in addition to masking any of their fellow participants, they were not free to discuss or even reference the meeting itself or anything that was said.

171 "there is a complete Doubleday sword"—Described at https://www.nyhistory.org/ exhibit/sword-belt-and-buckle-belonged-abnerdoubleday, found online August 27, 2020.

172 "If you don't have access"—For information on this new and more precise form of carbon dating, see Megan I. Gannon, "Long-Awaited Update Arrives for Radiocarbon Dating," *Scientific American*, September 1, 2020, found online February 10, 2022 at https://www.scientificamerican.com/article/long-awaited-update-arrives-for-radiocarbon-dating/.

178 "had already told the *Cincinnati Enquirer*"—As reported by Baseball History Daily at https://baseballhistorydaily.com/2014/04/09/ origin-stories/, found online August 27, 2020.

178 "Mills, however, was himself"—See https://omnibusmonuments.wordpress.com/ 2014/04/08/the-myth-of-abner-doubleday-andbaseball/, found online August 27, 2020.

178 "That honor guard was commanded"—See https://havechanged.blogspot.com/ 2017/12/madame-blatavsky-and-beginnings-of.html, found online August 27, 2020.

179 "And here's the smoking gun"—Block, pp. 42–45.

185 The text of Doubleday's journal entry is reproduced here to assist the reader:

> June 26
>
> Today I am a man of eighteen years. Father has determined that I shall enrol in the Academy at West Pointe next year, & that I must prepar

myself of both hed & hart. I have accompanied him here to Cooper's Town to meet with Maj. Wm. Duff, who is to form a military academy in this place. And who I wd add has a most comely wife. I shall stand tall in my handsome blue uniform, & perhps met one lik her.

Mr. Fenimore Cooper, recently returnd from Europ of which he had much ill to say, has made a pointe to met me, as both of our fathers served in the Congress. He shewed me his newe naval history. He invited me to join in a game of ball with several local lads. After we debated for some minutes over which set of rules to employ, there being many, Mr. Cooper himself proposed that, as it was my Birthday, I should design the game. The other fellows were enthusiastic, and I was so honord.

I decided upon four bases in a diamond shape at thirty paces distance. The throwing bar was to be twenty paces from the home base. There were eighteen of us in all, not counting Mr. Cooper, who chose jist to watch our exrtions, & fellows divided and placed themselves so as to protect as much ground as they might. Several other rules were established, & I was selected to be the first striker. The game was so succesfl that Mr. Cooper declared mine to be the finest of rules & said that he would writ them down in detail.

The Best: Mr. Cooper wrote the date on the ball with a Happy Birthday Abner wish, signed it himself, & gave it me as a keepsake of the day. I shall always treasure it.

Tmorrow father returns home, and I am to remain here for a time.

190 "One of the experts"—Schraufnagel, p. 3.

190 "Apparently, there are people in this world"—See the section of Hereford Cattle in Ritchie, found online August 29, 2020 at https://www.canr.msu.edu/ans/uploads/files/Breeds%20of%20 Beef%20Cattle%20Ritchie%20Jan2009.pdf.

190 The story of the Herefords' arrival in the US is accurate, but in reality, Clay shipped some cattle to New York State in 1839–1840, not two years earlier as indicated here.

191 "that was a somewhat common practice"—See https://en.wikipedia.org/wiki/Baseball_(ball), found online August 29, 2020.

192 "a new technique called thin-layer chromatography"—See https://www.azolifesciences.com/article/Utilizing-Thin-LayerChromatography-in-Ink-Analysis.aspx, found online August 30, 2020.

193 "something called Incense-cedar"—See the history of the pencil at https://pencils.com/pages/the-history-of-the-pencil, found online August 30, 2020.

197 "during the seventy-fifth anniversary events"—"Hall of Fame to Mark 75th Year with Special Events, Commemorations for Diamond Celebration," Press Release, National Baseball Hall of Fame and Museum, June 12, 2013, as cited by Wikipedia.

203 Quoted in Lekachman.

Sources Consulted

Algeo, John. "Reincarnation: The Evidence," Quest 89:2 (March-April 2001), pp. 44–50, found online August 12, 2020, at https://www. theosophical.org/publications/quest-magazine/1410.

Arenson, Karen W. "Chinese Tycoon Gives Columbia $26 Million," *The New York Times*, October 1, 1997, found online August 12, 2020, at https://www.nytimes.com/1997/10/01/us/chinese-tycoon-gives-columbia-26-million.html.

Beyrer, Jack. "MLB Ships Jobs To China To Build Closer Relationship With CCP," *Washington Free Beacon*, September 29, 2021, found online on that date at https://freebeacon.com/national-security/mlbships-jobs-to-china-to-build-closer-relationship-with-ccp/.

Birdsall, Ralph. *The Story of Cooperstown*. New York: Charles Scribner's Sons, 1917.

Blavatsky, Helena. *The Key to Theosophy: Being a Clear Exposition, in the Form of Question and Answer, of the Ethics, Science, and Philosophy for the Study of Which the Theosophiocal Society Has Been Founded*. London: The Theosophical Publishing Company, 1889.

Block, David. *Baseball Before We Knew It: A Search for the Roots of the Game*. Lincoln: University of Nebraska Press, 2005.

Block, Philip. "Abner and Albert, The Missing Link," in David Block, *Baseball Before We Knew It*, pp. 32–49.

Chafets, Zev. *Cooperstown Confidential: Heroes, Rogues, and the Inside Story of the Baseball Hall of Fame*. New York: Bloomsbury, 2009.

Dotinga, Randy. "Baseball's Greatest Myth Has Roots in Point Loma," *Voice of San Diego*, September 2, 2019, found online August 12, 2020, at https://www.voiceofsandiego.org/topics/sports/baseballs-greatestmyth-has-roots-in-point-loma/.

Douglas, Beatrice C., "Abner Doubleday, US Baseball's Pioneer Once Lived in Mendham: Cooperstown Letters Tell Of Life There," *Morristown Daily Record*, N.D. 1950.

Ellwood, Robert. *Theosophy: A Modern Expression of the Wisdom of the Ages*. Wheaton, IL: Quest Books, 1986.

Foster, Janet W. Historic Preservation Consultant, Mendham Borough, *Mendham Historic District, Morris County, NJ*, nomination document, 1984, National Park Service, National Register of Historic Places, Washington, D.C. Found online August 12, 2020, at https://npgallery.nps.gov/GetAsset/9e71ee6b-6644-4701-b10a-76f08a35370a.

Gilbert, Thomas W. *How Baseball Happened: Outrageous Lies Exposed! The True Story Revealed.* Boston: David R. Godine, Publisher, 2020.

Griffiths, Brian. "Rob Manfred Is Ruining Baseball, Not Preserving It," *Annapolis (MD) Capital,* August 10, 2020, found online August 12, 2020, at https://digitaledition.capitalgazette.com/infinity/article_share.aspx?guid=000c0bf6-faa9-4d08-81e3-fd32f59f0277.

Guinn, Jeff. *War on the Border: Villa, Pershing, the Texas Rangers, and an American Invasion.* New York, Simon & Schuster, 2021.

Gumpert, Bert and Emily, and David W. Anderson, "Abner Doubleday," Society for American Baseball Research, found online August 12, 2020, at https://sabr.org/bioproj/person/abner-doubleday/.

Karmik, Tom. "Origin Stories," *Baseball History Daily,* April 9, 2014, found online August 12, 20202, at https://baseballhistorydaily. com/2014/04/09/origin-stories/.

Lamster, Mark. "The Curious Architecture of Albert Spalding," found online August 12, 2020, at https://www.marklamster.com/index.php/2009/08/10/the-curious-architecture-of-albert-spalding/.

Lekachman, Robert. "Virtuous Men and Perfect Weapons," *The New York Times,* July 27, 1986, Sec. 7, p. 7.

Levine, Peter. *A.G. Spalding and the Rise of Baseball: The Promise of American Sport.* New York: Oxford University Press, 1985.

Mallinson, James. "A.G. Mills," Society for American Baseball Research, found online August 12, 2020, at https://sabr.org/bioproj/person/ a-g-mills/.

Martino, Andy. *Cheated: The Inside Story of the Astros Scandal and a Colorful History of Sign Stealing.* New York: Doubleday, 2021.

McMahon, Bill. "Al Spalding," Society for American Baseball Research, found online August 12, 2020, at https://sabr.org/bioproj/person/ al-spalding/.

Miller, Timothy. "Visionary Architecture of Utopian Communities," in *Revista de estudios Globales y Arte Contemporaneo* 4:1, 2016, pp. 79–122.

Otto, DSteven. "Answering Back: How to Reply to Slanders Against Theosophy," *Quest* 107:3 (Summer 2019), pp. 28-31, found online August 12, 2020, at https://www.theosophical.org/publications/quest-magazine/4683-answering-back-how-to-reply-to-slanders-against-theosophy.

Petsche, Johanna. "Gurdjieff and Blavatsky: Western Esoteric Teachers in Parallel," *Literature and Aesthetics* 21:1, June 2011, pp. 98–115.

Ritchie, Harlan. *Breeds of Beef and Multi-Purpose Cattle.* East Lansing, MI: Michigan State University, 2009. Found online August 29, 2020, at https://www.canr.msu.edu/ans/uploads/files/Breeds%20of%20 Beef%20Cattle%20Ritchie%20Jan2009.pdf.

Ross, Robert B. *The Great Baseball revolt: The Rise and Fall of the 1890 Players League.* Lincoln: University of Nebraska Press, 2016.

Ryan, Charles J. *H.P. Blavatsky and the Theosophical Movement,* second and revised ed. London: Theosophical University Press, 1975.

Ryczek, William J. *Baseball's First Inning: A History of the National pastime Through the Civil War.* Jefferson, NC: McFarland & Company, 2009.

Sources Consulted

Schiff, Andrew. "Henry Chadwick," Society for American Baseball Research, found online August 12, 2020, at https://sabr.org/bioproj/ person/henry-chadwick/.

Schraufnagel, Noel, *The Baseball Novel: A History and Annotated Bibliography of Adult Fiction.* Jefferson, NC: McFarland & Company, 2008.

Thorn, John. *Baseball in the Garden of Eden: The Secret History of the Early Game.* New York: Simon & Schuster, 2011.

———. "The Letters of Abner Graves," *Our Game*, February 20, 2013, found online August 12, 2020, at https://ourgame.mlblogs.com/theletters-of-abner-graves-8fc6 a4694419.

Vlasich, James A. *A Legend for the Legendary: The Origin of the baseball Hall of Fame.* Bowling Green, OH: Bowling Green State University Popular Press, 1990.

About the Author

J.B. Manheim is Professor Emeritus at The George Washington University, where he developed the world's first degree-granting program in political communication and was later founding director of the School of Media & Public Affairs. In 1995 he was named Professor of the Year for the District of Columbia. He learned his love of baseball watching Dizzy Dean broadcast the Game of the Week and huddling with his grandfather for warmth on July nights at The Mistake By The Lake, AKA, Cleveland Municipal Stadium, and renewed it when the National Pastime finally returned to the Nation's Capital. Manheim brings to life his expertise in propaganda and strategic communication through his fictional stories of baseball behind the scenes. His writing will lead you to question whether what you think you know about the history of the game and about the powers who control it is real, or whether it's just a carefully nurtured product of lies, deceptions, misdirection, and propaganda. JB Manheim is a member of the Society for American Baseball Research and the Internet Baseball Writers Association of America.

www.ingramcontent.com/pod-product-compliance
Lightning Source LLC
Chambersburg PA
CBHW011427010726
47494CB00011B/2543